A Love Like Blood

Marcus Sedgwick

A Love Like Blood

PEGASUS CRIME

NEW YORK LONDON

A Love Like Blood

Pegasus Crime is an Imprint of
Pegasus Books LLC
80 Broad Street, 5th Floor
New York, NY 10004

ISBN: 978-1-60598-949-5

10 9 8 7 8 6 5 4 3 2 1

Printed in the United States of America
Distributed by W. W. Norton & Company, Inc.

For MH

Sextantio, Italy

1968

Dogs are barking in the night.

He's somewhere in the broken village on the hilltop opposite me. I can just make out the line of the rooftops against the dark sky.

The air is hot and I am tired, but that's not why I'm waiting. Nor am I waiting to mark any moment of reflection either. Not even to honour Marian.

I've chased him for over twenty years, and across countless miles, and though often I was running, there have been many times when I could do nothing but sit and wait. Now I am only desperate for it to be finished.

I am acutely aware of every minute detail of the moment. The grime on my face and neck, the smell of the still-warm grass around me, the throb I still get sometimes from my ruined hand, the weight of the knife in my right pocket.

Many times, over the years, I was lost, alone, unsure how to proceed, not knowing where to turn next, but now I know, and I'm waiting for one thing only: for the right moment, so I can do what I'm going to do, unseen.

Despite my concentration on the few lights in the village, on the sounds around me, on what I will do, I cannot help but remember some of the journey.

This story begins a long time ago; twenty years ago at least; maybe more somehow, I see that now. Yet in another, fuller, sense, my story begins centuries, millennia ago, for this is a story that must go back to the moment when blood flowed from some ancestor of ours; hot, bright and red.

For me, however, it began in August of 1944, in Paris.

*   *   *

3

Still the dogs are barking.

One is near me, somewhere on the hillside, shut in a farm-yard, but across the valley in the dark town a dozen or more answer it, barking till they're sore, till they choke and splutter, and then start again. It ought to be disturbing, but it isn't. Nothing can break my concentration now, nothing can spoil my waiting, destroy my patience.

I wonder what they're barking at. At each other? Each being driven by the other into ever more frenetic howls and rages. I hear no voices, no shouts, no one seems to try to shut them up, and so they go on.

They bark frantically, not even in anger, but in wild desper-ation it seems, on and on, through the night.

ONE

Paris

August, 1944

Demons that have no shame,
Seven are they!
Knowing no care,
They grind the land like corn;
Knowing no mercy,
They rage against mankind;
They spill blood like rain,
Devouring their flesh and sucking their veins.

They are Demons full of violence
Ceaselessly devouring blood.

Assyrian incantation against the Seven Spirits

I

Paris was free, and I was one of the very few Englishmen to see it. I was twenty-five, a captain in the Royal Army Medical Corps, attached to 26 Field Hygiene Section, and were it not for the fact that our CO had a strange whim one afternoon, I would not have seen what I saw.

For anyone who lived through the war, or who fought in it, or, as I did, found themselves in the fighting but did not fight, a thousand new paths through life opened up every day. Of course, many of those paths led to death, whether on the front lines, behind a hedgerow in Normandy or at home under the fleeting shadow of a rocket bomb, and that instilled a certain feeling in many people, something new that few of us had felt before. I saw, time and again, what living with the quotidian possibility of death did to people; making them reckless, or adventurous, heedless that they had a future self, an older self, who was relying on them not to destroy their lives before they could become that person.

Because, I supposed, it was an old age that might never arrive, in which case what use was there in protecting it?

But there were other possibilities besides death, many of them. Other possibilities that led people to strange events or chance meetings that would determine their living destiny, or, as I was to discover, that led to an increase in fortune, or wealth.

It seemed to me, even young as I was then, that I had merely shut my eyes one day. At the time, I was a newly qualified house officer at Barts, six months under my belt, Cambridge life still in my heart; I still thought of my room at Caius as my home, not the digs I'd taken in Pimlico. Without time to take in what was happening, I was called up and sent to Oxford to join an RAMC military hospital that was forming in the Examination Building. A moment later and I was on the Isle of Wight, for two weeks' training on the Ducks. Then another brief moment, one of waiting, in the countryside above Southampton.

When I opened my eyes again, I was on Sword beach, watching the troops run behind the tanks pawing their way up the sand, making for the tracks the sappers had laid, all the while trying to get my trucks off the landing ship, for we, of course, came last.

I remember calculating that I was eighty-four days into my active service when I saw Paris. Less than three months, but already a lifetime, in that I felt I had changed, started to grow up at last.

While I would like to pretend that I saved the lives of one hundred, two hundred, three hundred soldiers as the Second Army fought its way across Normandy, that I saw death daily and grew fearless of its presence, I cannot. That was perhaps the case for other men of the RAMC, but life in the Hygiene Section was a different matter. It was our job to find safe sources of drinking water, to purify it if necessary, to set up showers and dig latrines. In its own way, our work was vital, for without these things an army quickly becomes ill and unable to fight, but there's no way of pretending it was a glamorous business.

In truth, I saw little of the wounded, and though from time to time we would run across a field hospital, I saw very little blood, which is in itself a strange thing for an officer in the RAMC to report.

Of course, I had seen enough blood during my studies; but of that, what can I say?

Maybe I should here admit to the first time I saw blood. By which I mean not a smear on a grazed knee in the playground, or a few drops from a bleeding nose on the rugby pitch, but lots of it. Blood in quantity. Which I first saw as I observed a simple operation on a man in his fifties in the theatre in Trumpington Street. I can remember that moment well. There were very few medical students in Cambridge in those days and that particular day there were just three of us who watched: an emotionless intellect named Squiers; Donald, who would become a friend of mine, and who fainted as the first drops welled under the surgeon's knife; and me.

I watched . . . how can I describe it? It seemed to be a dream that I was in, and I watched from within it as if I was witnessing something secret. As if I was seeing something I shouldn't; like seeing a couple making love. The colour, the sheer quantity . . . it seemed, quite literally, to be full of life, and I guess I began to understand something I have had much cause to consider since then: why it was that the ancients instinctively felt that life is in the blood. That blood is life.

None of that was clear in my mind, then. Then, I just marvelled at it, wondering if my reaction showed to those around me.

The surgeon and the nurses helping him barely stirred when Donald fainted – apparently that happened a lot – and neither did they seem to show much interest in the blood. I glanced at them briefly, reluctant to look away from the operation, and couldn't understand why they didn't seem to react to it, but were vaguely irritated by its presence, the awkwardness it gave to the procedure. Squiers was presumably making mental notes on the physiology, so I was left, taking in nothing medical at all, merely dreaming.

And yes, after that day, in my medical training and in France, I occasionally saw large amounts of blood. But none of the other times remains in my memory, until what I saw in a hole in the ground in Saint-Germain-en-Laye.

2

Like most young people, I had always wanted to see Paris. I had never been out of England before; my parents, while they had the money to travel, were not the adventurous type, and my childhood holidays had all been on the British coast – Brighton, Norfolk, Cornwall, Ayrshire. Scurrying on to the Normandy sand amid a German bombardment was not how I had imagined my first trip abroad.

Though we were there to fight a war, there is so very much of a soldier's time that is idle. This idleness meant that I had plenty of time to watch, to observe what I found around me. I looked closely at the villages we passed through, at their inhabitants, and I even tried to speak to them when I had the chance, though my attempts at French were timid and faltering.

For much of that time we were stationed in Plumetot, right by the Canadian Air Force base. The local people rewarded us with bottles of Calvados at almost every opportunity. Our CO, in return, attended to the medical needs of the villagers, something they were most grateful for. For the most part things were quiet. We watched the Engineers roll out a new asphalt landing strip alongside the existing grass one; we found supplies and purified drinking water. Of course, we never forgot the war; for one thing the German lines came very close to the far corner of the airstrip, from where snipers would take occasional potshots.

Once the German armies were routed in the Falaise, however, things suddenly sped up, and we decamped and began to move east rapidly.

Then, towards the end of August, we were about thirty miles to the north of Paris when we heard on the BBC that the city had been liberated. It's hard to explain how important it seemed, a cause for great celebration, a turning point; someone on the radio said it was the greatest day for France since the fall of the Bastille, and maybe it was.

That evening, our CO, Major Greaves, called me over.

'Ever seen Paris?' he asked. Clearly he knew that I had not. I don't know how old Major Greaves was. From the viewpoint of my youth I supposed he was ancient; from where I sit now I would guess he was in his late forties. I didn't know him very well, despite the time we'd spent together since grouping before D-Day.

He was a little shorter than me, with a slightly plump face, and there was always a little look in his eyes as if he'd rather be far away, doing something else, which I could easily understand. It showed in his voice, too, not really in the words he used but in the way in which he said them. I knew he'd fought in the First War too, and he must have been young then, and not a major. He would have seen some fighting.

'No, sir,' I said, anticipating what was coming next.

'Well, you'd like to?' he said, and I of course told him I would. 'Good. We'll take half the unit in tomorrow, you and I will stay overnight, and the other half will go in the day after.'

He stopped and waited for me to speak, but I didn't.

'Well? What do you say to that?'

I couldn't help the smile that suddenly burst out of me from nowhere.

'I'd say that was wonderful, sir,' I said. 'Really wonderful.'

'Well, we have some time to spare. We can either spend it here and stop the men from picking holes in each other, or we can give them a treat. I've made some arrangements. You sort out who's going on which day.'

*　　*　　*

I did, dividing the men more or less at random, and the next day I climbed into the Major's jeep, a private at the wheel, and we led one of our trucks with the men into the city through the Porte de Clignancourt.

It was unbelievable. Of course, I knew London well enough then, but Paris seemed something else. We rolled down from Montmartre, towards the opera house, looking for the hotel where the Major and I were to stay. The city was quiet, the streets almost empty, with very few vehicles on the roads. Occasionally we saw American or French soldiers, who seemed amazed to see our RAMC truck with its red cross on the side, and they waved at us. When I waved back, the Major kept looking straight ahead, but I could see there was a twinkle in his eye.

There were local people on the streets too, and I was amazed at them. I don't know if I'd been expecting scenes of starvation or desolation, but we didn't see them. Of course, the city was damaged in places, but nothing like the destruction of London. And the people had their dignity, seemed well enough fed, while the girls looked stylish to us and every one we passed attracted cheery whistles from the men, returned for the most part with equally happy smiles.

We trundled along the Seine that afternoon, seeing the Eiffel Tower and the Champs-Elysées, down which, just two days before, de Gaulle had marched triumphantly after von Choltitz's surrender. We learned later there'd been shooting from some high windows, no one knew who it was, but de Gaulle had just kept on striding along. I think we all felt like that; that the joy of the liberation made us all immortal, immortal for a short time. It was a strange visit, as if the war had never happened, was not still happening elsewhere, and yet it so obviously had, and was.

That evening, after we'd packed the men off to the rest of the unit, the Major and I headed back up towards Montmartre to see some nightlife. A couple of American soldiers we spoke to told us to try Pig Alley, which we soon learned was what they called Pigalle.

I had never seen anything like it. Here was life! Though it was of a rough and dirty kind, that didn't matter to us, we were simply glad to find that people were alive and having fun. Nor had I ever seen such things as the women standing on street corners and sitting in open first-floor windows, or such blatant drunkenness in the streets. Nothing had prepared me for these sights, but it only made me wonder, and the Major let a half smile spread across his face as we looked for somewhere to have a drink.

The Bal Tabarin and many of the most famous clubs were still closed, but there were plenty of smaller places open, doing good, fast business with the Americans. Once again I was struck by the strangeness of it all. A few days before, it would have been German officers who would have been here, though they must have known their time was at an end by then, felt as strange as we felt, though in a different way.

We found a bar, large enough for a small band to play in the corner, and to have people dancing. The Major bought us a bottle of wine and we sat to one side.

'Charles, isn't it?' he said, pouring us both a drink.

'Sir?'

'None of that tonight,' he said, looking very sternly at me. Then his face broke into a sly smile. 'For tonight you call me Edward. Yes?'

I nodded.

He pushed my glass towards me.

'Cheer-o,' he said.

'Cheers,' I answered, and we drank.

He put his glass down, and put a serious face back on, but I could see it was a pretend one. Suddenly I was seeing a new side to the Major; playful, almost childlike.

'I have a confession to make.'

I nodded, showing him I was waiting and willing to give absolution.

'My concern for the men's relaxation is only half the reason I wanted to come here. What are you doing tomorrow morning?'

The question surprised me just as much as our whole trip to Paris had. It was a question that seemed to suggest I was at home in London with a few vague plans for the weekend.

'Nothing,' I stumbled out. 'Why?'

'We should have a couple of hours before the rest of the men get here. There's somewhere I want to visit. The Musée des Antiquités Nationales. It's in Saint-Germain-en-Laye. I've always wanted to go there. They have the finest Palaeolithic collection. The Venus of Bastennes, for example.'

I must have appeared pretty ignorant, because I was.

The Major humoured me.

'Not your subject perhaps? There are other remarkable pieces too, if something more modern's up your street. Right up to the late Middle Ages. The museum itself is a chateau, with a long and famous history. James II lived there after his exile.'

The Major's idea of modern was amusing, but he didn't seem to notice.

'Wondered if you fancied coming over?'

'I'd love to,' I said, not because I had any interest in archaeology but simply because it would mean I'd get to see more of the city.

'Splendid,' said the Major, and it was settled.

It meant an early start, but that didn't stop us from staying late in the bar, talking when we had something to say, watching the dancing figures whirling to accordion, violin and piano when we didn't. We smoked and drank, and then drank some more.

I stole glances at Edward, as I was supposed to be calling him, watching him watch the happy people. He had a gentle smile on his face that never faltered, and I found it hard to remember that he was my CO.

Finally we made our way back down towards the Opéra and crawled into bed in the small hours.

I had drunk too much, and slept badly. When I did, I dreamed, and my dreams were happy ones, holding no hint of the horror that was waiting for me, just the other side of sleep.

3

The weather had been good to us since we'd arrived in the city; that morning was the same, and I was glad of it. The Major rapped on my door smartly at seven, and I dragged myself out of bed, hung-over, possibly even still drunk, for despite the frequent tots of Calvados at Plumetot I wasn't used to heavy drinking.

The Major smiled at me, spoke briskly.

'Captain Jackson? Shall we?'

I managed to nod.

'I'll see you outside in five minutes, then? Good.'

Our driver, the private, made a fairly blatant display of his displeasure at being up so early when he was supposed to be on leave and drove like a maniac through the empty streets, succeeding in making my hangover worse. From time to time he would briefly lurch to a stop to check a map he'd procured, and then we'd set off again with a squeal.

The Major showed no sign of noticing this; his good humour from the evening before remained, and in fact the fresh air and the sun started to help me feel much better, despite the private's offensive driving.

I don't know if the Major knew, but I certainly didn't, that the Chateau de Saint-Germain-en-Laye had been German Army headquarters during the occupation, not for the city, but for France and the Low Countries: High Command West.

It was an incredible sight – it was the first large French chateau

I'd ever seen, so regal, so ornate, so elegant, perched on the hill-side looking back down across the river to Paris.

It had been evacuated a few days before the liberation, and was now in the hands of the Americans. I started to doubt if the Major knew what he was about; a British officer arriving on their doorstep caused quite a stir.

While the private lounged in the jeep in the sun by the gates, I hung at the Major's heels while he explained what he wanted. As it slowly dawned on the American company commander what exactly that was, his mood relaxed, and then he waved a hand.

'Sure. Go ahead. The whole place is yours. Just don't take anything home with you, right?'

He laughed, and the Major gave a small, embarrassed nod, thrown by the directness of the American's wit.

'Won't it all have been taken away?' I asked. 'Put into storage?'

'Yes, some of it will, but they cannot possibly have moved everything. Look! You see?'

We walked through corridor after corridor, and the Major was right; on every side hung paintings and tapestries of obvious antiquity, but what the Major was after was many thousands of years older, and of that there was no sign.

For the first time since we'd arrived in Paris, his mood worsened, but then, as I began to think the whole thing had been a waste of time, a piece of luck.

As we stood at the top of a flight of stairs, wondering where to look next, a voice called to us.

'*Je peux vous aider?*'

We turned and saw an old man inspecting us from a doorway.

'*Messieurs? Vous cherchez quelqu'un?*'

The man was clearly nothing to do with the military, on any side. He was very short, had white hair and a slight stoop, and looked exactly like a museum curator should, which was almost exactly what he was.

The Major stepped forward, pulled his cap off his head, and stuck his hand out.

'Edward Greaves. So very pleased to meet you.'

Monsieur Dronne was, in fact, a caretaker, but there was something about the way he referred to the place as '*mon musée*' that told us he knew as much about the collections as the directors of it did. Probably more.

M Dronne confirmed for the Major what I had feared, that most things had been taken away and put in safe storage, but much had not, including items that didn't appear to be obviously valuable, among which was the Major's precious Venus.

The old caretaker led the way down to the lower levels of the chateau and into the cellars, where row upon row of cabinets stood.

By the feeble light of dim, bare bulbs overhead, the two men began to speak excitedly in a mixture of mostly French and some English about the pieces Major Greaves had come to see.

As M Dronne reverentially pulled out a drawer with a great show of drama, I could see the Major holding his breath.

'My word . . .' was all he said as M Dronne unwrapped it and placed it on the cabinet.

His Venus turned out to be a tiny piece of ivory, not two inches long, carved into the head and shoulders of a woman. I looked at it, and looked at it, but couldn't quite get excited.

The Major's hands, on the contrary, were trembling, and he was speechless, though not for long.

As he and M Dronne chatted away about how old it might be and where it had been found, who made it and how and why, they moved on to look at other pieces, and I, forgotten, dawdled behind them, gazing for a while at each one.

I looked again at the Venus; her face was a simple triangular shape, seemingly calm, with no sign of a mouth. Her hair hung in what seemed to be tight plaits. I looked harder and began to feel a little of its mystery, but there were other things to look at; more figurines found in the same ancient layers of earth as the Venus.

There was an engraved antler, the outline of a woman's body scraped into the flat of the bone. A series of markings that were thought to be fish. And then there came something that did arrest me.

Another figure of a woman, again in bone. The figure was headless, and the arms had either been broken off or never carved. The breasts were absent too, and so the only thing that showed it to be a woman was a gouge for the vulva. Something nagged me about it as soon as I saw it and then I realised what it was. The carving seemed effortless, so that it did not intrude at all upon the depiction of the body; it was almost as if the bone had been found that way, so smooth and subtle was the carving of the body and legs. But the cleft between its legs was deep and scratched, a little clumsily done. Almost frantic, I felt, though I knew I was probably imagining too much. I speculated that perhaps the mark that showed her to be a woman had been done later, by another, more forceful hand. There was the faintest splotch of colour there, too. Brown. Maybe red that had faded.

The only other thing I remember looking at was a bowl, apparently Assyrian, which M Dronne showed us as a curiosity. It was a dirty white bowl, mostly in one piece, upon the inner face of which was a sequence of figures. He pointed at one couple.

'*Ce pot, dit-on, montre la représentation la plus ancienne au monde d'un vampire.*'

I looked closer, thinking I must have misunderstood him. It was a gruesome little scene, picked out in red glaze, of a man copulating with a woman. I should specify, a decapitated woman. It was a highly stylised depiction; the woman was slender, with legs awkwardly long.

M Dronne explained that the female figure was a vampire, and that the image was a talismanic device to ward off such creatures; if they did not heed the warning, their fate would be that of their colleague on the bowl.

How any of this was known, M Dronne did not say.

My head swam, and in the darkness of the cellars I felt a return of the nausea from earlier.

'I'm going up for some air,' I called to the Major, but I don't think he even noticed me.

I climbed back up into the daylight and, suddenly feeling desperate for some air, found my way out into the grounds beside the chateau, overlooking the city.

In the distance I could see our jeep and the private with his legs draped over the steering wheel, so I turned away and took a walk around the park, breathing in as much of the gently warming air as I could.

That was when I saw it.

The bunker. In fact, there were several of them, two by the chateau alone, more in the park. I found out later that, as the HQ of Oberbefehlshaber West, Saint-Germain in general and the chateau in particular had had numerous concrete bunkers and air-raid shelters constructed there, but why I wandered over to the one I did, I have never known.

I wondered later if I'd heard something, but I don't think so, not consciously at least. Maybe I just picked up on something without really knowing it and that was what took me over to the bunker's mouth to look in.

Though it was a bright morning, little light penetrated beyond the open doorway, and yet despite this I felt compelled to enter. I put my foot on the first step, ducked my head under the low lintel of the entrance, and went down, into the gloom.

Then I did hear a noise, but it was very faint and I could not determine what it was. I trod quietly, the ground levelled off in front of me, and I took another step, waiting for my eyes to grow used to the dark.

There was that noise again, just a little way ahead of me, and without making a sound, I pulled a book of matches from my pocket.

I tore off one of the matches, lit it, and held it out in front of me, shielding my eyes from its light.

What I saw there . . .

What I saw there I saw only for the length of time it takes a single match to burn down, and yet it changed my life.

Crouched on the ground, just a little way away, was a man. He was hunched over something, and as I lit the match, he stopped what he was doing, and turned to look at me.

Underneath him, the lifeless body of a woman lay on a raised slab on the floor. Her head hung back off the stone step, her hair splayed out. She was dressed, mostly, though her blouse was torn a little around her neck and breast. She was young.

I saw that.

At the same time, I saw the man. I couldn't see what he was wearing – some dull uniform of sorts, but it was too dark to tell whether it was British or American. Or even German. His hair was short, dark, swept to one side, and from his mouth blood dribbled on to the woman's once white blouse.

His hand was on her left shoulder, holding back her clothing to expose a long and fresh wound from which blood flowed freely, and from which, I understood at once, he had been drinking.

I didn't move.

It might sound like madness, but I didn't move. I can only explain it as if I'd come across a giant wolf in the woods, and my body and mind had frozen from the fear. Somewhere, at the back of my mind, that's how I felt: frozen. And yet I also knew instantly that I was in terrible danger. As a medical officer, I was unarmed, but that was not the source of my fear; my fear came from the look on the man's face.

He'd been discovered in the midst of some appalling act, and yet he didn't even move, much less get up and run, or fight.

All he did was look at me, and it was the look that terrified me, for it was a look of amusement, but not at what he was doing.

He was amused by *me*.

All that, in the time the match took to burn my fingers, and then, though I am ashamed to admit it, I turned and ran from the hole, stumbling back up into the sunlight. I staggered away from the bunker to a bench, where I sat down and was sick.

I don't know how much time passed. Suddenly I felt afraid again, as I realised I was sitting with my back to the hole, though it was perhaps a hundred yards behind me.

I stood, and turned.

Below me lay Paris in the August sunshine. The morning was wearing on, and the heat was building. I could see for miles, beyond free Paris, maybe as far as land still occupied by the retreating German Army, I didn't know. Yet it reminded me that the war was still on, that this sojourn in Paris was some strange anomaly, not what life really was.

On the ground between my feet I saw the book of matches; I must have dropped it there. I stooped and picked it up, and turned back the way I'd come.

Forcing my eyes over to the bunker's mouth again, and knowing I ought to do something, I set off towards the hole. Even in times such as this, times of great stress, the mind is still able to throw up irrelevant details. I noted the grim coincidence of the picture of the vampire I had just seen, and what I'd seen the man doing, and then I wondered if I'd imagined it all; if my tired and drunken mind had shown me things in the shadows that weren't really there.

I think I was about halfway there when my steps began to falter and my legs to tremble. I stopped, forced myself on again for a few feet, and then stopped again.

'Captain?'

I turned to my right and saw the private a few paces away. He appeared to be less grumpy now he'd had a bit more sleep in the sunshine.

'The Major's waiting. Time to go, sir.'

I nodded, but didn't move.

I hesitated. 'Private,' I said. 'Do you see that bunker there?'

'Sir?'

'Would you . . .'

I stopped. Wondered what exactly I was asking.

'Would you . . . take a look in it?'

'Sir?'

The private stared at me.

'Are you well, sir? You don't—'

'I'm fine. Just do as I ask, will you? You needn't go far in.'

The private nodded, seeming to think it would be faster to accede to my strange request than question it. He set off towards the hole.

Watching him about to enter, I felt a sudden pang of guilt at my cowardice. What was I doing, sending this man instead of me?

I caught up with him and, afraid to make any noise, made a dumbshow that I would come down with him.

At once the look on his face changed.

'No, sir,' he almost barked at me. Disgust spread to his mouth. 'I'm not like that.'

He held my eye for a moment, and before I even realised what it was he thought of me, he turned.

'I'll wait for you at the jeep,' he said. 'Sir.'

The penny dropped and my face burned.

'No!' I cried after him. 'No, no, I—'

But he was gone. My shoulders hung, and I turned to face the hole again.

I waited, glancing at the chateau, where I could see the Major talking to the private.

My breathing had almost stopped, my chest tightened as, with shaking hands, I pulled out the matches from my pocket again, striking one as I rushed down into the hole.

There was nothing there. No one.

I began to doubt myself further, wondering if I had indeed had some strange hallucination, and I called out.

'You there!'

There was no reply but a tiny dead echo.

My match went out and I lit another, approaching the place where I'd seen him, and then I knew I wasn't losing my mind, because there was blood on the ground.

But no woman, and he had gone, too. Vanished.

My second match went out, and I lit a third, turning around.

I saw I was in a corridor, with the mouths to at least three other passages leading away to total blackness, into which I gazed for a moment or two, my heart beating hard.

Then my nerve left me, and I turned and ran up into the sunshine again, slowing to a walk when I saw the Major, climbing into the jeep beside him, sitting in silence as the private drove us slowly back into town.

I don't remember anything else about my time in Paris, nothing in detail. I suppose it was around then that the men began to whisper about me, nudging each other and winking when they thought I wasn't looking. The private had obviously been talking.

But I didn't care about that. I had few friends amongst the men; I'd never found it easy to be one of them, as some of the other officers did. I'd always been set apart, and this gossip made little difference to me.

We left the city in the early evening and returned to station. Amid the noise and activity of the unit, it was easier to hide my silence. A torpor and introspection settled in me, and that night I lay half awake, replaying the scene I'd witnessed, again, and again, and again.

Of course, I hadn't even dreamed yet of the full horror of the situation. That this moment would cling to the rest of my life, weighing it down, crippling it, pulling it in a direction I would never have wished it to go.

No, then all I could think about was the woman on the ground, the man squatting over her.

In my mind she became more beautiful every time I replayed the scene, though thinking back now I'd seen her in less than half-light, for a few seconds, in a moment of great shock. Maybe she had been very beautiful, maybe very ugly, I don't know, but there had been an elegant curve to her jaw, finely shaped eyebrows, waves of thick dark hair, and I'd seen her as attractive.

I berated myself. Would it be any less terrible if she'd been hideous? Of course not.

And the man. Him.

I'd seen his face most clearly in profile, and then, as he turned slowly to look at me, in full. His nose strong but not big, his dark brows, his eyes, mocking me.

I could not understand everything about the way he had looked at me; that would come later. For the whole of that first wretched night, I was consumed by other, more immediate questions.

Who was he? Who was she? Was she someone he knew, or some poor girl he had lured into the hole in the manner the private thought I had been trying to?

Had he killed her? That seemed likely, but maybe not. Maybe he'd just found her, and . . .

What?

Cut her body and drunk her blood?

I questioned again if that's what I had really seen. It was ludicrous; it was, as I've said, something I should not have seen, something wrong. Not just violence, not just murder, but something even more depraved than those acts.

My mind turned over and began to sink beneath these awful thoughts, but still sleep did not come till the very early hours, as daylight returned. And yet, even in sleep, and as I forced myself awake again, and as we struck camp that morning, and even as we began to roll further east chasing our men chasing the German forces, one question rose to dominate all my other thoughts.

It was the question that drove me to where I am today, that ate away at my sense of self for year after year, and it was this.

I said that the young woman's body was lifeless, but even on the way back to the city in the jeep, I had begun to realise that that was an assumption I'd made. It was dark. It only lasted a few seconds. I saw a terrible and shocking thing.

I'd assumed she was dead.

But what if she wasn't, what if she'd still been alive when I'd found her? What then?

4

In March 1951, I went back to Paris.

After the war, I'd returned to London briefly, but then took a specialism, telling myself that it would offer a better career, though in truth it was more something that happened than something I chose.

The chance to move back to Cambridge was all I thought about, and when a position arose in the small Department of Haematology, I took it.

I had further studies to do, and I did them diligently. I worked hard, but I also enjoyed being back in the place I felt was home, with some old friends around me; people like Hunter, an English professor who was a lifelong family friend, almost an uncle to me, and Donald, who'd become a clinical psychologist, because, as he told me, it would mean he wouldn't have to see blood any more.

I, on the other hand, both in the department and in Addenbrooke's Hospital, saw lots of it, though mostly it was unrecognisable as such, mere smears of stained erythrocytes between two glass slides, under a microscope.

I became a consultant by the age of thirty-one, and was immediately disliked by my older colleagues at the hospital for making them feel stupid, though to a man they were all distinguished doctors. I made some efforts to break down their hostility but whatever I tried failed and so I withdrew into my work. There at least I made good progress; so much so that in the early part of 1951 I was invited to speak at a conference on leukaemia in Paris.

I was sitting in my office in Trumpington Street when I opened the letter of invitation. As I looked at it, I stood up, slowly, and then looked out at the cold Cambridge morning.

Students on bicycles hurried by, striped college scarves wound tightly around their necks; the bare spikes of trees stuck their fingers into the sky; the steps of the Fitzwilliam were still damp with melting snow. My mind was far away, on the edge of a piece of parkland by the chateau of Saint-Germain-en-Laye.

I tried to work out how I felt, and then realised that that in itself meant I felt nothing. But it was a strange kind of nothing.

I sat down and wrote a letter to the organising committee, telling them I would be delighted to accept, querying what expenses would be covered, and outlining what I would like to speak about.

At the back of my mind, of course, the memory of Saint-Germain lingered, but it did not bother me seriously. By the time the war had ended I had seen my share of horror, more than my share perhaps, as the fighting grew more intense as we made it further east into Germany. I saw worse things than I'd seen in that hole, if one can possibly compare one horror to another, and I'd seen enough to make me realise that what I'd seen was not unique; that war makes men do monstrous things, and that those things were not my fault.

Anyway, I was excited. I had achieved the rank of consultant almost embarrassingly early; I'd been invited to an international conference; and Paris was, I reminded myself, a beautiful place. I had never flown; even that excited me.

If anything, I saw the trip as a chance to make things better. I know now that I believed that if I could go back to Paris and feel normal, it would lessen the meaning of what I'd witnessed in 1944. Just one more awful thing among the many that had happened during the war.

5

Paris was more or less as I'd remembered it, but cold and wet. It was a miserable March morning when my plane touched down at Le Bourget.

A car had been sent for me, with a driver and an aide, a young Frenchman. Lucien was polite, had excellent English and explained that he was a medical student and had volunteered to look after me during my five-day trip. He was quiet, spoke only when spoken to, but answered my many questions about the city graciously.

I was asking him about how things had changed since the war, but there was a look in his eye that made me think he would perhaps rather not speak about it.

I could see for myself that there was more life in the streets, a few more cars on the road. Clothes were a little more colourful, food was better, and in short, Paris was Paris. But over the course of my first couple of days there, I began to sense in my conversations a certain malaise in the people.

I knew immediately what it was, because it was the same back home, especially in London. It's hard to imagine now, now that war is far behind us, but back then, on a trip to town, something had become clear to me.

I'd been to the theatre in London to see a rather bad play at the Criterion, and stopped over for the night in an even worse little hotel in Half Moon Street.

Walking down Piccadilly, watching the people rushing past, noses to the pavement, shoulders about their ears, I suddenly knew what was wrong, wrong with them, with me.

How ill we were! How sick our lives were, how empty, how grey. Without the war to tell us that life was precious, what were we? Threaten to take something from us and we grasp on to it with desperate desire; give it back to us, and how soon we grow tired of it! So we are left with our flat, ruined lives; humiliated, humiliated by many things. That we are alive when our friends are not, that we struggled through the dramas of the war only to end up in a dull, broken and impoverished world, that we had felt noble in the face of the dangers of life, and now we sat in a pile of ugly rubble, knowing we had turned German cities to rubble too.

It was confirmed to me the following day as I sat in a café in Shepherd Market. I sat by myself in a corner, feeling less alone here than I had at the theatre the night before. Even at such an early hour, shattered and deteriorated tarts loitered in doorways, cigarettes hanging from their mouths, their faces floating white bags. Behind me I heard a man reading a paper remark to the waitress, 'The headlines are so dull, aren't they?'

I could almost hear him think to himself, *if only one could hear the buzz of a robot bomb.*

And it was the same in Paris, and maybe it was doubly so for them, for they had had *the enemy* in their midst, had served them meals, made their beds, cleaned their clothes. Some of them had presumably slept with them, and all had wrestled daily with notions surrounding dignity and fear and survival.

For them, there was no antidote to the ennui, and although Lucien was kind enough to accompany me out to Montmartre on my first, free, evening, and although there were people dancing, and the large clubs had reopened, I found myself longing for Major Greaves to pour me a glass of house wine and tell me to call him Edward.

The next day I gave my paper.

I was as nervous as hell, and it was a disaster. This was my first experience of the world of medical academia in conference, and after I finished speaking I was assailed by dozens of questions. We quickly became bogged down in a fruitless argument about methodologies and I grew flustered and began to sweat, despite the chill of the big salon in which the presentations were taking place. It wasn't so much the questions themselves that bothered me; it was something underneath them, something in their delivery. I sensed resentment in everyone, as if they were jealously trying to find fault with me. Not with my paper, but with *me*.

I left the auditorium, Lucien at my side, and when we stood on the steps of the hotel, I could see something had changed about Lucien too. He asked me if I wanted him to take me anywhere for lunch, or what else I wanted to do, but he couldn't look me in the eyes, and I knew that, in his estimation, I had been humbled.

When I'd arrived, I had been a shining example of what he perhaps hoped to be; now he wasn't so sure.

I mumbled something about taking the afternoon off. There was nothing I had to do, and I couldn't face the glare of my colleagues, not yet.

Lucien offered to arrange a car for me to look round the city. I began to refuse and then something slipped into my mind, and I accepted the offer.

Half an hour later, I sat in the back of a comfortable Citroën, heading for Saint-Germain-en-Laye.

My driver spoke no English, so we fell into silence.

As we pulled up the hill into the town, I had a sudden urge to be alone, not be tailed all day.

'*Il y a une gare ici?*' I asked the driver.

He said something fast that I took to mean there was at least one station, and so I had him drop me off, and sent him back into town, presumably to take the afternoon off too.

*   *   *

Did I know what I was doing?

Perhaps I did. I'm not sure, in all honesty, what took me there, but it was one of those times when you feel impelled to do something, to act your way through a scene or two of your life that has already been written for you. You find yourself walking somewhere almost without thinking, as if unseen forces have a hold of you. Or maybe you do know what you're doing, deep down, but it's so buried in your unconscious that it feels automatic.

Within minutes, I was in the park beside the chateau. The building itself hadn't changed, but outside there were small signs to show it had returned to its former role as the Musée des Antiquités.

Briefly, I remembered the Major, and his passion for the ivory Venus. I remembered old Monsieur Dronne and wondered if he was happily taking care of 'his museum' once more, but my mind was on something else, and I found myself heading for the edge of the park overlooking the valley, the river, towards the city.

I had to look at myself, at my arms, to see the black wool of my suit in order to remind myself that I was not in uniform, that the war was over, and that this was 1951, for the park looked just the same, or so I thought at first.

But, though I looked and looked, I could not see the bunkers in the park. They appeared to have been removed. Seven years had passed, my memory might have distorted things, but . . . no, I knew I was in the right place, at the side of the chateau and before the first avenue of trees.

The only thing different, as far as I could see, was a new little bandstand. I wandered towards it, trying to remember, and then I understood that what I was looking for *was* the bandstand; it had been built on top of the bunker, the entrance to which was now a small wooden door, firmly padlocked. A small window had been punched in the front side, right underneath where a bandleader would stand, and I crouched down on my hands and knees, trying to see inside.

I couldn't. It was too dark, and the glass was grimy and mud-splashed, being so low to the ground.

A couple passed by me on bicycles, looking at me strangely, and I tried to give the air that this was something one did every day, but I stood nonetheless, and walked back towards the town.

I found a large and noisy brasserie and was pleased to get a table to one side, where I could observe both the cold square outside, and the diners in the restaurant.

And there it was that I saw him.

6

Him.

I knew at once it was the man from the hole. He was turned in profile to me, sitting across a small table from a young woman, in her early twenties I guessed.

I remember that for a moment I questioned myself, told myself I was being fanciful, wanted to dream up this powerful coincidence in an attempt to destroy the ennui that pervaded me just as much as everyone else, but it was, unquestionably, him.

My first impulse was to run, but the waiter appeared in front of me. I looked up.

'*Je peux manger quelque chose? C'est trop tard, peut-être . . . ?*'

'*Pas du tout,*' he said, and began setting out cutlery for me, placing a large card menu on the table. Adding in English, 'In Paris, you can eat at any time.'

I looked across at the man again, and realised he had not seen me, and probably would not see me. I was fractionally behind him, and I could watch both him and the girl easily without drawing attention to myself. While I was glad I was not too close to them, I soon regretted not being able to hear what they were saying, although I could hear enough to know they were speaking in French, and fluently. I would most likely not have understood them even had I sat at their table.

The girl was striking. Not beautiful, but there was something about her. She had a slightly pointed nose, but it was fine and gave her an air of nobility. Her mouth was noticeably wide, but the most striking thing about her was her hair; long auburn ringlets hung beyond her shoulders, quite unlike the short French fashions.

Though I couldn't hear what she was saying, she spoke in an animated way, using her hands a lot, something that again made her very different from the few women I knew in Cambridge. Her gestures were quick and vivacious; I could see she was at ease, thinking quickly, moving ahead with her thoughts. She wore a black blouse and a bright red skirt, and low black heels.

I looked from the girl back to her companion. He bent down to one side, brushing something off the hem of his trouser leg, and as he straightened again I was given the same view of his face I'd seen seven years before, three hundred yards away, in a hole in the ground.

It *was* him.

Those eyes, that dark brow, and yes, his hair was a little different, and he had grown a thin moustache, but it was him.

Who was he? What was he doing here, so close, as I put it in my head, to the scene of his crime?

He was dressed well, very well in fact, better than any other man in the place. He wore a dark grey wool suit with a waistcoat. Silver cufflinks gleamed when he reached to pour the girl another glass of wine. His shoes were expensive, spotlessly clean despite the weather.

I tried to judge his age, studied the small lines around his eyes, possibly a grey hair or two in the temples of his slick black hair, and guessed he might be ten years older than me, maybe less. His hands were somehow both elegant and strong; he appeared to be tall.

He was very different from the girl; where she was all movement, he was very still, and when he moved, he moved slowly and with great deliberation. He spoke deliberately too, with the occasional firm gesture of his hand, or just the flick of a fingertip, as if he did everything with great precision.

Then, without warning, he stood and walked right towards me. As before, I froze as he met my gaze, but then he looked right through me and walked on to the Gents, somewhere behind me.

I breathed again, realising he didn't know who I was, which was confirmed to me when he returned from the lavatory without so much as a backward glance.

He rejoined the girl and they renewed their conversation. Their waiter served them coffee and I noticed the extra deference he paid to the man, and the girl by extension, going so far as to give a slight bow as he left them.

My food arrived. I ate almost nothing, but I must have drunk a little too much wine, because when they stood, having finished their coffee, and got ready to leave, I decided to follow them.

I called my waiter over quickly and left far too many francs as a tip in order to avoid waiting for change.

They were at the door, the man almost a full foot taller than her, and I loitered for a moment putting on my coat, giving them a slight head start, and then pushed out through the heavy doors into a light drizzle.

I hesitated again, feeling light-headed, then, pulling the collar of my raincoat up around my ears, I walked as casually as I could after them, keeping to the opposite side of the street.

I must have looked pretty stupid; it was a wet Thursday afternoon, Saint-Germain was empty save for them, and me, but they were too occupied with each other to pay any attention to whoever might be behind them, and anyway, I didn't follow them for long.

In the very next street they stopped at a doorway, and the man pulled a key on a chain from his pocket. They disappeared inside, leaving me in the rain. I crossed the street to pass by the door, and saw there were several brass plaques fixed to the stone, and though I didn't want to linger I had time to read a couple of them. They were professional nameplates.

Cabinet de Chirurgie, read one. *Salon de Psychothérapie*, another.

I knew the kind of thing; a private address with one or more private physicians of various kinds and dubious qualities, no doubt helping rich women overcome an array of troubles during a course of expensive and frequently unexpectedly prolonged treatment.

London had the same addresses.

But which nameplate belonged to him?

I felt I'd paused too long at the door and I moved on, but not before one name caught my eye, just because it was more exotic than the rest. It read, quite simply: *Verovkin, Salon des sciences de l'Orient ancien.*

I walked on to the end of the street, and then suddenly felt idiotic. What was I doing? Did I hope to find something, or prove something? I don't know; I think I acted purely without thinking. My morning at the conference had been terrible, but that was far from my mind now, and I think I was acting upon impulse alone.

It was an impulse that had brought me back to Saint-Germain, a coincidence that had taken me to the very restaurant where he was eating, and an impulse that had led me to his door.

I stood under the porch of a doorway as the drizzle turned to rain, and just as I was wondering what to do next, the girl emerged from the door, halfway down the street.

She set off, away from me fortunately, and telling myself I might be able to discover more about him by approaching her, I followed.

7

It was beginning to get dark as I followed the girl through Saint-Germain, trying to move slowly enough not to catch up with her, for she was not a fast walker.

She walked through the wet streets, and soon I realised where she was heading: the station, where she made her way on to the platform for Paris. Seeing this, I ducked into the ticket office and bought a single to the Gare Saint-Lazare.

There were few other people taking the train that afternoon; I tried to stand near enough to a man around my age that it might be thought we were travelling together. I congratulated myself on this little strategy, and briefly felt like a detective in an American movie, a gumshoe trailing a suspect, a thought that amused me, though the fantasy quickly paled as I grew colder and colder on the platform.

Finally, the train she'd been waiting for arrived. I dallied a little as she chose a carriage and just as the whistle blew I climbed in after her, walking down the corridor past the compartment she'd chosen, taking the next one for myself.

The sun set as the train rumbled slowly down from Saint-Germain and twisted towards Saint-Lazare, a journey much longer than it should have been. At each stop I left my compartment and walked slowly past hers. Finding her always in the same position, reading a book. She was very different now that she was alone; she seemed rolled tight into herself, unaware of anyone or anything around her.

I didn't know if she would leave the train before the terminus, but she stayed on till the end. I allowed her ten seconds' head start, then hopped down from the carriage, and saw I'd made a mistake. The station was crowded and she had vanished in the sea of people in front of me. For some reason this loss worried me, and I felt desperate not to let her go. Then, there she was, bobbing through the passengers heading for the station gates.

I pushed past people in an effort to catch up, got within a few feet of her, and kept it that way.

She walked more briskly than before, out of the station and up towards the Place de Clichy, after which she turned into a street within sight of a big cemetery. I had been thinking she would be heading home, but instead she went into a bar and sat down at a table by herself.

I hesitated, but knew I could not do so for long. Either I had to follow her in as if it had been my destination too, or walk on by.

I went in.

I chose to sit on a stool at the bar, and ordered a cognac; by that point I genuinely needed a drink, not just from the damp cold.

'*Vous êtes en train de me suivre?*'

I didn't hear her approach me, but I turned and there she was, looking confrontational, if not exactly angry.

I was too embarrassed to say anything at first, then blurted out a denial.

'*Non, non, mademoiselle. Je*—'

That threw her somehow.

'You're English,' she said.

I stood up.

'Is my accent that bad?'

She nodded. 'And your dress sense.'

I felt a slight easing of the situation, as if she felt having an Englishman follow her was better than if I'd been French. Perhaps she was just interested, her curiosity aroused. I decided to press ahead with the slight chance I saw.

I held out my hand.

'Charles Jackson. Your English is very good.'

She looked at my hand for a moment, then took it and shook it lightly and briefly.

'Or do you mean, not bad for an American? Marian Fisher.'

It was my turn to be thrown.

'You're American?'

'Are all Brits this slow? So, are you going to answer my question, or not? Are you following me?'

I took a risk.

'Yes. Yes, I was. I apologise.'

She didn't seem to react.

'Let me buy you a drink. Let me explain? I assure you I mean you no harm.'

She looked at me then for the longest time, during which, I suppose, my character was being assessed.

'OK,' she said. 'Cognac. Would you like to join me?'

She nodded at the little table she'd taken, and a minute later I carried two glasses of cognac over to her.

That was how I met Marian.

8

I should say that I think I fell in love with Marian that first time we met. We became friends and she liked me, I believe, a lot; though I nearly ruined any chance at that first meeting by not being honest with her, something I learned she valued very highly.

We became friends, and for that I have to thank Hunter, my old family friend.

Hunter Wilson had been at school with my father, and they'd gone up to Cambridge at the same time. Hunter had eventually become a professor in the Faculty of English at Sidney Sussex, while my father had gone into property to make a fortune. Although he wasn't actually family, trips to visit Hunter when I was a boy had made him feel like an uncle to me, all the more so as I had no real uncles, my mother and father both being only children.

Through my time as an undergraduate, Hunter was a regular part of my life, and I think we both enjoyed the way that the gap in our ages didn't seem to exist, let alone to matter.

Hunter had brought me many things in life already, by that tender age. It was he who gave me a love of music, and of reading, and now, in an indirect way, he gave me Marian.

'So,' she said. 'Let's have some answers. Who are you? And why are you following me?'

I was at first thrown by such directness, though I came to like it very soon. It made it so much easier to know what your companion was thinking and feeling, instead of footling around with English correctness.

'My name is Charles Jackson,' I said, 'and I'm a haematologist.'

I hesitated for a moment because I was used to people asking 'A what?' whenever I told them what I did. Marian didn't, and waited for me to go on.

'I'm here for a conference. On leukaemia. It's something we're working on in Cambridge just now.'

'You live in Cambridge?'

I nodded. I thought I might be managing to steer her away from her other question, but I was wrong.

'And you're following me because . . . ?'

I did something foolish. I contradicted what I'd already admitted.

'No,' I said. 'I'm not following you. I—'

She stood immediately, making to leave.

'You were in Saint-Germain earlier. I saw you at lunch. And on the train. I thought you weren't going to lie to me, so I'll wish you good evening—'

'No!' I said, perhaps a touch too forcefully. I softened my voice. 'No, wait. I'm sorry! I only meant, I wasn't really following you, not to start with at least. It's your . . . friend.'

She stood, waiting, but did not sit down again.

'Anton?'

I now had a name; I had to assume it was my quarry's.

I nodded.

'Why?'

'I'll explain. Won't you sit down? Please?'

She sat. The bar was filling up steadily with locals, mostly single working men stopping for a glass of Pernod on the way home. Night had come on, and the rain was a drizzle once more, snaking softly down the window glass.

I said I would explain, and yet I never did. Not really. What could I tell her? Not the truth; that I thought he was a murderer at worst or some demented pervert at best. I saw how stupid that would look, and I didn't want to lose the chance to use this connection I'd found to the man. I might be able to find out more about him if I didn't give her cause to be cautious. Besides that, I realised I already didn't want this conversation with Marian to end quickly. I found I wanted to say something that would make her stay a while longer, and her cognac glass was already empty.

I downed mine and held it up.

'Another?'

She paused for a moment, then turned and waved at the barman, who wandered over and refilled both our glasses.

He smiled at her.

'*Ça va, Marian?*'

She smiled back.

'*Merci, Jean, assez bien. Et toi?*'

So I knew this was a local place of hers, but I marvelled at this strange American girl who drank in bars by herself often enough to know the barman by his first name, and call him *toi*. She intrigued me more and more. I sensed she was not someone who stuck to the rules, the rules of society, at least.

She turned back from Jean, who returned to his counter.

'So?'

'Oh, it's nothing really,' I said, as casually as I could. I'd decided that was my best strategy. 'I just thought I might have known him, a while ago. In the war, in fact, but I couldn't quite find his name, or where I met him, and . . . well, I didn't want to make a fool of myself.'

She nodded.

'So you thought you knew him?'

'Yes. In the war, I—'

'And you followed me instead.'

It was a statement, not a question. She stared at me, waiting for an explanation.

'Yes, I . . . I couldn't remember his name, or where I'd seen him. You see, I was stationed so many places, we met so many

people, in different units, in the French forces, the American . . .
And so then I wasn't sure, and as I say I didn't want to make a
fool of myself. You know us Brits . . .'

'I'm starting to,' she said.

She had a simple way of unnerving me but I tried to ignore it.

'Well, in fact by that point I began to think I had made a
mistake. That I didn't know him at all.'

There was some truth in that. Somehow, I could not equate
any companion of Marian's, such a personable, likeable young
woman, with that creature I'd seen in the bunker in 1944. So I
was beginning to doubt myself.

'So instead you decided to follow me?'

She didn't let things go easily, I'd learned that much already. I
tried to act sheepish. It wasn't hard.

'Well, you can hardly blame me for that . . .' I ventured.

'Oh, you liked the look of me. Why didn't you just come right
out and say it? The British thing again? It's a wonder you guys
ever get as far as having children.'

She laughed, but it wasn't malicious. A thought crossed her face.

'Do you have children?'

I shook my head.

'Married?'

'No, not even that.'

She drank her cognac, and I followed suit. It wasn't the best,
but it wasn't bad, and a hot rush shot through my veins. Of
course, I felt a little bolder.

'You're a long way from home,' I said.

'I am,' she said simply, as if that was all I needed to know, but
I wasn't going to let it drop.

'What are you doing here?'

She sighed, looking at the table for a while, then lifted her
head and smiled at me, half hidden behind a slant of red hair.

'Sorry,' she said, brightly. 'I guess you get to ask me some
questions too. I'm researching. For my doctorate.'

'At the Sorbonne? What's your subject?'

She sighed again, but this time with a playful smile on her face.

'French and Italian medieval literature.'

'Really?' I said, a spectacular reply.

'Really,' she mocked, her eyes wide. She laughed.

'Sorry, I didn't mean it to sound like that.'

'Like what?'

'Like . . . I don't know. Like I was surprised.'

'But you were, weren't you?'

'Everything about you is surprising,' I said. 'A single girl, all the way from America, studying for a PhD at the Sorbonne.'

'Who said I was single?'

That threw me but I tried not to let it show.

'Is Anton your . . . ?'

She smiled.

'No, he's not my boyfriend. He's my *patron*.'

She used the French pronunciation.

Now I did look surprised.

'Your patron?'

'Yes, how do you think I look after myself here?'

'I didn't think about it,' I said, truthfully. 'Rich parents, perhaps?'

'Yes, I have rich parents. Rich parents who wanted me to marry the first officer they could set me up with, and who did not permit me to come to Europe to study what I wanted to study.'

'So you came anyway?' I asked. 'I'm impressed.'

'The folks weren't. I'm the first Fisher not to behave herself. They cut me off.'

She looked me right in the eye, daring me to pity her. I didn't know how to respond, so changed the subject slightly.

'And Anton? How did you meet him? You don't just look up patrons in the phone book.'

Her wide mouth spread even wider with her smile and I decided I liked it. The noise and bustle of the café couldn't compete with Marian's presence, which had captivated me.

'No,' she said, nodding. 'I had some money of my own. Rich parents . . . And so I had about a year. I worked as well, in the evenings. In bars, like this one. My French was OK. It got better quickly. And then about six months ago, just when things were looking bad and I was thinking I might have to go back home cap in hand, I met Anton.'

I tried to sound as relaxed as I could.

'Who is he?'

Could she hear my heart thumping hard in my chest? I thought the whole bar should be able to hear. She didn't notice.

'Anton? He's a very rich man, who likes to support the arts, so he says. We met in a bar I was working in, not far from here, in the fall. He's a count, sort of . . .'

'A count,' I said. 'Sort of?'

'A margrave, actually. That's a kind of count, isn't it? I'm not sure.'

I shook my head.

'I don't know. I think so.'

'The Margrave Verovkin!' she declared, like a little girl, suddenly. 'My Estonian count!'

I wanted to ignore the possessive pronoun and picked up on something else.

'Estonian?'

'Yes. I had to look that up. It's part of the Soviet Union, or it is now, anyway, on the Baltic Sea. He said he lived in exile as a boy with his family, in Austria, I think, and then in Switzerland when the war broke out. After the war he moved to Saint-Germain and took over a ruined palace. A small one, on the edge of the park.'

'So . . . he didn't fight?'

The man I had seen had been in uniform, some kind of

uniform anyway. Maybe he'd been an officer. For a moment I was distracted, but Marian was still answering me.

'He's a count!' she said. 'Counts don't fight. Do they?'

She looked puzzled and very comical, and I laughed.

'No, I suppose not. And he's paying for you to finish your studies?'

'Yes, he is, and don't think I'm some charity case. I'm teaching him English in return. He's not bad but he gets simple things wrong still. That's where I've been today.'

'And what does he do? In that office?'

'My, you really were spying on him, weren't you?'

She looked at me fiercely and I was about to defend myself when she smiled, and I knew she was playing with me again.

'He's a doctor. Of an amazing kind. He's studied oriental philosophy and medicine for many years, and is a great thinker. He's adapting some of his findings and applying them to a new medical science he's creating.'

I said nothing. I had put this together with the words I'd seen on the brass plaque. *Verovkin, Sciences de l'Orient ancien.*

'You're a doctor, too?'

'Of sorts. A haematologist.'

'Yes, you said. So you won't buy any of this I'm telling you. But don't worry. It's your mind that's closed. That's all.'

I started to feel a little nettled by these remarks, especially because she was right. It sounded like a load of hokum to me.

Yet I didn't want her to go. I tried to think of something that might keep her interested in me.

But she was already standing.

'Listen,' she said. 'I'm tired. I better go. And you have to go back to your conference. And then home to Cambridge, I guess?'

'Cambridge awaits me,' I confirmed, solemnly. 'After the weekend. And you, you have to go back to your studies. To Saint Eulalia, I suppose?'

She stopped putting her coat on when I said that.

It was a lucky guess, something I'd plucked out of the air that I'd once heard Hunter talk about. I knew no more about it than the name and that it was the story of an early Christian martyr.

'Isn't that the sort of thing you're studying, the Sequence of Saint Eulalia? That kind of thing?'

'Oh, so you're not as uneducated as you make yourself out to be?'

'I've read a book or two,' I said, feigning modesty, apparently quite well. I decided to confess. 'Something my friend Hunter spoke to me about.'

She suddenly looked more interested.

'In Cambridge . . . ?'

'Yes, why?'

'What's your friend's surname?'

'Wilson. Why?'

'You know Hunter Wilson?' she said, in genuine surprise. '*The* Hunter Wilson?'

'I don't know about "*the*", but he's one of my best friends. Why?'

'Because he's the greatest living Dante scholar, that's why.'

That surprised me in turn, but I knew I had an advantage to play and I didn't want to let it show. I knew Hunter had a passing interest in Dante, had written a book or two on him, outside of his work in the Faculty of English. Almost as a hobby.

'Yes,' I said. 'He writes on Dante. Why do you ask?'

'Yes, well, I ask because my PhD is on a particular motif in Dante.'

She looked thoughtful for a while.

'Anyway, I have to do some reading before bed. I'd better go . . .'

She hesitated, and I stood, smiling.

'Listen, Charles. Maybe you'd like to meet for a drink over the weekend? Yes? It would be nice to chat some more.'

I smiled, and told her that would be lovely, and though I already knew she only wanted to see what she could find out about Hunter, I didn't care. We arranged to meet the following day, Friday, outside the museum in Saint-Germain. She had an English lesson to give first.

'You're more interesting than you look,' she said, her teasing nature returning, and I didn't mind at all, because I could see it was good-natured. 'Are all Englishmen like you?'

I laughed.

'Yes,' I said. 'More or less.'

She left, and I sat down again, watching her go.

'More,' I quietly said to myself, 'or less.'

I emptied my glass.

9

The weather on that Friday started no more kindly than the day before, and up at Saint-Germain the wind sliced through the town, and me.

As soon as the conference had finished for the day, I'd headed for Saint-Lazare again, ignoring the invitations to dinner from various delegates. I doubted their sincerity anyway, wondering if I would be the slaughtered calf at some dinner party to further my humiliation, and I didn't relish the thought of dragging my way through an evening of more of that. Lucien came up to me and tried to persuade me to join him, but I had decided not to be taken in. Just because he was smiling then didn't mean I was going to be welcomed back into the fold after my disastrous paper.

Instead, I went up to Saint-Germain early, well ahead of the time Marian and I were supposed to meet. There were things I wanted to look at.

It was already growing dark as I got to the park, a long, long piece of old estate land that stretched away from the chateau, along the ridge overlooking the river and the city, before spreading out 'inland' and becoming the Forêt de Saint-Germain.

I recognised the first stretch of manicured parkland as an old riding gallops, and set off that way. The only road was far behind me now, away to my left. From time to time a motor car trundled along it, sending long shadows of tree trunks raking across the park like dark fingers. Otherwise, I was alone.

My hunch was right: at the far end of the ride stood a small chateau. Dusk had come and gone and the lights of the building twinkled warmly, a gentle orange spilling from each one across the wet grass towards me, where I stood at the tall black railings. Even in the dusk I could see that though the chateau was old, it had been refurbished very recently, and I knew it was almost certainly the margrave's.

Knowing that in the growing darkness I could not be seen from the house, even if someone were to look straight at me, I stood and let my gaze wander over the small but grand building. I don't know what, if anything, I expected to see, but I considered the story Marian had told me.

Anton Verovkin.

An Estonian margrave, to boot. His life in exile presumably began as a small boy on the outbreak of the Revolution – maybe the troubles in 1905, maybe 1917. I knew nothing about Estonia, and that was a problem. There was nothing I could find fault with in her account of her patron's life, but that was perhaps simply because I was ignorant. I didn't even know if Verovkin was an Estonian name. It sounded more Russian to me, but almost the only thing I did know about Estonia and all the countries in that region was that they had been fought over and owned by many different rulers in their time, Swedish, German, Russian, and so the names of nobility might therefore descend from almost anywhere, and might have been altered half a dozen times as battles were fought and lost and allegiances changed.

I didn't even know what a margrave was. Was that higher or lower than a count? I had no idea, royalty not being something I had ever taken much interest in.

I stared at the chateau.

There was a little movement inside, and one or two curtains were drawn.

I shivered. There was nothing to be found here, and I turned back to the town, walking briskly to try and get warm again.

I had an hour before I was due to meet Marian, and as I came back past the Musée, I saw it was still open.

I headed inside, to warm up as much as anything else, and wandered around the museum, remembering my last visit there: the American soldiers amused by the Major and me, and little Monsieur Dronne.

Lost in reverie, I realised I'd wandered into a room of Palaeolithic artefacts. A museum guide stood a couple of feet away; a middle-aged woman looking tired and bored, flexing her ankles uncomfortably from time to time.

'*Monsieur Dronne travaille toujours ici?*' I asked, and had to ask again because my accent was so poor.

The guide looked vaguely puzzled.

'*Je ne vois pas qui c'est,*' she said.

So he'd retired, or maybe he had died. It was only seven years, but it was very possible.

An impulse entered me. I wanted to find those little figures I had seen with the Major that day.

'*Madame, s'il vous plaît, la Venus de Bastennes, où est-elle?*'

The guide looked at me strangely then. I had obviously said something that changed the way she thought about me, and she seemed even more puzzled than before.

'*Non, monsieur. Elle a été perdue. Pendant la guerre. Pendant la guerre, nous avons perdu beaucoup de choses. Trop de choses.*'

I opened my mouth to argue with her, trying to scrape the correct French together to tell her that I'd seen it, that I'd seen the Venus of Bastennes with my own eyes, and had held it, and other pieces, in my own hands, but then I thought that maybe it was best not to tell her. Who knew what had happened in the last days of the war?

Maybe old M Dronne had retired and now had a private collection of his own, kept in secret in his little apartment somewhere. Or maybe it had just been stolen one day.

I left, thanking her for her trouble, and as I ambled on through the museum, I realised something else; that what was wrong with the Venus was what was wrong with the margrave.

The end of the war, the end of any war, was the perfect place to hide, to change yourself, to become something and someone else. There are far too many other things to worry about, as an occupied land is restored and repaired, to question the validity of every story you're told. And after all, Paris in 1944, I knew, must have been full of many stories stranger than the one about the Estonian count suddenly rebuilding a tiny ruined chateau at the edge of a park.

He might well be the Margrave Verovkin, once of Estonia. Or then again he might be anyone else at all with a knowledge of Russian and a large amount of money.

10

I met Marian in the brasserie where I'd first seen her with Verovkin. I caught sight of her as she crossed from the other side of the square, by the steps of the grand church opposite the museum, and watched her come towards the restaurant, walking slowly through the steady rain despite the fact that she didn't have an umbrella.

She seemed tired and cold when she arrived, so I ordered cognac again, which she drank quickly.

She smiled.

'What are we eating?'

'You're the local, you tell me,' I answered and watched her as she perused the menu. She looked just as lovely as before; still, I thought, not beautiful, but her face was fascinating to me. As she read, drops of rainwater formed on the end of a ringlet by her forehead and, having become too swollen, dripped on to the table. She noticed and drew her fingertip through the water in slow circles. The drops of water clung to themselves, rising from the dark red lacquer of the varnished tabletop. It was, somehow, incredibly erotic, and I had to pull my eyes away for fear I might embarrass myself.

'Bouillabaisse,' she said firmly, and I ordered that and some red wine.

'How're the English lessons coming along?' I asked. It was the most innocuous way I could think of to get her to talk about Verovkin. I wondered again whether I should tell her my suspicions about him, warn her that she was in danger, but the time wasn't right. Even to me it sounded fantastical and I needed to wait until I knew for sure. If I let her talk she might tell me something that would confirm it for me, one way or another. So I let it lurk in the back of my mind, unsaid.

'Well,' she answered. 'Very well. It's good for me to learn how to teach. It will make my writing better too, I think.'

'Yes, that could be true,' I said. 'So, what's his first language? Russian? Estonian? German maybe, if he grew up in Austria and Switzerland?'

'He speaks lots of languages. I've never heard him speak any of them really, apart from French, of course, though occasionally he says something to me in Russian. Just little pleasantries I suppose. I don't know if he speaks Estonian, he left when he was a boy and the nobility spoke Russian or French, didn't they? His vowel sounds are hard to place. Maybe that's the German mixture in there . . . I'm no linguist.'

'Yet you speak excellent French.'

'So would you if you lived here for a couple of years.'

I conceded that point.

'How is your conference?' she asked politely.

I thought about it. It struck me that something had changed. I had seen this conference as an exciting opportunity, as the start of my career proper, as a chance to make my mark. Instead, it had been a failure for me personally, and even more disturbing than that, I realised I didn't even care. Something *had* changed. The coincidence of seeing Verovkin had pushed all thoughts of my work aside, and now I found myself thinking mostly about one person.

Maybe for the first time, I actually questioned whether being a doctor was what I wanted to do. Or whether it was just something I had found myself doing.

'It's good,' I said. 'There were some very interesting discussions today on the differential diagnoses between acute lymphatic and acute myelogenous forms of the disease.'

I stopped.

'Really?' she said. Her eyes were holding mine, shining. Her hair dripped again and she shook her head to flick off the water.

'Yes, really,' I said, laughing. Then, 'No, not really, not at all.'

Our wine arrived and our food not long after that and as we ate, Marian began to grow more lively again, more animated.

'Just the thing for a damp day outside.'

I agreed, and saw her come to life before me, waving her hands around as she spoke, talking about the places she'd seen in Europe, the places she wanted to go next.

'And Paris,' she said. 'There's still so much to see here. God, I love this town.'

'Where do you come from?' I asked. 'Where's home?'

She darkened slightly at the memory of her family.

'New York. The Hamptons.'

And though I knew little of American geography, I knew that meant that when she'd said her parents had money, they had serious money.

'It's my sister I miss the most,' she said, suddenly, bluntly.

'I'm sorry. I didn't mean to make you think of painful things.'

'That's OK. I'd fought too much with my parents to stay. It had to happen. They were never going to understand that the world has changed, that it's not the one they grew up in. Even Amagansett. I just miss my sister.'

'Do you write to her?'

Marian nodded.

'But I don't often hear back. It's possible they're hiding my letters.'

'They'd do that? I'm sorry.'

'Thank you,' she said, and suddenly looked so miserable I wanted to put my hand out to touch her. I didn't.

I poured her some more wine.

'So, what do you want to know about Hunter?' I asked, smiling.

She laughed. 'Was it that obvious?'

I nodded.

'So, you know, I've been thinking. Easter is coming and I have some time off. I've never been to England, well, apart from the stopover at London airport . . .'

She trailed off, for once seeming unconfident, and I decided to help her out.

'Would you like to meet Hunter?'

She almost exploded with joy.

'Oh yes, yes, I would, very much. Do you think he'd mind? Do you think you could arrange it?'

I held up my hand.

'It would be a pleasure. I'll call him as soon as I get back. And, you know, Hunter is also a very good host. We'll dine well.'

So it was settled that Marian would visit. I would find her a room in Caius if I could, or Hunter might be able to swing something at Sidney.

After a while, she began to grow tired again, though we spoke for a little while more, about her studies and the doctorate. It seemed Marian felt she'd get her PhD effortlessly if she just once met the great, as she called him, Hunter Wilson.

It amused me to see someone I thought of as just a good friend idolised in this way, and I asked Marian if she would be able to speak in his presence.

'You try and shut me up,' was her reply.

'Anyway,' I said, 'you haven't really told me anything about this research of yours. Just that it's something to do with Dante.'

'Blood,' she said.

'I beg your pardon.'

'It's about blood, how blood is used in *The Divine Comedy*. What it means.'

'What it means?'

She nodded, but I wasn't really listening to her reply, because two other thoughts had hurried into my mind.

The first was this: blood. Of course it would be blood.

And the second made clear something that had been nagging at me ever since Marian had sat down with me that evening. That she looked paler than the day I had met her. Much, much paler.

11

Almost as soon as I boarded my flight home, a few bald thoughts hit me, the main one being this: what on earth was I doing?

I'd flown to Paris with dreams of a glittering career in medicine; I'd come home feeling decidedly jaded about academia, and having invited the friend of a man I suspected to be a murderer to visit me, but the trouble was that I wasn't sure about anything. It was true that I had begun to doubt what I had seen in Saint-Germain, both on my present trip, and even in 1944. If that sounds odd, believe only that I have often pondered the nature of memory; the way in which we can distort our memories over time, so that as the years pass something is exaggerated, added to, subtracted from, or otherwise twisted to the point where it no longer has much basis in reality. Sometimes, perhaps, these changes are not significant, but at other times a whole memory can be effectively destroyed, reduced to nothing – or created from nothing.

And as time passes, the mind can play various tricks. I once had a memory, for example, of something that I was sure had happened in my childhood: of falling from an apple tree and my father catching me. Years later, my mother told me it was a dream I'd reported having at the age of six; that it had never actually happened. Yet I still remember telling it to my friend Donald when we were undergrads as though it were the historical truth, because somehow in my mind it had become just that.

I wondered if I had done something like that with my encounter in the hole in the ground, but then there had been the blood, the blood on the ground when I went back for a second look. I could still smell it if I closed my eyes, and sense its warmth.

Still, it was too late by then. Marian had my phone number and we had arranged a tentative date for her arrival. To meet the *great* Hunter Wilson.

Hunter himself guffawed at that when I phoned him the evening I got back, but said he'd be delighted to help if he could, and at the very least he had a recipe for pork belly that he was keen to try out on me.

Though it had been cold and wet in Paris, Cambridge was, as so often, a couple of degrees colder than anywhere else, and I shivered as I climbed into bed, wondering when spring would come.

I dreamt.

In my dream, it was dark, or at least, I was not supposed to be seeing anything much, at first mostly just hearing something. I was in a small warm space, I knew that, and I was somehow hovering near, very near, the naked body of a woman.

I was excited. So was she, for she was softly moaning, her head tilted back, hanging over something, her lips apart as small cries of pleasure escaped; gentle, high cries of pleasure.

She seemed dreamy, unaware, as if drugged, high on some opiate, hallucinating perhaps, or maybe just her senses dulled.

The dream continued, and now sight began to play a bigger role. Her cries increased in volume and in frequency, she began to arch her back, her mouth opened wider, and her eyes scrunched up tight. Her long hair flowed wildly back from her head, as if blown by the wind. Her moans began to come in small, heaving gasps; I could feel her breath on my face, and I pulled away from her a little more.

And then I saw the truth.

The moans were not cries of pleasure.

She was in pain, in torment. There was a knife sticking out of her stomach, from which blood flowed and flowed. She was softly crying in terrible pain, from the knife, and from the man who was forcing himself into her, again and again.

I woke, screaming, and knew that I'd been dreaming of the girl in the bunker being tormented by that terrible figure, that man, that beast. And that I was the beast.

12

Immediately upon waking, I knew what the dream meant. It meant that I felt guilty, that by doing nothing when the woman might still have had a chance, I had as good as killed her myself.

It took a long time for the horror of that dream to pass off, several days in fact, during which my mind was not really on my work and every night I feared I might have the same dream.

I went to see Hunter one evening, late.

I scurried from Caius over the cobbles of Green Street to Sidney, through the ever-present cold Cambridge wind, and, nodding at the night porter who knew me by sight if not by name, I wound my way up to Hunter's rooms and knocked on the heavy door.

It swung open. He stood within, and as he often did roared a greeting at me as hearty as any prodigal son could ever have had.

'Charles!'

'The great Hunter Wilson, I presume?'

He pretended to shut the door in my face.

'Not today, thank you. I gave a statement to the press yesterday . . .'

I barged my way in then and after some small chit-chat, we took chairs either side of his little fireplace, in which a small pile of coal was burning brightly.

'That's welcome. I haven't been warm in months, it seems. I should be used to this place by now.'

Hunter poured some whisky and handed the glass to me.

'I've been here a fair bit longer than you,' he said, raising his glass, 'and I'm still not used to it. You know they say the monks chose Cambridge for their new university because of the cold. They thought a warm climate was distracting to the concentration.'

'Is that true?'

'That's the story. It's still true, for want of a better word, isn't it?'

I wondered what he meant for a moment, but was used to such things from Hunter. I knew what he was saying; that it didn't really matter if the story was just a story, because it still had the truth in it.

It reminded me of what I'd come to talk about, and I must have suddenly looked serious, because Hunter sat deeper in his chair. He was a big man, not fat, just tall and broad, and his age had done nothing to change that. He had lots of hair still, all white now, though when I'd met him as a boy it had been a dark grey-brown. He fought regularly to try and stop it looking crazy, when what it actually needed was a trip to the barber in All Saints Passage.

He considered me for a while, judging my mood.

'Ah,' he said. 'Ah! Go on then, tell me.'

I swilled the whisky round in my glass.

'There's something I never told you,' I began.

'I knew it!' he cried. 'You're queer! No? A communist? No? Wait, I have it, you're actually a woman! Yes?'

'Hunter, stop it,' I said, though I smiled. I never knew how someone his age had managed to stay so boyish. It was what I liked best about him, but I wanted him to listen to me seriously.

Bless him, he did.

'In the war . . .' I tried again to focus my thoughts. 'I didn't tell you much about the war, but not because I was trying to hide anything from you, or anyone. It just seemed better when it was over to move forward and get on with other things.'

He nodded.

'But there is one thing I was hiding. Not just from you, but from everyone. Something I saw in Paris.'

Hunter, though he frequently played the fool, was the smartest man I had ever known. He was already making connections.

'You never told me you were in Paris in the war. I thought the French and the Yanks liberated it . . .'

'They did. Our CO took us for some leave, just after the liberation.'

I could see he was amazed by this. He raised a finger.

'And you have just returned from Paris and now your mood is bad and you've come here to drink whisky late at night. What happened?'

That was what I'd come for, the Hunter who cared, who made it easy to talk, to discuss things.

'I saw something. Someone, rather. It was . . . a coincidence, I suppose. That's all. I was in a restaurant in Saint-Germain—'

'Lovely. I know it well.'

'No, not Saint-Germain-des-Prés. Saint-Germain-en-Laye. To the west of Paris itself. It's a suburb on a bluff that looks over the city. I went there one day. I'd had a really bad morning at the conference. I wanted to clear my head, I wanted . . .'

'You wanted to go back somewhere, I think.'

I nodded.

'Yes. I wanted to go back, I don't really know why, to the place where I saw something in 1944.'

'Which was?'

So I told him the whole story, of the Major and his Venus, of M Dronne, of the bunker and what I'd seen there. And then I told him about my recent trip, and about the margrave and about Marian. When I'd finished, I was very tired and it was very late. I'd drunk too much whisky and I felt on the verge of tears, but I didn't want to cry, and especially not in front of Hunter.

He listened without comment as I spoke, and nodded slowly when I'd finished. It was a relief just that he seemed to take me seriously, that he believed what I was saying, because I wasn't sure I believed it myself.

For once, he didn't have much to say.

'I was lucky not to have to fight,' he said, quietly. 'And you, you tried to help people, but you still saw more than anyone's fair share of suffering, I suppose. Don't punish yourself for that.'

I didn't answer, but smiled to show I was grateful to him.

'You know, Charles, I've known you since you were a boy. A very bright boy, but a dreaming boy too. And now you are on the verge of being a brilliant doctor. But I wonder whether you are still too much of a fantasist to be a very good scientist.'

'Maybe the best scientists are the biggest dreamers,' I argued. 'The ones able to think of something no one else has thought of before.'

He inclined his head and I knew I'd won that point, but it was his subtext that bothered me more. It meant that perhaps he didn't believe me after all.

He stood and put a hand on my shoulder.

I stood too. It was time to go.

'And Marian?'

'Marian sounds delightful from everything you've said, and I suspect that even if this man were to turn out to be some kind of criminal, she is nothing to do with it at all.'

'What do you mean? "*If*"? You don't believe me?'

He held up his hand, shaking his head, and was clearly searching for the right words.

'No, that's not what I'm saying. All I'm saying is try not to worry. Get some sleep. Go home now.'

I did. And I did feel better, because an hour with Hunter was like a confessional in some ways, and a holiday in others; you always came away feeling better, about both yourself and the world.

And I did feel better, because for the rest of that night, and half the following day, I was able to believe the lie I'd told Hunter and so wanted to believe myself: that the girl was dead when I found her.

13

What is blood?

Around the time of my visit to Paris, and Marian's trip to England, there were many excellent men and women trying to answer that question, trying to understand its composition and its nature in order to better fight the diseases and disorders of the blood. For a while I was one of them, and yet I had an unspoken question at the back of my mind all that time, one that even now I can only formulate like this: why is blood?

Why is it like it is, and what does it mean to us?

In our modern world, I knew, bright colours are not so rare, but that is because we have synthetic dyes and pigments. Long ago, in those caves in France where the Venus of Bastennes and other figures like her were carved, bright colours must have seemed magical; most of the world was soft browns and greens. The strongest colours would have been the autumn leaves, the blue of the sky on a summer's day, and even these would seem to have no permanence, for the leaf that is golden one day is on the ground the next, the sky that is blue one day can be grey the day after. There would be some brightly coloured berries and fruit, I suppose, too, but the one splash of colour that could always be relied on to amaze, to impress, to shock, maybe even to delight, would be blood. In every culture I knew of, red symbolised danger, presumably because of the link with blood; we are programmed to react to it, because that might save our life.

And though more blood was perhaps spilled in those distant days, it must still have been a rare moment, and when blood was seen it would have been such a contrast to the everyday world, such an extraordinary, magical, mysterious thing. And as someone bled to death and their life bled away with that blood, it must have been obvious that blood is the source of life, that without it we are nothing; its colour must have seemed chosen by the gods, as if to say, 'Look! This! This is important, for this is what you are!'

I learned at medical school how the colour of blood changes with its state of oxygenation, from dark, almost purplish, through to the brightest lurid red, but whatever its precise colour, our earlier selves must have formed a deep relationship with it. Relationship, that's the only word I can use, and still, after all my time thinking about it, I cannot find an answer to the question of blood.

14

At some point after my return from Paris and before Marian's arrival, I was called in to see the Head of Department, Dr Downey. My boss.

Although he didn't refer to it once, it was obvious that I had not impressed in Paris. Somehow word had reached him of my performance at the rostrum, and I wondered if he also knew I'd skipped a couple of sessions. All this sat unspoken on his desk between us, and I was unable to defend myself, for the accusations were not said aloud, and they were all the more damaging because of that.

Downey was a forbidding figure, old school, of uncertain age, probably in his late sixties, though I speculated idly about whether he'd been a classmate of Darwin, he was so antediluvian. He spoke to me in the kind of way that made you think he added *Listen here, young man* to everything he said to you, though it was done just with his eyebrows and his forefinger.

He sat before me in the gloom of his office and after some ambling around, saying nothing really, he got to the point.

'You're going to have to make up your mind what you want in life,' he said. I sat up a bit straighter. This sounded like plain speaking – something I had rarely heard from Downey. 'Do you want to be a consultant for the rest of your life, or do you want to try something different? God knows you've got there at a frighteningly young age; that's going to mean a long career in the hospital, practising your art. The board has approved the plans to move to a new site. In about ten years from now there'll be a grand new hospital to work in on the edge of town. We intend it to be the finest in the country. So you can work there, putting into practice everything you've learned, or you could do something else: you could be the one to move on our sum of learning, the one who discovers the laws that others will learn.'

He was, of course, selling me only one choice, and I knew what he expected.

'Is there an area that interests you? Something you'd like to look into? Think about it. I'll give you a small team of researchers. Just bring me something we can be proud of.'

I stumbled out of Downey's office feeling as though I'd been told to invent gravity, but by that evening, over drinks with Donald, I realised it wasn't so bad. Off the top of my head there were at least four interesting areas in haematology at the time, and I just needed to pick one that would interest me, and that I had a chance of cracking.

I think it was that evening Donald told me he was moving to London, to set up in private practice. He had got married earlier that year, and although I liked his wife, she certainly had expensive tastes.

'She wants children,' he said, matter-of-factly, 'and I need more money.'

I was sad that Donald was leaving, but just then it didn't bother me too much, because I had something I was anticipating, greatly.

Marian.

When she arrived I went to meet her at the station. She'd wired her arrival time, and the train was punctual.

When I saw her step down from the carriage, it felt like a small physical blow, as if something had knocked into me from behind. I think I actually caught a breath, then told myself to act as coolly as I could and went to meet her, my arms frozen to my sides, though I wanted to put them around her. And by the time we walked into town, me carrying her bag, and we got to St

Andrew's Street, I knew I was in love with her, and I felt sick, because I didn't get the slightest impression that she was in love with me in return.

I felt swept along, out of my depth in waters I knew little about. My experience of women was limited; I had been to a boys' school, so my first encounters with any girls of my own age apart from my sister had to wait until I came up to Cambridge. In the war, in France, there were those times when the men queued underneath a red lamp on some filthy street corner, but I chose not to accompany them. One more thing that set me apart from them. I pretended it was because I was wary of disease.

So the mere presence of Marian was almost too powerful for me. The click of her heels on the cobbles, the smell of her hair as it brushed near me, the warmth of her hand on my arm.

Marian talked away happily, and I found it was all I could do to answer her. She was fascinated by Cambridge, and had a hundred questions for me about this building and that church, and I quickly remembered what a remarkable place it rightly was to any visitor, let alone a young American on her first trip to England.

'I found you a guest room at Caius,' I told her. 'It's not far.'

'That's your college?' she asked.

'Yes, but I don't live in the Old Courts any more, I have a flat now, by the cricket ground. Here we are. Look, just wait here while I get your key.'

We ducked into the gates of Gonville Court, and I set Marian with her case just inside while I went into the porter's lodge. My heart sank. The porter was one I knew well, a curmudgeon from my own time as an undergraduate.

'I've booked a room for a visiting academic from Paris,' I said. 'Fisher.'

I waited while the porter made the slowest job possible of looking up something in a large book, all without saying a word to me. He glanced up again, and was just about to turn and start a presumably equally laborious hunt for a key when he saw something over my shoulder.

Marian had drifted into view, her case in her hand.

'Monsieur Fisher is a lady?' the porter asked, sarcastically.

I groaned.

It took half an hour of wrangling before they agreed to let Marian use a guest room in the all-male college, even just for one night, until other arrangements could be made.

'I'm so sorry about that,' I said, as I found our way to the third floor and unlocked the room.

Marian didn't seem to mind; on the contrary, she found it amusing.

'What century is this, anyway?' she laughed.

'You'd be surprised. I'll have a word with the Master. He likes me because I was a good student. Did them proud, you know?'

'Were you a good student, Charles?' asked Marian, her eyes twinkling, teasing me.

She walked round the large but simple room overlooking the courtyard. It was quiet, most students were down for Easter, and as dusk fell over the rooftops, it suddenly seemed rather spooky.

'Will you be all right here?' I asked, quite seriously.

'As long as you keep that dinosaur off my back,' she said, laughing again. 'Well? Were you a good student?'

'One of the best,' I said, quietly. 'Or so they said. And this is a college with strong links to medicine. That goes all the way back to John Caius himself, though he would admit no student who was blind, dumb, deformed, maimed, or otherwise diseased. Or Welsh.'

Marian looked at me sharply.

'Is that English humour?'

'Sadly not, it's true. Or so they say.'

'So they say. So they say. I can see I still have a lot to learn about Englishmen.'

Suddenly I was powerfully aware that we were alone in her room. The door stood open still, her bag just inside, and yet there was a strong sense of seclusion, of intimacy. She stood by the large window, almost in silhouette; beyond her, the roofs of the college were cut out against a light grey sky. Everything was quiet. I noticed her waist, so slim, and the curve of her hipbone through her dress, and for a fraction of a second, I pictured myself on my knees before her, kissing her stomach.

The moment seemed to stretch on, but was broken as someone clattered past in the corridor heading for the stairwell. The footsteps receded.

'Can we eat?' Marian asked.

'Yes,' I said.

It was the closest we ever were.

15

The following evening, I took her to meet Hunter and of course they got along famously.

They spoke about Dante Alighieri, and his work. They spoke about things I had little or no understanding of, and as they spoke on, it was as if I grew invisible, so forgotten had I become.

We sat in Hunter's rooms in Sidney, and as he poured generous libations for his guests, he peppered Marian with questions.

'Charles tells me you want to write on blood in Dante. What on earth possesses you to do such a thing?'

The question seemed impertinent, challenging, but Marian was not intimidated, or if she was, she did not show it. While she gave a long and reasoned and somewhat passionate explanation of what it was she wanted to do, Hunter sat and listened. Even I, knowing him so well, could not tell for a moment what he was thinking. When she was finished, Marian leaned back slightly in her chair and at last I saw a trace of nerves. So, she did care what the great Hunter Wilson thought, and what he thought was this:

'Brilliant,' he said. 'Quite a brilliant notion. To show that for Dante, blood is not simply a metaphor, but that it is, at times, *literally* the seat of love, or of fear, or of bravery. Wonderful. As far as I know, there is no one else in the world working in this way.'

He looked up and sideways slightly, something he always did when quoting from memory.

> '*Vedi la bestia per cu' io mi volsi*
> *aiutami da lei, famoso saggio,*
> *ch' ella mi fa tremar le vene e i polsi.*'

'From the *Inferno*. "She makes me tremble, and the veins in my wrists." So beautiful,' Marian said, nodding enthusiastically. 'Or consider when he sees Beatrice, miraculously alive, the first time after her death. *"Men che dramma, di sangue m'è rimaso che non tremi: conosco i segni de l'antica fiamma."*'

Even I could understand the thrust of that without Hunter saying, '"What drama! There remains blood in me that does not tremble. I recognise the signs of an ancient flame."'

And if I understood it, I understood it because it made clear what I'd felt at the station when I saw Marian again: a stillness amongst the trembling of my blood. And that, I thought, is why we turn to the great poets of our world, because they simply say these things better than we do.

Their conversation deepened, and I faded more and more into the background of the room, but I was not jealous, because Hunter in full flow was always a thing to behold, and it gave me more of a chance to look at Marian without fear of censure.

They spoke in greater detail about what it was that Marian wanted to do, which, as far as I understood, was to link Dante's work to his understanding of Aristotelian medicine, to show how his use of blood went far beyond the metaphorical.

'He has this concept, *sangue perfetto*, and I believe it lies at the heart of everything he does, that it links everything from the creation of a human being to their development and nourishment, to the relationship between body and soul, to their relationship with God.'

Hunter agreed.

'That's true. *Sangue perfetto*. According to Aristotle, this perfect blood was the source of all the body's fluids, from mother's milk to semen. They are just distillations – mere purifications – of that blood. He even supposed there was a vein of love, the vena amoris, that ran all the way from the heart to the fourth finger . . .'

'Which is why we wear a wedding band there even today,' Marian said.

If I'd thought before that she was not beautiful, I was wrong. That evening, as she lost herself in what was for her a thrilling conversation with Hunter, she had a beauty deeper than some surface show. She loved what she spoke about, and she loved that Hunter knew as much as she did, more in fact. It gave her a kind of honesty, an openness. A kind of innocence, as she forgot to pretend to be the cool American girl who had been tough enough to leave home and lose her parents in doing so, and instead became a young soul marvelling at what the world had put in front of her. And that was beautiful.

'But,' said Hunter, after a while, 'you still haven't answered my first question.'

Marian didn't reply. She seemed as mystified as I was; wasn't that what they'd been talking about for hours?

'My original question was why? *Why* do you want to study this thing about blood? Not *what* do you want to study . . .'

Still Marian didn't reply, and I could see that the question had hit home.

'I . . . I have no idea,' she said in such a serious way that a moment later all three of us burst out laughing. 'Really, no one's ever asked me that. Not even me.'

'Is it something you've always been interested in?' I suggested.

'Yes,' she said. 'No. Not really. I just enjoyed reading Dante and . . .'

'And you came up with an idea that no one else ever has,' Hunter proffered. That was one of the things I admired in him: he was generous, intellectually generous, in a way that so few people are, and even fewer academics.

The evening wore on and the conversation drifted away from Dante and to other things. I told Hunter about the veiled ultimatum Downey had given me.

'What do you think?' he asked. 'Is there anything which grabs you?'

'One or two things. There've been big advances in the use of plasma since the war. Improving its synthesis would be something. Or I might do something with clotting abnormalities. There's still a cure to be found.'

'For haemophilia? It always seemed such a stupid word. Literally: the love of blood.'

'You're not alone in that view,' I told him. 'It used to have many names, of course, before it was understood. Our modern name comes from haemorrhaphilia, which makes more sense.'

Marian leaned forward.

'The love of bleeding . . . ?' she queried.

'The tendency to bleed would be more accurate, but yes, that would be a direct translation.'

'Well, you'd better do something quickly,' Hunter said. 'Or you'll end up a fusty old academic like me. And no one wants that.'

We both protested and I could see that Marian and Hunter liked each other a lot. It made me happy to see that he thought she was as wonderful as I did.

'Come on,' she said, 'you seem to have a pretty nice set-up here.'

'College life? Yes, it's one way of being. But what have I seen of the world? I spent two months in France at the end of the war in 1918, and apart from that every summer I sit on a balcony in Florence watching the young people fall in love. I've no children, I've never married. Those are the things one ought to do with one's life, aren't they?'

He wasn't bleating; he just had a way of being very matter of fact about his private life. He didn't mention it often, but when he did, it was as if he was discussing a problematic passage in a text; fascinating yet ultimately of no great worth.

Maybe he was just one of those people who put all their emotional energy into their work, and it made me wonder where I was heading in my own career, what that future would hold. It did not then occur to me to extend that thought to my life in general.

Marian was having none of Hunter's self-deprecation, though, and began to tell him just how much she wanted a life like his, of study and of books, but though he did it politely, I saw him move the direction of the conversation away from himself and back to her.

'And what of your home?' he said. 'The United States? Don't you want to return? See your family?'

Hunter's openness must have infected all of us that night, because Marian didn't seem to mind telling him what she'd told me about the way she'd had to leave, the rift with her parents.

'And you have siblings? Are there any more like you at home?' he said, winking.

'Hunter!' I said, pretending to chastise him.

He wagged a finger at me.

'Come on, old boy, it's a fair question.'

Marian laughed.

'I have a sister. I miss her, but we write from time to time.'

'A younger sister, eh?' said Hunter, continuing his attempt to be comically lecherous.

'She's older actually,' Marian said, and suddenly stopped. Her face changed, and then she said, 'And I had a younger brother, too. But he died when we were very young.'

'Oh, I'm sorry,' I said. And without thinking it might not be the best thing to say, I added, 'How did it happen?'

'It was an accident. He found a knife in the kitchen and cut himself. Badly. Well, that goes without saying, doesn't it? My mother was upstairs, sleeping. Two young children in the house, you know . . . My sister was at school. I found him screaming on the kitchen floor in a pool of his own blood. He died on the way to the hospital.'

She stopped, looking down, unable to go on, unable to meet our gaze.

We were both speechless, because there weren't the words, any words at all, that would be worth uttering. She looked up, brightly.

'I wonder, Hunter, if I could use your bathroom?'

'What? Yes, oh yes, down the hall there. On the right.'

Marian stood, and we watched in silence as she slipped out of the room, gently.

We turned to look at each other, and we knew that the same thought was on both our minds. I was the one who said it.

'And she says she doesn't know why she wants to write about blood.'

16

I only saw Marian twice more after she left Cambridge that Easter.

I couldn't bear to let her go without arranging to see her again, and yet I couldn't bring myself to say aloud what I was feeling. Of course, I thought about it. But the more time I spent in her company, and the more I liked her, the more unreal my suspicions about Verovkin seemed. Marian, Hunter and I ate together every night, but the time I loved the best was the short walk back to her room when we were alone. These walks were mostly silent, which seemed strange after the flowing conversations of Hunter's rooms, and yet I cherished those brief moments more than anything.

The day I set her on the London train, and handed her her bag, I hesitated. Once again I thought about warning her, and once again I failed to do so. I'm not sure why. By then I thought I'd established enough trust for her not to just laugh in my face, or refuse ever to talk to me again. I think it was because of Marian herself. In Cambridge, she seemed so well. We'd eaten good meals every night, thanks to Hunter and the dining hall at Sidney. We'd drunk well too, and she could handle it. She was full of life and had been working with Verovkin for months. If he were a monster of some kind, he would have already taken his chance with her. So I dismissed my fears.

We made arrangements that I would come to Paris when I could, which she seemed happy enough about, if not as excited as I wished she might be.

As things fell out, it was the beginning of the summer before I was able to travel again, this time by train and ferry since I was paying for my own tickets.

The heat had returned to Paris, the heat I'd found on my very first visit, which had been so notably absent that spring. But if heat had returned to the city, what little heat there had been between Marian and me seemed to have vanished.

We had been writing intermittently, and her letters were friendly, talking about her work, both at the Sorbonne and, from time to time, as a waitress. She never spoke about the pupil to whom she gave English lessons, and I never asked. Instead she asked after Hunter, asked me how I was, said she was looking forward to seeing me, but I saw no sign of that when we were reunited.

One sunny Friday afternoon in June we met near Saint-Lazare.

In retrospect, she didn't seem herself, but at the time, I was too wrapped up in my own selfish feelings to notice anything much beyond the fact that she didn't appear to want to spend too long with me any more.

I tried to take her to the theatre or the cinema that evening, but she said she had to go home early. She was tired, and that I couldn't argue with. You could see it on her face, a great tiredness, as if everything was taking twice as much energy from her as usual. She was paler than before, by which I mean, paler than the last time I'd seen her in Paris, because in Cambridge she had seemed full of life, and in good health.

So she went home, but I managed to get her to meet me in Saint-Germain the next morning.

The town was humming that morning with a market in the square; the trees in the park were in full and fresh leaf; the sun was strong; and everyone seemed in good spirits – everyone but Marian, who barely smiled when we met, who talked little, and who cut short our meeting, saying she had to go earlier than expected to her English lesson. It was the only time that she mentioned him, and even then she didn't name him. It was merely by implication that he stood between us.

She was about to leave, and then I did something stupid.

I couldn't bear the way she was, and in a moment of rashness I decided that the only thing was to tell her how I felt, to show her. I put my hand on hers, and she turned to me.

'What is it, Charles?'

By way of answer I leaned in towards her quickly and clumsily tried to kiss her. She lurched away and my lips just brushed her cheek. She looked at me, glaring.

'I have to go,' she muttered, and turned.

'Wait!' I cried out, loud enough to stop her. She turned back, her face impatient, perhaps even angry.

'What?'

'It's him,' I said. And then I said the rest, without thinking, because my desperation had made me careless. 'He's dangerous. You're in danger, Marian. I'm sure of it.'

I wasn't sure of that at all, but I needed to convince her, and of course I needed to convince myself too.

'Dangerous? Who's dangerous?'

'Verovkin.'

'Anton?' She laughed. 'What on earth are you talking about?'

'I saw him. It was years ago. He killed someone, I think.'

'You *think*?'

The outrage outweighed the impatience now.

'You think? What are you talking about, Charles? No, wait, I'll tell you – you're talking nonsense. That's what. I have to go.'

'Marian, please. Wait, please, I—'

'No,' she said, 'just leave me alone.' Then she turned on her heel, and walked quickly away. I sat as if she'd slapped me across the face, doing nothing but watching her go. Watching her hurrying back to him.

As she reached the edge of the square, I stood up, way too late . . . way too late. I took a step, but she was gone, and I had let her go.

On Sunday I returned home, a long and tiring journey, during which I brooded, feeling forlorn, feeling that I'd lost something, though I wasn't sure what. Marian had not once spoken of any feelings for me, and I realised what a fool I'd been.

Nevertheless, I was worried about her, and when I got back to Cambridge, and my own selfish pain lessened, I saw that perhaps she was genuinely unwell, or something worse, something that I couldn't even put into words.

I spoke to Hunter about it one evening, and he could put it into words.

'My boy, are you trying to tell me you think this man is a damn vampire? You really are too much of a dreamer!'

'No,' I said, defending myself, 'I'm not suggesting that at all. I . . . I don't know what I'm suggesting. Just that she seems pale and ill and she seemed worse in Paris than she was when she was here.'

I could see Hunter was being patient with me.

'Charles, you're the scientist here. You know better than me not to judge by coincidence. You've only met her a handful of times, perhaps she is generally unwell.'

I nodded. He was right. I was thinking of fantastical things, and I knew that she'd been energised by her trip to Cambridge simply because of Hunter, her idol, and maybe some more regular meals than she was used to.

I had to wait a little while, but I had the proof of what Hunter said later that summer.

I'd written a couple of times to Marian, and she'd written back.

In my first letter I'd tried to apologise, but I was careful not to make any mention of Verovkin. I merely said I was sorry for being so forward and so clumsy and when she replied Marian ignored everything I'd said and enquired after my health, and Hunter's, as if she was an aged aunt. I got a couple more letters from her like that, both equally dry and dead. It was almost more frustrating than if she had been silent.

Then that was what she became. I wrote, and wrote again, and as the weeks went by and I still heard nothing, I grew worried, and then desperate. Finally, in August, I cleared a week-end, and made the rail trip to Paris once more, booking the cheapest hotel I could find near Saint-Lazare.

As soon as I'd dumped my bag in my tiny, dirty room, I set off towards her flat, somewhere I'd never been, having only ever written to her there. Her address was an apartment on the top floor in Rue Ballu, grand on the outside, but I guessed run-down on the inside. There was no answer to the bell, and deciding to return later, I sloped back to my hotel.

On the way, another possibility occurred to me, and I headed to the bar in Rue de Parme. I recognised the barman at once, and dug to remember what Marian had called him. I failed, but I could see he recognised me, and I took my chance.

'*Bonjour, monsieur,*' I said. '*Un pastis, s'il vous plaît.*'

I hated the stuff but I wanted to seem as much of a local as possible, not some clumsy Englishman on holiday. He poured me a measure and left me a jug of water, and I diluted it slowly, watching the clear liquid turn milky. He served one or two other people, and then, as he wiped the countertop, I summoned the courage to ask him where Marian might be.

I tried to sound as casual as I could, and maybe it was just my bad French, or maybe it was the question itself that made him look strangely at me.

'You are a friend of Marian's, yes?' he said, in English. It was half a statement, half a question that sought reassurance that I was bona fide.

I nodded.

'Yes, but we've been . . . out of touch.'

He considered that for a moment.

'Then you don't know that she went back to America. Because of her heart.'

I was too surprised to say anything at first; in fact, I was unsure what surprised me more, that Marian was gone, or that there was something wrong with her.

'Her heart?' I asked.

At first, foolish as I am, I thought the barman used the word in its metaphorical, romantic sense.

'Her heart?' I repeated.

'You didn't know about her heart?' he said, and he said it in such a way that I knew he was telling me I couldn't have been much of a friend.

'Marian has a heart condition. She has gone back to America to have an operation, which her parents will pay for.'

I finished my drink quickly and staggered back to my hotel. I didn't go out that night, but lay on the filthy bed, trying to take it all in.

She had never told me about the problem with her heart, and why should she have done? Maybe she felt weak about it, or maybe it depressed her too much to think about. Whatever, it must have hurt her pride deeply to have to return to her parents in order for them to pay for the surgery. I could see the deal they would have struck: give up that silly life in Paris, and come home. And we'll look after you.

I cut short my trip. I thought about trying to spy on Verovkin in Saint-Germain, but something stopped me, and that something was a deep misery over Marian that had risen out of the ground and threatened to swallow me. Instead, I returned home the very next day, and wrote a long letter to her. I knew her parents lived in Amagansett, and when I asked an American colleague of mine he told me it was a small place. Her family was wealthy and would surely be known; a letter addressed to her there would almost certainly reach her.

Amongst many other things, I apologised once more for my behaviour, for being foolish about Verovkin. I asked if she was well, and what her future held for her.

I sent the letter, and got no reply.

17

I wrote again, a few weeks later.

Still no reply, and I presumed that along with her life in Paris, she had been ordered to cut everything else from that time too. That was what I told myself to start with, but as the weeks turned into months, I suspected there was another reason. I had let her down, forcing myself on her; she was clearly not interested in me in any other way than as a friend, someone she'd run into once, who had got her a meeting with her hero.

I didn't like that explanation much, for it belittled what I felt about her, and to be honest, made me feel inadequate and unlovable. I had been nothing to her, when I wanted to be everything.

The only other explanation was that the letters were not getting to her, either because of the US postal service, or her parents' intervention.

The months started to mount up on each other, and I forgot about Marian, in time.

It became a foolish episode in my youth. I was approaching my mid-thirties, and began to work on haemophilia as I'd promised Downey I would. I decided to put it behind me. Not just Marian, but everything. Paris. The war. Everything.

Ten years passed.

In the first of those, I met a woman called Sarah, in the second, we got married, and in the third, Sarah died.

I mourned for a while, and before the age of forty I found myself to be a widower, and childless.

That's how things would have stayed. The years passed. My forty-second birthday came and went. And I would have grown older still, in ignorant bliss, and worked hard, and become respected in my field at last, but for the fact that one fine spring day, I received a letter.

As I sat at home opening my post over a late breakfast, I saw among the other envelopes an airmail one, from America. It was thin, so you could almost see through it, and as I held it my hands began to tremble, and the envelope with it. It had been sent to my old address, and forwarded on to me by the new tenants there.

I looked at the postmark, the stamps; they seemed so utterly foreign, so far away, so remote.

I slit the flap with a buttery knife and three folds of paper dropped out in front of me, and I read.

Dear Mr Jackson,

I don't know if you'll have moved by this time, or indeed whether you will get this letter, but I hope you do, because you sound like a kind gentleman.

You wrote to my daughter, Marian, ten years ago, and from your letters, I can see that you two were friends during her time in Paris. You will have to forgive that when we received those letters, my husband and I were not in a position to answer them, nor, I must add, did we understand what you had written.

My husband died a few months ago, and since then I have started to go through old papers and so on, and last week I found your three letters to Marian. We had only opened the first one; the second and third we put in a box with the first and then forgot about them.

Mr Jackson, I will be honest and say that my husband, though he loved Marian very much, did not show that love very well. He could be a difficult man and he took it badly when she left us to go to Paris. Many things in this house were run the way he wanted them to be run, but I mourned for my daughter, for her leaving us with such bad blood. My husband never accepted that she wanted to live her own life, her own way, and I was too scared to do anything differently, so I obeyed my husband. He is gone now, and I am old, and I start to see things differently, and I realise the mistakes I've made.

But that is not why I'm writing to you. As I say, you seem like an honest fellow, and I want to set you straight upon a couple of things, so that you do not have to go through life wondering about them.

The first is this: it seems you feel you made a fool of yourself in Paris in some way. On that note, let me tell you that Ann, Marian's sister, told me she once had a letter from Paris in which Marian spoke of meeting a lovely Englishman, that she was going to Cambridge to see him, that she wondered if she might fall in love with him.

The second is, I'm afraid, harder to tell. You seem to think there was something wrong with Marian, her heart, I think? That she came back to the States to have an operation here? Both of these things are not true. She was quite well, there was nothing wrong with her heart, nor, for that matter, was there anything seriously wrong with her, ever. And she never came back home. We received word that she died in Paris in 1951. She was buried in a cemetery there. I do miss her so very much. So now there's just Ann and me, and she's a married mom and always busy, though happily she lives nearby and I see her every week.

My! You don't want to know my life story; I just wanted you to have the truth so you never had to think, what if . . . ?

Thank you for caring for my daughter. Even if it was for a short time, it makes me glad to know somebody loved her.

Sincerely yours,
Margery Fisher, Mrs.

The letter dropped from my hands on to the table, and I realised I could not read any more, could not see, because my eyes had filled with tears.

TWO

Avignon

August, 1961

The Saviour of Men appeared to Catherine while she was praying.

And placing the right hand on Catherine's neck, he drew her to the wound of his sacred side, saying to her, 'Drink, daughter, that luscious beverage which flows from my side, it will inebriate thy soul with sweetness.'

Catherine, thus placed at the very fountain of life, applied her mouth to the sacred wound of the Saviour; she drank long and with as much avidity as abundance; in fine, she detached herself from the sacred source, satiated, but still eager.

From *The Life of St Catherine of Siena* by Raymond of Capua

After the same manner also he took the cup, when he had supped, saying, This cup is the new testament in my blood: this do ye, as oft as ye drink it, in remembrance of me.

I Corinthians 11:25, King James Bible

I

A week passed, at the end of which I realised I had been waking from a dream, a dream that had lasted a decade.

I did not take the truth about Marian's death easily; it was as if I could not admit it *was* the truth. Yet I read and reread her mother's letter a hundred times, and as I did so, question after question piled upon me, until I could not breathe.

One morning, I woke at four o'clock, yelling a wordless sound, just from fear. I lurched out of bed, my heart pounding, and though I went for a long walk in the yellow dawn light, I could not shift an unnameable terror inside me.

Looking back, I think that might have been when I started to change, but I cannot be sure. Maybe it had happened long before that. Maybe it had begun in a hole in the ground in Paris in 1944.

And who knows? Could there have been other, still older things I had not even thought of as yet that might have lain at the root of my motivations? I had not begun to have such thoughts; these were places of which I was not yet aware.

In those ten years, I had almost totally forgotten about Marian. She had left, angry with me, or so I thought; she had wanted nothing more to do with me. I had written her three letters; she had replied to none.

As I reread Margery Fisher's letter, questions I had stopped thinking about years before were joined by new ones. How had she died? Really? The letter didn't specify. Where was she buried exactly? And why in Paris? Surely they'd had the money to have her body brought home to the States. There were these, and

97

many other, questions, but the one line in the letter I read a thousand times raised the biggest question of all. Was it really true she'd thought she might fall in love with me? Had she?

If not, what happened that stopped her, why did she change her mind about me? And if she had fallen in love with me, then why did she pull away? If I closed my eyes, even after all that time, I could still see her pale skin that day I tried to kiss her, when anger crossed her face, when she walked away.

With some pain, I brought back an image of her that morning, tried to see the emotion there once again.

She'd said one word so forcefully: 'No'.

Now I wondered what she meant by that, exactly. That she didn't want to kiss me, that I should stop, was obvious, but why? Why didn't she want me to kiss her when once she'd felt she was falling in love?

I grew angry as I woke from this ten-year dream, and suddenly felt useless. I was forty-two and I felt as though I was at the end of my life, that I had sailed down a series of dead-end paths without even having my eyes open.

I had few friends. There was Hunter, of course, and I suppose he was more than enough friend to make up for having so few. I rarely saw Donald, who now had three children, and though we met occasionally on my infrequent trips to London, he was as busy as I was. And I *was* busy. I had set up and was running a small research unit, trying to develop better ways to help haemophiliacs through improved plasma products, if not actually find a cure. We had some small successes, and started to see that we were on the verge of emerging from a dark age, a very long dark age, for the sufferers of that illness. When I began the work in the unit, there was still not even a proper definition of the disease; its name, 'love of blood', seemed a powerful link to a time not so far back when the various awful cures for the 'bleeders', as they were known, included mercury and leeches. Even as I started my work, I learned about a similar unit to ours in

Oxford where they were working with snake venom. It was preposterous to me that we seemed to be no better off in our consideration of a cure for the disease than were the doctors of that most famous sufferer of all, Alexei Romanov. It had taken a witch doctor to keep him alive, and without him Alexei's death had been only a matter of time. Lenin's bullets had cheated the disease of a famous scalp.

The work was slow and to many people would have been very boring, but it occupied me, hour after hour, as I stared through the lenses of the microscope at pink-stained slides of haemo-globin in various anomalous states.

Every night I would go home, to my large empty house. Many years before Margery Fisher's letter arrived, I had moved from the college flat to a bigger place of my own, on Hills Road, so I would be near the new hospital when it was opened. Sarah, my wife, and I had chosen it, imagining we would fill its many rooms with children, children that never came. When Sarah became ill, that thought evaporated, and she went quickly. She died before we even completed on the deal, but I moved there anyway, not knowing what else to do, and in that big house I rattled around, living, I could see now, like a ghost.

I had no children, my wife was dead, and I hadn't met anyone else since her death, though in fact I wonder now if I was even looking.

I had been dreaming.

For ten years, I had been dreaming, and now a letter from America had pulled me awake into a reality I didn't want to acknowledge, because if it was true that I had been dreaming, I had woken into a nightmare.

2

At the end of that week of waking, I went to see Hunter.

It was a beautiful and hot day in early May, and we left his rather stuffy and dark rooms and walked out to the Backs. The trees towered above us, in full bright green leaf, and students and tourists eyed each other on the river.

We saw none of that, as I told Hunter about the letter. He had all the same questions, and I told him that I'd written to Marian's mother, asking how she had died, and where exactly she was buried. And about the Estonian.

'When did you send it?' he asked.

'I haven't yet. I wrote it last night. I'll send it later today.'

'Are you sure you want to?'

He stopped walking for a moment, which I took to be a sign that this was an important question.

'Yes. I think so. Why?'

'Consider the old girl, Charles. There she is, sitting in her big house, sad, but happy in her memory of her daughter, and she gets another letter raking up the past. Are you sure you want to do that to her?'

I can see now that he had a point. I didn't then.

'She said herself in her letter that she wanted me to know the truth, so I didn't have to live not knowing. I'm only doing the same for her.'

'But she does know. Or she thinks she does. She presumably thinks her daughter was run down by a motor car, or drowned in the Seine, or whatever they told her. She's dealt with that and, from what you've said, it sounds like she's come to a point of peace with it. And you want to tell her the truth, the real truth, but you don't even know what that is. That some man you saw in a tunnel in the war killed her?'

I shook my head.

'I don't know. I . . .'

I stopped. I found it hard to think, let alone to explain.

'You don't know what happened any more than she did. Are you sure this Estonian was even the man in the bunker? What makes you think he had anything to do with Marian's death, however that happened? You have no proof of that.'

There I had to disagree with Hunter.

'No, on the contrary, I think it highly unlikely that Marian died in an accident when she was also consorting with a murderer. That's the most likely explanation.'

'The two are not connected,' Hunter persisted. 'You're displaying false logic. It's just as likely that she died from some other cause as by his hand, and anyway, there is absolutely no evidence to show he had anything to do with her death. Tell me! What would you say if you walked into a French police station? That some man you once saw just once, mark you, dining with the young lady, is a murderer? Why? They'd laugh at you. It was all so long ago, Charles. Why don't you leave it be? Wouldn't that be better?'

'It's not a question of better,' I snapped at him. I regretted it immediately, but I could see my anger had hurt him.

'I'm sorry,' I said. I stared at the punters on the river as if I was looking straight through them. 'I'm sorry, Hunter.'

We parted soon after that, and I was left thinking about what Hunter had said. Why not just let it go?

He was right, it would probably be better to do so, but it wasn't a question of what was best. It was a question of what I had to do.

I'd mourned Sarah when she'd died, of course, but it was only with Marian's mother's letter that tears had come, and now it seemed they would not stop.

I had to find out what had really happened, and though Hunter was right that I had nothing I could ever report to the police, I knew that Verovkin was in some way connected, was responsible.

How did I know?

All I had to do was shut my eyes, and think my way back to a hole in the ground in Paris as the city erupted in jubilation, and there, in that hole, was that man.

Looking at me.

And it was that look that told me I was right.

He had killed Marian.

3

At the end of May I managed to get away to Paris for a few days. I had in the end sent a revised version of my letter to Margery Fisher, in which I asked for details of Marian's death, but said nothing of my fears.

Arriving in the city by train, I began to hunt around the Place de Clichy, but I found nothing. No one at Marian's old address had ever heard of her; Jean, the barman in her local, had moved on too, no one even remembered him, though strangely, in that frustrating way in which memory often behaves, after ten years I had been able to recall his name when before I couldn't.

I went out to Saint-Germain, to the street where Verovkin had had his practice, and though my heart began to pound even at the end of the road, it was an unfounded fear. The little brass name plaques were still there, but Verovkin's had gone. There were even four little holes and a rectangular patch of stone of a different colour where it had been, yet that strange nothing comforted me, let me know I was not imagining it all, because it meant he had moved on.

I set out to find him, but I failed.

All my searches came to naught and I had to return to Cambridge before Monday's round of lectures.

A week slipped by, a week more, and I sulked in an uneasy mood, downcast and angry at my impotence. I ghosted my way through my working day and every night I sat in a chair in my living room, staring at the hearth, though there was no fire lit, listening to the Third Programme and whatever it chose to broadcast into my home.

I heard none of it. All I could hear and see in my mind were a series of voices and images, memories of Marian, and dreams of what might have become my life, had she not been killed. This state of affairs continued without an apparent end, until one night when I got home from work and found, at last, a reply to my letter to Marian's mother.

Slipping off my coat and shoes, I carried the letter into the kitchen, and tore it open.

It was much shorter than the first one and, I felt, less friendly. I wondered if I had given some offence, but I put that aside, because Margery Fisher gave me the name of a Parisian cemetery.

As I read the letter, I felt something warm tap my stockinged feet.

I looked down, and saw that the toes of my brown sock were dark and wet, and for a moment I stood staring stupidly at them, until I saw another drop of blood fall. I turned my hands over and saw I had given myself a large paper cut along the side of the left ring finger. I must have done it as I opened the letter, and in my state of mind not even noticed.

Another drop welled from the cut and slid down my wrist now that I had turned my hands over. I dropped the letter on the table and shoved my finger in my mouth, only now noticing that I was in pain.

With my finger still in my mouth I went to the cupboard under the stairs and awkwardly, with my right hand, fished out the box where I kept first aid; and as I did so I sucked the blood.

I remembered something we'd been told when I was a medical student, that the taste of blood – that supposedly metallic taste – only arises when blood comes into contact with skin, as an oxidation reaction occurs between the fats of the skin and the iron in blood. *What then is the natural taste of blood?* our lecturer had put to us, telling us it would be different, and I remember darkly wondering how he knew, because who has drunk enough blood to be free of that metallic reaction with the skin?

A strange thing, though, I thought, as I moved back into the kitchen with the first-aid shoebox: why are we happy to taste our own blood, when other bodily fluids we do not rush to taste? And yet to Dante, so Hunter and Marian had told me, these other fluids – mother's milk, to nourish the newborn; semen, the seed that creates the newborn in the first place – were but the various distillations of that one divine substance, *sangue perfetto*. Blood was at the heart of it all. At least for Dante, and Aristotle, the source of his theories.

But it made me think: who has not put their finger to their mouth and tasted it? I remembered that as a boy I used to have a lot of what I would describe to a colleague as epistaxis, but which to me, at the time, were nosebleeds, prolonged and heavy. I would lie on my back while my mother slid a key down my neck to draw the blood away. I think even then I doubted if that was doing any good, but meanwhile I would press a flannel to my nose and wait until the bleeding had stopped, pulling it away to reveal a clotted nose and a white facecloth drenched in red. I must have tasted a lot of my own blood then, but I couldn't remember what it tasted like.

All these thoughts rumbled along in my mind while I fiddled with the plasters in the shoebox, fumbling with my right hand to find and place a sticking plaster on my left ring finger. Being left-handed, it was my clumsy right that was given the job, and I botched it the first time, and the second. Trying for a third time, my eye fell on Margery's letter again, and I saw I had dropped it face down on the table, and that it continued on the back.

I saw one word and stopped what I was trying to do with the plaster and my bleeding hand. All thought of that was gone as I saw that one word: *beast*. I must have stared at the paper as if the words upon it were on fire.

I snatched it up again, and I read that Marian had been found, murdered, it was thought, by a killer who had struck before in the area, and whom the press had dubbed 'the Beast of Saint-Germain'.

Margery said little more than that, and I could see my letter had dragged up old sufferings. Hunter had been right, and I felt awful, but I didn't regret what I'd done, because it had given me two pieces of information I needed desperately.

Firstly, I knew that Jean, the barman, had lied to me. He had told me Marian had a weak heart, and had been obliged to go home to the States. Why had he done that? The only, the obvious, conclusion was that he was known to Verovkin, was an ally of his, and I decided that I would perhaps do better to pick up his trail than that of the elusive margrave.

And secondly, I knew where Marian was buried, and I wanted that so much because I wanted to be close to her again. Even just once, though she had been dead under the grass for ten years, because I knew now that she'd been taken. She had not gone naturally into death. She had been taken, against her will, and with horrible violence.

Anger suddenly poured out of me, rising from nowhere so that I cried out and swept the back of my left hand across the table, smashing the shoebox, sending it flying across the room to the kitchen wall, where it scattered its contents on the floor. I hung my head and looked at the mess I'd made, not failing to see the drops of my own blood that had splattered the white wall.

I stood waiting for the anger to subside and of course it did, but it did not disappear altogether. Rather it turned into a sort of determination, so that three weeks later I grimly found my way to Paris again.

I located Marian's grave, I stood in front of it, and I wept. I hunted in the libraries and found old newspaper cuttings of her death, as well as of two others reported to be the work of la Bête. And I made a nuisance of myself in Saint-Germain itself, asking around, being nosy, accosting anyone who would listen to me, and so it was that one day I had a conversation with an old working man, a local odd-job man, who told me that around eight or nine years ago, he couldn't remember, he had been paid five hundred old francs to shift boxes from the *petit palais* at the end of the park on to a small *camion*. He told me that although no one had told him where the boxes were heading, he had heard the drivers moaning that it would take three days to drive to Avignon.

So I had it. He was in Avignon.

4

I arrived in Avignon in August 1961, having had to wait until I could take more leave without raising too many eyebrows. I had tried to take a sleeper from Paris, but not having booked, I had to wait a night and take two trains to Avignon the following day. The evening I spent in Paris I was anxious and restless. I had no business there any more. I had taken all I needed from it, and I had paid my respects to Marian at her graveside.

She was buried in Montmartre, just a short walk from where she had lived. It had taken me three hours to find her grave the first time I went, but this time I walked straight to it: a small plot with a simple but decent headstone, which simply gave her name and her dates. It spoke of nothing more. It gave no hint of the horror of her death, of how she had been stabbed repeatedly, at least seventeen times according to the extract from her post-mortem, large sections of which had been faithfully reprinted in *Le Figaro*. I'd read that article again and again, awful though it was, because it was the last mention of Marian in the world that I had, not counting her mother's letter. Though it was torture to do so, therefore, I pored over it many times, even forcing myself to reread the description of the state of her body; the mass of stabbings, both in her body and in her face. Her face. I felt sick as I read that, but there was worse to come. The surgeon who conducted the autopsy had concluded that the murderer had inflicted these wounds with a knife, but not a particularly sharp one. He guessed it was something like a table knife. Aside from the wounds, her body displayed the marks of teeth on the shoulder, neck and breasts. He had bitten her. He had torn her skin, deeply. Finally the report spoke of the mutilation of her breasts and genitals with the knife. Interestingly – that was how the paper put it – there was no sign of sexual assault. How they could not consider that mutilation of the genitals was not a sexual assault, I was at a loss to understand. I supposed they meant there was no sign of him on her, his semen. That he had not actually raped her.

Interestingly.

Every time I read that word, I wanted to march into the offices of the paper, cause some terrible atrocity, and ask them if they found it interesting. Why is it, I wanted to ask them, why is it that with some dreadful crime, a brutal killing like this, that the newspapers feel they need to make every explicit detail a thing of public record? Why not leave these things unspoken, why not leave them to the bereaved, these things that should remain private? Something vaguely connected in my mind: reading these gruesome details, I felt as I had when I stood in the operating theatre in Trumpington Street; as if I was seeing something I shouldn't see. Blood, like the physical act of love, like murder.

So why expose these things? The answer, I can see now, is money, but at the time I was too full of rage to see so clearly and it made me want to storm their offices.

But I didn't, of course, and anyway, I knew where the source of my anger really lay. It lay in Avignon.

In Paris, I considered going to the Sûreté with what I knew, but I hesitated, because, after all, what did I know? Nothing, really. A name, and with that name a link to an act of horror I'd seen during a time of general horror. I would be throwing wild accusations around, and I knew it. I wondered if I was doing the right thing, but I must have walked past a half-dozen police stations in Paris that day, and entered none of them.

I stood at Marian's grave, and I wept angry tears, and found that it did not help to do so. I stared at the earth, trying to stop myself from picturing what was underneath, and wondered if that was why Marian's father, rich though he was, had not wanted to bring her body home. What was there, in that dark soil, that was worth bringing home? I imagined that was what he'd said to Margery. I imagined them arguing about it, and in the end the grieving mother must have done all she could just to get him to pay for a respectable headstone in a corner of Montmartre.

As I stood at her grave, terrible images surged into my mind, unbidden and unwelcome, as I saw him attacking her, cutting her, biting her, ruining her. I tried to force them out, tried to find peace by remembering Marian's face as I had known her, but though I attempted to paint a picture of her, I could not manage to do so. I knew I had constructed no more than a caricature of her; that I couldn't really see her any more in my mind; that she'd gone. In her place was only the evidence of my eyes – the letters cut in the stone in front of me.

That evening, the evening before I left Paris for the south, I ate in a small bistro just down from the cemetery. I ordered almost without thinking, some food, some wine. I sat in a corner and watched the customers come and go, watched the two young waiters and one waitress go about their evening's work quickly and professionally. My waiter brought my food; I ordered some more wine, watching a little performance between the waitress and two old Parisian gentlemen. I watched, not even really able to hear the words, the ritual they enacted. The bringing of the food, the noises of delight and gratitude from the men. The waitress, inclining her head, do you need anything else? The glance between the men, old friends presumably, no, nothing, thank you. We have everything we need. The smallest curtsey from the waitress, thank you gentlemen.

It struck me as a small mime show, one that would be repeated this evening in Paris alone many thousands of times.

But there was something further that interested me, and it was a story even older than that of food: it was one of lust. I saw the way the old men looked at the girl when she wasn't looking. As her eyes turned to one man, his friend would take his chance to stare at her. She was pretty enough, perhaps that was why they gazed. Then I realised that she wasn't pretty, not really. What she was, was young, a thing so often mistaken for beauty. Her skin was pale and smooth, her eyes bright, her lips red, and her hair was, in fairness, spectacular, a mass of blonde curls.

Perhaps it was just habit that made these men in their seventies look at her cleavage, and at her bottom when she left them. Perhaps they genuinely harboured desire for her. As she returned to enquire how their food was, I saw one of them take his chance to steal another look at her, but this time he looked not at her breasts, but at her neck. The carotid, I noticed, pulsed slightly, and the man had seen this. She turned to him and he smiled into her eyes instead.

She smiled back, and was gone again.

I stayed a long time in the restaurant, picking slowly at my food, drinking more wine than I should have. Eventually, the waitress came over to me and looked at my plate.

'*Ce n'est pas bon?*' she asked, seriously concerned.

'*Si, si, c'est très bon. Mais je n'ai pas faim.*'

I smiled, but I could see she wasn't convinced, and I felt the need to offer her, and therefore the unseen chef, some further encouragement. In stuttering French I tried to explain that it was very delicious, and that I liked the sauce in particular. Only now did I notice what I was eating: coq au vin.

Now she smiled, broadly, and I knew I had done the right thing. '*Oh, c'est le sang qui donne ce bon goût à la sauce; il la rend beaucoup plus riche. C'est le secret du chef.*'

She winked at me as if to show that this was a secret she regularly shared, and I kept the smile on my face until she'd gone, then pushed the plate away from me.

Le sang? It was the blood that made the sauce rich. What little hunger I'd had vanished. I quickly swallowed a lot of wine and staggered into the hot night.

So the following day, when I arrived in Avignon, my mind was already cloudy with dark thoughts, with words from the article about Marian's death, which I continued to play in my head like a tape recording with the accounts of the two other murders in the district around the same time, all presumed to be the work of the same hand.

I had booked a hotel with a travel agent in Paris. I took a taxi from the station, and found myself being driven across the river, out of the city. My hotel turned out to be across the Rhône, in Villeneuve-lès-Avignon, not the city itself, but a small town directly facing it.

The Hôtel du Rhône was a crammed and squalid place; the room was tiny and didn't look at the river but at a train line and a brick wall. It was unbearably hot, with a window that barely opened, so as soon as I'd dumped my old holdall on the bed, I set out for the city itself.

I didn't feel like I was in France any longer, it felt far too sultry and southern to me, as if I'd crossed the border into Spain, though I had never been there either. It was dusk. A strong and hot wind blew into my face as I crossed the river towards the city, so warm and dry it almost made me gag.

The city seemed to have an almost perfectly intact wall, medieval I supposed, and the whole skyline inside was dominated by the crenellations of some large castle or palace, the towers of a cathedral.

The sun set behind me as I crossed by a new suspension bridge, seeing to my left a massive old fortified bridge that ran halfway across the river, then stopped, and I knew it must be the one from the nursery rhyme I'd sung as a boy.

L'on y danse tous en rond . . .

Everyone dances in circles. I had never understood why, what that meant, until that point. The bridge, or half of it, must have collapsed or been destroyed at some time, making it a road that went nowhere, only to the seemingly furious waters of the Rhône below, leaving its passengers to dance in circles. Maybe I was imagining all that, but I could see them anyway, figures dancing, swaying, swinging perilously near to the waters.

I reached the end of my bridge, and stopped.

For a brief moment, I wondered what on earth I was doing. It was no longer a fantasy, finding this man. It had become real, here and now, in Avignon, and I was about to enter the city where I believed him to be hiding. If I had any second thoughts, now was the time to pay them heed. But that only lasted for a second, because I knew what I was doing, and why; I had no second thoughts.

I was going to find Marian's killer.

It was the how that worried me, not the why.

Not then.

5

That first evening in Avignon overwhelmed me.

I have tried to work out what it was about the city that disturbed me so, but right from the very start, as I passed through the old walls, I felt unsettled. It sounds melodramatic to say I felt as if I was entering a giant beast of some kind, but that is the first impression I had – of walking into a living, breathing monster, one that had streets for veins and buildings for organs. I think, too, that I had the immediate sense that I did not belong. That I was a transgressor. Not just because I was English, and pale, when almost everyone around me was speaking French and bore tanned skin. It was something more than that; it was because I could not understand why I was the only one who seemed to feel the oppression and imminent violence of the place. I couldn't understand why everyone else was strolling, smiling, eating, joking, flirting and enjoying themselves, when it seemed apparent that a storm would break at any moment.

I entered the walls by the gate at the Place Crillon, and, without the breeze that had scoured me raw outside the city, the heat grew worse. The square was crowded, heaving with people on all sides, and everyone seemed to be in couples or groups. I felt very exposed, as if everyone was looking at me, though at the same time I felt utterly invisible. Everyone was hurrying somewhere, or just standing and chatting, or walking arm in arm to a restaurant. It felt very different to Paris, in a way that I could only pinpoint with one simple word: danger.

I crossed the square and took a small street that led from the far corner. Within five minutes I was lost as I found myself in a network of twisting alleyways and small cobbled roads that turned around and in on themselves, cutting between high blank walls of stone with only occasional windows, which were frequently barred.

A strange fear crept into me that first evening, and it never left me. There was something about the city I could not place, some oppression, some terror.

I don't know how much of it was my state of mind. I was tired, very tired from the journey. I had not eaten much. The sudden, more intense heat of the south, that hot wind, was blowing in my eyes, across my lips, and all the while, the thought lingering at the back of my mind of what I was doing there, and why.

But maybe there was more to it than that. The city did have an air about it. It felt alive, it felt dangerous. It felt old, somehow older than Paris, somehow more primitive, despite the various grand buildings I saw.

I passed out of the network of alleys and stumbled into a large open square, at the far end of which I saw a building I took to be the Palais des Papes; beyond it, the Cathedral.

Again I found myself a paradox, both invisible and terribly exposed all at once, and I ducked down another small street, trying to look like I knew where I was going, avoiding eye contact with everyone.

The walls around me grew higher, leaning in towards each other at the top, almost touching. They turned about and I found myself taking dead ends, having to retrace my steps. It seemed as if no path ran straight for more than twenty paces, and the hot and foetid air from kitchen doorways blew on to me, again making me want to retch.

My mind began to dissolve.

The city had become the entrails of the animal that I'd entered, through which I was walking, or struggling to walk. I heard footsteps behind me and quickened my pace, taking turns at random until I suddenly realised I was in a small street I'd been in five minutes before. I stopped, and made my way to look in a jeweller's window, dark and barred now, and with nothing on view. Feeling foolish, I turned, and bumped into someone.

He cursed at me but walked on and I mumbled an apology to his back, in English. By the time I managed to turn it into French, he was gone.

I found myself hurrying down more alleys whose walls were black with age and covered with obscene graffiti, images of rampant penises and hanging breasts. In red paint were scrawled words that I could not understand, and which I took to be dialect, or curses.

At one moment I was jostling for room past thronging crowds, and the next I was alone in a long narrow street that curved gently like the back of a bow, with high blind walls, making me feel as if I was walking through a canyon.

I stopped, my breath heavy, my feet sore, and tried to decide what to do.

A figure stepped into view in a pool of lamplight at the end of my street, a thin woman. She walked quickly down the street towards me, staying on the opposite side, and I thought she was coming for me, but she gave me no more than a glance as she passed me by, a look that told me not to look back at her.

So I began a retreat to my hotel, eventually finding my way to the city wall. As soon as I stepped outside the old town I felt better. I felt in less danger and there was that breeze again, which had at last cooled enough to provide a little relief. Tracing the wall round to the river, I found the bridge by which I'd crossed the Rhône, and hurried back to my hotel, my head bowed into the wind.

I snatched my key from the night porter and locked myself in my room, where I fell asleep almost immediately.

Yet my sleep was not good. The heat of the room and the rumble of freight trains just yards away from me woke me frequently through the night, until my dreams and my waking thoughts became one long disturbed vision, and it was a vision of the city.

It started from the feelings I'd had that evening, and I saw the city as a beast, though one of stone. I kept walking around inside it, more lost than if I'd been in a maze, and I felt that it had a dark heart, which for some reason I was looking for, but would never find.

The little history I knew of the place fed my delusions. I knew that Avignon had been the home to the antipopes who had rivalled Rome for a while, and my dream saw it become home to the opposite of the light of the Church. Here was darkness, filth. If Paris was glory, Avignon was squalor, depravity and cruelty. Here, crusades were launched not just against the infidel of the Holy Land, but against Cathars and other heretics. Here the Inquisition came and extracted confessions of witchcraft and devil worship from the screaming innocent.

Here blood had flowed, and would certainly flow again.

6

I woke the following morning, late, and somewhere in the night I had had enough sleep to feel better. I felt embarrassed with myself for the way I'd become so jumpy the night before, but what I felt above everything else was hungry, terribly, terribly hungry.

I ate a vast breakfast, and washed it all down with strong coffee, so that by the time I headed back into Avignon in daylight, I was no longer afraid or paranoid. The morning was cooler, though the wind across the river was ever-present. My fear was replaced now by determination, and I took in the city in a single glance as I crossed the bridge.

He was here, somewhere, I thought. In front of me was the whole city, and he was here.

I wondered how to start, how to find one man in a city of tens of thousands of people. All I had was his name, so that was what I used to begin my search.

Given his wealth and his status in Paris, I made the assumption he would be living in a large house at the very least, something grand. It might be in the city or, I supposed, outside, in a chateau or villa.

I began at the central post office, where I explained as best I could that I was trying to deliver a parcel to the Margrave Anton Verovkin, but was not sure of his address. Either my French was bad, or the woman behind the desk did not feel like helping, for I left not even knowing if she hadn't understood, or had refused to help. She just lowered her eyes at me when I pushed, and said 'Non, non,' repeatedly, until I left the counter.

There was a telephone booth in the corner of the bureau de poste. A telephone directory sat glaring at me, and I scoured it every way I could think of, but found nothing.

In desperation, I went to the Hôtel de Ville, and asked if they could help me find an eminent local person. A man at the enquiry desk was a little more helpful and told me it was not something they could do officially, but that, for my information, he had never heard of such a person.

By mid-afternoon I sat in a café in Place Crillon, and wondered if I had been defeated. I had tried everything I could easily do, and I wondered what was left to me. That the clerk at the Hôtel de Ville had not heard of Verovkin proved little, but it did make me start to doubt everything, and I supposed, with an awful lurching feeling, that the margrave could have changed his name. In fact, the more I thought about it, the more likely that seemed. It appeared he had done his best to cover his tracks after Paris; the very least he would do in Avignon would be to take a new name. With his money, who would doubt him? The super rich have no need to prove who they are, though I supposed that if he left France he would have to have a passport in some name or other, but what name?

I sat in the café for a long time that afternoon, until the sun began to lower in the sky, and I felt a return of the oppression of the night before. I scuttled back across the river and ate in the hotel, possibly the worst meal I'd ever eaten in France, but I felt better there, on the far side of the running water, as if that would somehow stop him from knowing I was there, stop him from finding me. I felt better. I felt safer.

I went to bed, and was woken every hour by the rumbling of trains behind my head.

7

I had been in Avignon a week. I had found precisely nothing, despite all my efforts to locate him, and I was in a terrible mood.

I was physically exhausted from walking the streets every day, checking the little brass plaques of every professional doorway in the city. I had made two excursions out of the city to nearby villages by taxi. I had asked not just those taxi drivers, but several others if they had ever heard of the margrave. None had.

I made my questions more vague, not asking after him by name, but asking if they knew of a foreign nobleman who'd arrived in the city around eight years before. I asked in taxis, I asked in bars, cafés, shops, hotels, and people began to look at me as if I was mad, and I, in turn, began to wonder if I was.

Then, one afternoon, four days before I had to return to England, I went into a café in the Place de l'Horloge, near the palais, which I had not visited before, and as the waiter approached me, I knew him.

I cannot believe that he didn't recognise me, or that even if he didn't it wasn't obvious from my reaction that I had recognised him. It was the barman from Paris, Jean, who had claimed to be Marian's friend.

A decade had passed, I had changed a little, but I suppose that he was not expecting to see me, and it was that which made me unrecognisable.

'Monsieur?' he asked, and I ordered a coffee, trying to keep my voice calm, to ignore the way my heart was beating erratically, the way my blood seemed to have suddenly grown cold.

I wondered whether to make a bolt for the door before he returned, but stopped myself. Wasn't this why I had come? To find *him*, or someone who led to him. And Jean had not recognised me. I determined to be strong and see if I could use this meeting.

As he returned, I thanked him, as casually as I could, though I didn't meet his eyes, and it was that that led me to see something. As he placed the coffee cup on the table, his sleeve rode up above his wrist, and I saw he had a strange tattoo there.

I saw it for only a moment, and saw it was an animal of some sort, though I could not be sure what.

He left.

I drank my coffee, wondering what to do next.

If he was here, I knew I was right. The margrave was here somewhere too; they must know each other, or it was too great a coincidence. It confirmed that the barman had lied to me when he told me about Marian leaving Paris. I wondered if it was a story he had been told to tell anyone who'd asked after her. Or whether I had been the only one.

There seemed to be only one thing I could do, which was to leave the café, return when it closed, and follow him. If that did not take me to Verovkin, it might take me one step closer.

As I thought these things, another waiter came by, an older man, and he began to clear some cups from a table next to me. Like Jean he was short-haired and thin. He had a striking face, with two deep lines in his cheeks that might once have been dimples but which were now creases as long as his fingers. He was dark-haired, had black bristles for eyebrows and heavy stubble, and I was immediately afraid of him.

I lowered my gaze to his hands, and, looking hard at his wrists, I saw that he had the same tattoo as Jean, though still I could not make it out exactly. He turned to me, and saw me looking at his tattoo.

I downed my coffee, left some coins on the table, and hurried out of the door, trying not to break into a run as I did so, but not stopping until I was once again lost in that maze of alleys.

I leaned back against a wall, trying to catch my breath, staring at but not seeing more strange graffiti opposite me. Suddenly a gang of four young men bowled down the alley, loud and drunk though it was still only the late afternoon. They bawled something at me as they passed that I didn't understand and was glad not to, and I decided to keep walking.

I walked for a long time and found myself at the river, where I stared deeply at the passing waters.

I forced myself to wait there until my heart rate had subsided, and my mind had settled again, though in truth it felt as turbulent as the river, which was muddy and full of competing currents.

They were here. The margrave. A cohort of his. And the other waiter, I realised now, could almost be an older brother of Jean's; they even shared the same tattoo.

Sometimes, when you dream, you have a series of symbols presented to you, but though you know they must have meaning, you do not see what that meaning is. And then, much later in the day, as if from nowhere, that meaning will leap at you, and you see that the room you dreamt about is in fact a representation of your head, your mind. That one room, the one you couldn't get into in the dream, is that part of your mind you can't access, can't understand. Or maybe you dream of a boat at sea, but only later that day do you understand that you are the boat, and that the sea is your confusion.

It was like that with the tattoo. In truth, I *had* seen the animal, and I had seen it clearly, but it took some time for me to process it, until suddenly, as I stared into the brown waters of the river, I knew what I had seen, though unlike the revelation of a dream, I did not yet understand its meaning. For that

I would need help, but I now knew that what I had seen was a bird. And a strange bird at that. I had seen one in London Zoo as a boy. A pelican.

8

'A what?'

I could picture Hunter's face as he barked down the phone at me from Cambridge.

I stood in the small booth in the lobby of the post office, the only place I could find to make an international call. It was costing me a fortune in francs that I had balanced in a tower on the counter in the booth, and was shovelling into the greedy mouth of the machine.

'A pelican.'

'How's your holiday?'

'Indescribable. Listen, Hunter, I just need to know. What does a pelican mean?'

'What does a pelican *mean*? Are you feeling all right? Probably best to drink bottled water down there, you know?'

'Hunter! What does a pelican symbolise? It's a symbol of something, isn't it? What does it mean? Hunter, hurry, I'm running out of francs.'

There was a silence, and again I could see his face as he dredged up what he knew about the pelican.

'It's a heraldic device, for one thing. A vulning pelican.'

'A what?'

'Vulning. From your Latin, Charles! What did they teach you at that expensive school of yours? *Vulnerare*. To wound. The Ancients believed that the pelican was so attentive to its young as to wound itself to give them blood to sustain them. It's a religious symbol too. For the Eucharist, obviously.'

'Obviously,' I said. 'Hunter, you're a genius, how do you know this stuff?'

'It's the symbol of Corpus Christi, in both Cambridge and the other place. One gets to know these things. Take my place, for example. We have a blue and gold porcupine, which—'

'Never mind the porcupine, Hunter, stick with the pelican. Is it ever used as a tattoo, or body marking?'

'Jesus, man, what kind of holiday are you having?'

'Hunter! I'm running out of coins. I—'

And there the conversation ended.

Corpus Christi. The name of a college, but literally the body of Christ, as eaten during the Eucharist, during which wine is also drunk. Wine that symbolises his blood. Hence the pelican.

That was why I'd phoned Hunter, because he was the sort of man who knew something about everything, and a lot about some things.

But it told me little else, except that I knew I had to follow either Jean or his 'brother' and see if something would lead me to him.

I forced myself to waste a couple of hours because I didn't want to sit down to dinner until late, and I had already decided where. There was a restaurant with a terrace beside the café. I would eat late, and spin out my drinks, and wait for the café to close.

And then?

After that, I wasn't sure.

9

I walked back to the hotel to fetch a pocket Kodak camera I'd brought with me. I wanted at the very least to get a photograph of Jean, and the other man whom I presumed to be his brother. That would feel like I was doing something, like I was making progress.

I walked slowly to kill time, and that was easy enough, because it was another stifling evening and I was already tired.

When I recrossed the river and made my way to the Place de l'Horloge, the clocks were chiming nine and I had a little trouble getting a table where I wanted, outside, but facing the café next door.

It didn't take me long to realise that neither Jean nor his older friend were there. After fifteen minutes had gone by, I saw every waiter in the place come out to the customers outside, and I knew they weren't working that evening.

Angry with myself, I ate quickly, knowing I'd have to come back the next day and start over again.

I paid, leaving a large tip to apologise for being so rude as to take such a short time over my meal, and had set off back to my hotel when, in a narrow street that ran down the side of the Palais des Papes, I saw both men walking straight towards me. Instinctively I turned into the doorway of a tourist shop, still open despite the hour, and saw I was in a bookshop.

I grabbed a book from a narrow shelf inside the door, pretending I was fascinated by it. From the corner of my eye, I saw them pass the shop entrance and stop. I set the book back on the shelf, and ducked further inside.

They didn't seem to have seen me, but were smoking and talking; the shop was at a small junction and I guessed they were about to separate.

'*Vous voulez quelque chose?*' asked a voice. I turned to see a young woman behind the counter, eyeing me suspiciously.

'No, thank you,' I said in English, without thinking. I went blank and couldn't think how to say I was only browsing.

'*Je vais fermer le magasin maintenant.*'

'Oh, yes,' I said, and began to make for the door but saw that Jean was still outside. I had to stall in some way or I would walk right into them. I grabbed the first book that came to hand. The shop was a mixture of new books and second-hand, and seemed to have lots of a religious nature, aimed at tourists to the cathedral, I assumed. In my hand was a volume called *My Servant, Catherine*. I handed it to the girl, and said I wanted to buy it.

She took my money and was again making to shoo me out, but the two were still outside.

'*C'est un cadeau,*' I said, hurriedly. I made a dumbshow of wrapping the book. She frowned at me and then understood.

'*Non. C'est pas possible.*'

I hesitated, and she must have thought I was arguing with her.

'*C'est pas possible. Bonsoir, monsieur.*'

She indicated the door, and with relief I saw the two men walking together, as it turned out, along the street that led away from the shop.

'*Merci. Bonsoir,*' I said, and as she held the door open for me, as Jean's had earlier that day her sleeve dropped back to reveal a strong, fresh tattoo of a pelican, pecking its breast. A drop of tattoo-blue blood fell from its beak.

I stared.

'Where did you get that?' I asked, again, stupidly, in English.

But she must have understood, because she hesitated for a moment before saying, '*C'était une blague.*'

It took me a while to remember the word, by which time I found myself on the street once more. *Une blague.* A joke.

The tattoo didn't look like any sort of joke to me, but I put that from my mind as I realised that Jean and his friend were out of sight. I hurried away down the street after them, shoving the book I'd bought in one jacket pocket, and checking the camera in my other.

As I made the corner, I saw them again, and followed them round two corners, and a third, and found myself at the *place*, where they walked straight back into their café.

'Damn it all,' I said under my breath, and knowing I couldn't very well take up a place in the neighbouring restaurant again, looked about for an answer.

I couldn't just sit out on the steps of the Hôtel de Ville for hours; the square was emptying of tourists, and I would easily be seen from the café.

The answer turned out to be a hotel with rooms that looked down on to the *place*, but also, on one side at least, the café.

I took a deep breath, and pulled out my wallet. I was already spending way too much money on this trip, but I had come too far now to back down. The main thing was that I had my passport; for security I had decided to keep it on me and not leave it in the crummy hotel across the river.

This place was a different beast altogether. One night would probably cost me as much as the five I'd spent in Villeneuve. The carpet was thick, chandeliers twinkled, a piano played in the bar across the hall, and all in all I decided I liked it.

At the reception desk they looked at me a little strangely when I asked if they had a room on the south side. I explained it was because of the bells from the cathedral. They took my passport with the usual promise to return it the following morning, and checked me in. They asked after my luggage and I explained it had been lost and would follow later in the week.

I made my way up to the room with the porter, tipped him, ordered a coffee from room service, and checked on my view.

It was perfect.

From my window I could not only see the terrace of the café: I was on the side of the building and could see their kitchen door, a little way down the darkened street.

When my coffee came, I pulled a chair to the window, set my camera on the ledge by the window, which I opened a fraction, and switched off the light.

Then, I sat down to wait.

10

I began to doze.

Despite the coffee, with the room comfortable and warm, the chair soft, my eyes grew tired. Needing something to keep me awake, I pulled the book I'd bought from my pocket and opened it at random.

Many of her thoughts have the beauty of the wild flowers we admire without asking whence they came or wondering why they bloom in this field of corn, or that meadow . . .

I turned at random to another page.

Her enthusiasm was warlike; she demanded a struggle to the death against the infidel, and a generous spilling of blood.

I wondered what it was I had bought and turned to the beginning, and as I read the title page I saw that it was a biography of Saint Catherine of Siena. The book was a recent reprint, only a few years old, of a book that had been written long before that. Centuries before that, in fact.

I read on, all the while keeping half an eye on the street below me, and whenever I was content that Jean was still busy serving, I relaxed again.

I found the book strange, and shocking.

She began by whipping herself with a little cord; then she persuaded some other little girls to join her, and they used to meet in the most hidden corners of the house to pray and to discipline themselves. She directed the little group. She scourged herself, ate less, prostrated herself and prayed very much – and, in an impulsive outburst, said to Christ, 'My Lord Jesus Christ, I promise thee and give thee my virginity, that it may ever be thine alone.'

I wondered at it all. I had been brought up in the Church of England, though not with any great devotion. I knew little about Catholicism, and less about the saints, and as I read about her life, I read the story of a young woman who at a very young age devoted herself to Christ, and who, from the earliest age, seemed to have an obsession with blood.

From drawing blood by scourging herself as a young girl, to receiving the head, and the blood, of a executed man literally in her lap, to her deathbed, where it was said she cried out 'Blood, blood!' as her last words, her whole life was sprinkled with the thought of it, the worship of it. I read how she had had a vision in which, after many years of starving and punishing herself, Christ appeared to her and married her.

He offered her his wound from the lance, the Holy Lance, the Spear of Destiny, and gave her the blood to drink from his side, and she drank.

'I desire blood,' she said. 'And in blood I slake, and shall slake, my soul.'

I thought about Marian.

I thought about the woman in the hole, and the man with her. Had I really seen him drinking from her wound, drinking her blood? Was it possible that such people existed outside the pages of Stoker or Lefanu, or had I just imagined it, in my horror of the scene?

I turned back to the life of Saint Catherine, but everything I read only disturbed me more.

It was as I read about this strange and obsessive individual that I saw the last customers leave the café, that I watched Jean and his friend close up and leave by the kitchen door, and that I, with nothing more than a camera for protection, made up my mind to follow.

11

What is it that we fear the most?

I didn't think I could witness anything more unsettling than what I'd seen during the war, but I was wrong to think that. That night in Avignon, I began to see a whole new world of awful profanity, and yet, could I call what I saw profane? Because what I witnessed appeared in the guise of deep religion, albeit a religion of horror.

It was easy enough to follow the two men through the twisting alleys of Avignon. It was close to two in the morning, and no one else was around. I let them out of my sight, and followed only by listening for their footsteps ahead of me, loud on the cobbles, while I trod softly behind them. At each corner I would stop and poke my head around cautiously, and so it was, as the narrow streets suddenly closed right in, that I saw them enter a door in a wall.

I held my breath, counted to thirty, and then followed, creeping right up to the door, a large and old thing that I suddenly realised was the entrance to a church, tucked right in among the jumble of buildings. The passageway I was standing in was no more than a few feet wide, and it was all I could do to step back a way and see the high windows, from which a soft light flickered.

I licked my lips, and noticed my mouth had run dry. I couldn't just enter by the same door, but I risked peering through a large and ancient keyhole, and saw figures moving inside. Just inside.

I threw myself back against the wall and waited again.

Still nothing, still no one. Growing more and more certain that I had found something that should not have been found, I crept along the passage to where the end of the building suddenly dropped away and I saw an iron gate leading into a courtyard. The gate was locked, but I was still young enough in those days to climb over it, and moments later was kneeling in a small porch at the back of the building. Again I peered through the keyhole, and this time saw not into the church, but a small vestibule of some kind.

I tried the handle. It moved. I put my weight against the door and opened it as slowly as I could and quietly crept inside, leaving the door slightly ajar in case I wanted to leave in a hurry.

It took a short while for my eyes to adjust to the near darkness in the hall, and when they had, I saw a thick curtain hanging across another door, and knew it led into the church. I had no way of knowing who was on the other side, or if anyone was looking in my direction. There was nothing for it but to move the curtain a fraction, and see if there was any reaction.

I lifted the foot of it to one side, and waited, and still there was nothing. I slipped inside the church, and keeping low, moved to the side of the nave, pressing myself into the shadows and taking one tiny step at a time.

I suppose that all this had taken me longer than I'd thought because when the first people came into view, they were already in the middle of their activities.

I saw a group, maybe a dozen, lined up in front of the altar.

Candles lined the altar and cast a strong light on their faces, and I felt a little safer in the shadows. The people were dressed in nothing special; I saw Jean and the other waiter had changed into looser clothes, but otherwise I saw nothing unusual. I moved another fraction along the side of the nave, all the while keeping the pews and pillars between me and the group, but I need not have worried, for they were all looking towards the front, towards the altar, though I couldn't see what they were looking at.

I moved again, and I saw.

It was him. He had his back to me, but I knew it was him, from his height, from his stance. He wore some kind of robe, the robe of a priest, long and black, loosely tumbling to his ankles. His back was towards me, and then he turned, and I saw his face for the first time in ten years. He had aged a little, it was true, but it was him.

He held something in his hands, held it aloft for the others to see.

Something lurched inside me then, and I was almost sick, because I recognised what it was. It was a tiny thing, so tiny, and yet even as far away as I was, I knew it. It was the figure from the musée. Not the Venus of Bastennes, but the one with the red slit between its legs.

As he held it, his followers, or disciples, for I suppose that is what they were, stared open-mouthed and in wonder, and then at some unseen signal they each came forward in turn and kissed the figure, between her legs, where I remembered that smear of reddish-brown pigment lay.

I watched, dumbstruck, and even in that moment it was not lost on me to wonder what else the margrave had stolen from the museum in Saint-Germain. What other things had gone missing? Golden things perhaps, valuable things, with which one could, with but a little trouble, easily amass an untraceable fortune.

I watched, my head thumping, and I counted the people. A dozen. Twelve. Surely no accident, that.

They were moving again, and I knew I might have little time. I pulled my camera from my pocket and began to fiddle with the settings, worrying about how loud the shutter was, trying to work out what light was available, regretting the slow speed of the film I'd chosen, and then I forgot all about it, because something took place in front of me that stopped every other thought.

He spoke. Strange, really, that it had taken so many years for me to even hear his voice. It was a strong voice, deep, and he spoke in French, but I knew what he was saying.

'*Faites ceci en mémoire de moi.*'

Do this in remembrance of me.

He spoke slowly, and there, once more, was that look on his face. A look I still didn't understand, but it was the same one he'd turned on me in that hole in Saint-Germain, the same eyes, the same turn of the mouth.

A young woman had stepped forward in front of him and pulled up the left sleeve of the light dress she wore. Verovkin had stepped to the altar and now turned back, holding a cup, a brass chalice, and a small knife. She moved slightly and now I saw it was the woman from the bookshop, with her pelican tattoo.

He handed her the knife, and I watched aghast as she pressed the tip of the blade into the inside of her left wrist. I heard her give a short gasp, which caught in her breath, and then blood welled down her arm. She quickly lowered her hand, letting it run into the chalice that he held out for her.

She handed him the knife, stepped back, holding her wrist to stop the bleeding, and the next stepped forward. An older man this time, and now I saw the same tattoo on his wrist, that same tattoo. The pelican. They all had it. And they pierced it with the knife, each of them in turn allowing their blood to run into the cup.

I realised I was shaking, hard, and made an effort to still myself, tried to breathe freely, but I could not, because as the last of the twelve stepped back, he held the cup aloft, and spoke again.

'*Puis, prenant une coupe, il rendit grâces et la leur donna, et ils en burent tous. Et il leur dit: Ceci est mon sang, le sang de l'alliance, qui va être répandu pour une multitude.*'

He lifted the cup to his lips, and he drank. Not a sip, but a mouthful.

Each of them stepped forward, and each took a sip of their mixed blood, and as each did so, he repeated the liturgy.

'*Ceci est mon sang, le sang d'alliance. Faites ceci en mémoire de moi.*'

I lifted the camera to my face.

I held it there, then set it on the corner of a pew, and tried once more to summon the nerve to press the shutter release.

'*Ceci est mon sang, le sang d'alliance. Faites ceci en mémoire de moi.*'

He repeated it again, and again, and the seventh or eighth stepped forward to drink. It was now or never.

'*Ceci est mon sang, le sang d'alliance.*'

This is my blood. The blood of the covenant.

I pressed the button, but my timing was wrong. The small click rang out in a moment of silence as a middle-aged woman drank, and everyone froze, and then looked towards where I crouched. I burst from my hiding place, knowing they couldn't really see me, knowing it would give me a small head start.

I sprinted for the curtain and burst out of the door while they were still taking in what had happened, trying to work out what to do, but even as I clambered over the iron gate, I could hear steps in the porch. I had been seen now, in the faint lamplight of the city, but I paid that no attention, and landing on the far side of the gate, I hurtled down the street and took the corner before anyone could follow.

I took as many turns as I could, and though I heard no one behind me, I didn't stop running until I reached the door of my new hotel.

The night porter looked at me strangely, but I merely smiled and made my way up to my bed, where I lay all night, fully clothed, clutching the camera to my chest.

I listened for sounds of pursuit in the streets below, but all I could hear was my heart pounding, and his words in my head.

'Do this in remembrance of me.'

I lay for a long time, and my thoughts drifted as I grew tired, exhaustion washing into me. If the city was a beast, I had penetrated its very centre. Seen the heart, in which was a thirst. If the city was a beast, it was now, for a short time at least, a sated one, bloated and content with its offering of blood.

Still; his words, in my head. I couldn't get them to leave me.

'Do this in remembrance of me.'

12

When finally I slept, it was early morning.

At noon I left the hotel and took my camera to a small photographic shop I'd seen a few days earlier. I asked the shopkeeper how soon he could develop the photos and at my insistence he told me that, for a price, they could be ready later that afternoon.

I spent the day trying to idle time away, nervously pounding the streets, stopping for coffee once or twice. Every eye I caught I looked away from immediately, but I knew that I was safe really. No one had seen my face, no one knew who I was, what my name was, even what my nationality was. At most they had seen a figure about my height and build. I'd returned to the hotel in Villeneuve to change my clothes, trying to make myself as different as I could be.

Finally, I went back to the photographer's. The afternoon was wearing on, and I wanted to get to the police station as soon as possible, but only once I had evidence.

As I entered the shop, I knew something had changed. The man greeted me, but in a surly manner, and I should have fled there and then.

I didn't. Instead I asked for my photos, and he told me there were none.

I told him there must be some mistake, and he spoke very rapidly in French. I asked him to slow down, insisting that he give me my photos, and again he repeated that there had been nothing on the film.

I got angry. I was desperate, and he was playing me for a fool, though I knew it was possible nothing had turned out. The light was poor; the film was wrong; I had only taken one shot. Yet I felt a little uneasy too. I was good with a camera, I knew what I was doing. This failure reminded me of those stories of ghosts, or other creatures of fantasy, that cannot be captured on film, or seen in a mirror.

One or two other customers left the shop, and he held up a hand to placate me.

'Monsieur?' he said, and indicated a curtain that led to the darkroom behind the shop, I assumed. '*S'il vous plait . . . ?*'

And still I did not understand what was going on. I thought he wanted to take the argument out of his shop, though in fact it was now empty. And so, like a fool, I ducked under his arm and into a back room.

He opened a door that I saw led outside, and nodded at me, showing that I should go out into the alley behind the shop.

I hesitated, and as I turned, he shoved me in the back and I stumbled outside. The door slammed behind me. Two rough men faced me. One of them was Jean.

I opened my mouth but the first fist hit me before I could speak.

I fell immediately and it was all I could do to cover my head as the kicks began to fly into me. I don't know how long it lasted, but it seemed to go on for ever, until suddenly I heard shouts, and the sound of footsteps running away, and more approaching.

I rolled over, in great pain, and saw two policemen staring down at me.

'*Monsieur? Monsieur? Mon Dieu!*'

Of course, by the time I was able to explain what had happened and take the police around to the front of the shop, it had shut. No sign of anyone in the shop, or the flat above.

They spoke no English, and I was having great trouble communicating anything, let alone French, but I got them to understand I wanted to go to the police station, where I demanded an immediate audience with whoever was in charge.

The captain, a polite, middle-aged man called Leclerc, had a paunch and good English.

'But monsieur,' he repeated again and again, 'you should go to a hospital.'

I agreed with him. My nose was bleeding still, I could barely move my neck, there was a cut behind my ear, I hurt everywhere. But I refused to go anywhere until I had told my story.

And what a story it was.

Of a murderer from Paris, of a blasphemous cult in the city, drinking blood in a church whose name, I now realised, I didn't even know. I could take them there, I assured them, only I couldn't show them photographic evidence because they had destroyed it and beaten me up, and in fact, if his two men hadn't happened past, I would probably be dead, or something very like it.

I stopped.

The captain smiled at me.

'You don't believe me,' I said, stupidly.

'No, monsieur, I am of course very happy to hear what you have to say. But I think right now you are a little excited, perhaps. Maybe you could go to the hospital, get cleaned up, and come back tomorrow. And we can sort all of this out.'

He smiled at me again, and glanced at the blood I was dripping on his carpet.

'But you can't just ignore a crime!' I protested. 'I can show you the shop, I can—'

'Monsieur? No one is ignoring you. But you are not well. Come back tomorrow, and we can talk.'

I felt idiotic. I felt like apologising for ruining his carpet, and I felt my anger subside, and as it did, I realised that I hurt. So I did what he said. I let them take me to the hospital, wondering whether it was standard police procedure. Shouldn't they have at least taken a statement?

I hurt too much to care about it for long. So I got cleaned up. I went back to Villeneuve and checked out, and moved all my stuff to the hotel in town.

I ate early, drank a lot, and went to bed, where I passed out in my clothes.

And in the middle of the night, they came for me.

13

What is it we are most afraid of?

Is it that harm will come to us, or that harm will come to those we love? Of the latter, I had had my share; of the former, my share was about to come.

What can we say of pain? Why do we fear it so? Why is it that we are unable to remember it when we are well and happy, just as we are unable to remember joy when we are sad?

When I woke, it must have been as my hotel-room door was kicked open. I felt fear then. Even as I struggled to wake and understand what was going on, I felt some kind of primitive fear, something that must have been planted in us aeons ago, and I rolled out of bed before they got to me. But it was no good. Strong arms held me and someone struck me on the head from behind, not enough to knock me out, but enough to make me retch and stagger.

I was dragged on my tiptoes out of the room before I could make another sound, and down a flight of stairs at the back where the night porter held a door open, nodding at the men who dragged me out and into a car right outside the hotel.

We didn't drive far, to just outside the city walls, where the car stopped. The three men pushed me out, and tumbled after me, giving me another crack on the head to keep me in line. I tried to stand and my legs gave out. I watched the car speed off into the night, and I wondered what was going to happen to me.

They dragged me off the side of the road and down a bank, underneath the arch of the modern bridge by which I'd crossed the river every day.

And there they began to beat all hell out of me. Their fists flew at me until I could no longer stand, and then they started to kick again, and I was too weak to do anything to stop them.

But they did stop, because a voice called out.

I rolled on to my back, groaning as I did, and a torch shone in my face.

The torch flashed away and I saw him above me.

'Who are you?' he said, and I noticed that he used English. He already knew something about me, then.

He turned to the leader of the three, who I now saw was Jean, and whispered something.

I didn't answer. I couldn't. My lips were bleeding and already swollen, blood was in my mouth.

There was some discussion and then someone reached down and began ferreting in my pockets, pulling out my wallet, some other small things. There was more discussion and I dimly saw my bag. They must have brought it from the hotel. They began rummaging through that too, throwing everything on the ground, and then they found my passport.

He, Verovkin, took it and studied it.

'Charles Jackson . . .'

He spoke with hardly any accent, and what little there was, I couldn't place.

I moaned, holding my hands above my head. It was a truly pathetic gesture, a gesture of supplication, and it meant that I begged not to be hurt any more.

'Who are you?'

Again I said nothing, just squinted up into the face above me, desperately trying to think what I could do.

'Do I know you?' he asked.

I was too terrified, in too much pain, to even speak, but his question told me something. That unless he was playing games, it meant that he, like Jean, hadn't connected me to Marian, and that gave me a little hope that they would leave me alone, once they'd done enough damage, once they'd scared me enough. But I was wrong.

'I don't know you,' he said. 'You're no one.'

He turned to Jean. For some reason, presumably to scare me, he spoke in English.

'Kill him and put the body in the river.'

He began to walk away, and Jean pulled out a knife from inside his jacket.

I began to squirm backwards in the dust under the bridge, and then there were more voices, and lights.

From underneath the bridge, I could even see the flash of a blue light winking on the stonework.

There were voices and I rolled over, Jean hovering above me, knife in hand.

A voice called out and Jean stepped away, slipping the knife back inside his pocket.

Verovkin had stopped, and was talking to a man by the entrance to this little tunnel under the bridge. A policeman stood next to this man, but as I watched, the man waved him away and the light caught his face and my vision cleared, and I saw it was Captain Leclerc, though he was not in uniform.

Thank God, I thought, feeling like I would just sink into the dust. They believed me. They've come for me.

I watched, waiting for Verovkin to run, or to be arrested, but neither of those things happened. Nor did Jean and his two accomplices back away.

Verovkin was waving his hand in Leclerc's face, pointing at him. In return, Leclerc held his ground at first, though even hurt as I was, I could see him take a small step backwards as Verovkin pressed in on him. Then Leclerc stabbed a forefinger on to Verovkin's chest, speaking quickly but all too quietly for me to hear.

Verovkin was still as he listened to the captain. He became a statue, then turned away rapidly.

Leclerc came and stood over me, and Verovkin kept his distance.

'So,' said Leclerc, 'I think it's time you left Avignon, yes?'

I rolled on to my side, and managed to prop myself up on my right arm a little.

'What?' I said.

'Time for you to go, monsieur. You are not wanted here. You should count yourself lucky that I was informed. And that I got here before anything could happen.'

'Happen?' I spluttered. 'Something has already happened! Aren't you going to do anything about it?'

Every word hurt and I had to drag breath into my lungs even to say those few.

'Yes, monsieur. I am going give you a hundred francs, and drive you to catch the night train to Paris, and you will never come here again.'

With that, Leclerc nodded at Jean and the other two, and I was hoisted up and taken from the bridge. Verovkin glared at me as I was carried away, but I just stared back, wondering what on earth was going on between these people.

A short, agonising car ride and I was dumped at the station. Leclerc stood over me while we waited for the train, where I was put on-board in second class, in a deserted carriage. The others left the train, and Leclerc threw some money and my passport at me.

I had recovered enough to catch his arm.

'But aren't you going to do something? That man—'

'No crime has been committed here. I strongly suggest you do as I have told you. Goodbye.'

The train began to pull away as he jumped to the platform, and I stared at the walls of the carriage as the train rattled me hundreds of miles north, in appalling agony all the way.

14

I arrived in Cambridge three days later, having made a spectacle of myself on the way.

A hundred francs had been enough to get me to Paris and on to the coast, but I had had to buy some cheap clothes as mine were ruined and covered in dried blood. With that taken care of it was enough to explain I'd been in a car accident and was making my way home, poring over everything that had happened in Avignon. Who was Verovkin, and what power did he hold that he seemed to be able to act with impunity there? Leclerc had saved me, but how had he known what was happening? Maybe the hotel's night porter had made a phone call. Clearly there was a powerful group of people in the town, and Verovkin was at their head. Leclerc had merely talked him into not committing murder on their patch, it seemed, and but for that, I would have been a body in the river.

I was two days late reporting back for work, and I think only the extent of the cuts and bruises on my face was enough to keep me out of trouble.

Of course, I told Hunter, and only Hunter, the truth, and asked him what I should do.

'Drop it,' he said, flatly.

'What?'

'Drop it. No good can come of it. If you want my advice, just drop it.'

I told him I couldn't and I explained why. It was Marian, I said, I couldn't just give up on her, just let it be. I went further and asked him for help, because, being Hunter, I knew he would know someone who could help, and he did.

He knew a magistrate.

'You can't just walk into a police station in Cambridge or London and report a crime in Avignon, and a possible murder in Paris. You won't be taken seriously.'

He was right, and so began my first, and last, attempt to solve the matter using what Hunter described as 'the proper channels'.

He had his magistrate friend write to a chief inspector with the Met, who managed to get someone in Interpol to 'make enquiries' to the prefecture of Vaucluse.

Eight weeks later, through this circuitous and painfully slow route, I got a reply.

In long-winded terms, it boiled down to this:

No such person as Verovkin has ever been heard of in or around the Avignon area. Furthermore, Captain Leclerc is an officer of the highest standing, and a decorated veteran to boot. The other individual we believe you are referring to (no name was given) is a member of local society and a noted philanthropist. The accusations you have made are wild and fanciful, but (it was pointed out to me) even if true, neither blasphemy nor the willing imbibition of one's own blood are a crime, and no further enquiries are to be made.

The matter was closed, though there was one strange thing.

I had reported, also via Hunter's magistrate, that I suspected that Verovkin was the murderer known as 'the Beast of Saint-Germain'. Though the reply from the prefecture addressed everything else I'd accused Verovkin of, there was no mention at all of the incidents in Paris. Not a single line.

I had learned a little: that Verovkin was using a new name, and that most likely he had some of the police department in his pocket, if not actually in his control. Maybe some of them were part of that group I'd seen in the church, drinking their own blood. Maybe Leclerc was one of them too, one of those who were cutting themselves for him.

And how should I describe them? His followers? His acolytes, his disciples? His church?

For it was clearly a cult or sect of some kind, which had usurped a church in the backstreets of Avignon for its more sinister actions. Whether anyone outside the cult knew what was happening in the small hours of the night, I had no idea. Perhaps the priest there was involved, perhaps the warden had been scared into silence. Perhaps people had gone missing, and too late I wondered whether it would have been useful to check if there had been any murders in Avignon along the lines of the activities of the Beast in Saint-Germain. Somehow I doubted it; Avignon being a much smaller place than Paris, a series of brutal deaths would draw too much attention, arouse too much outrage, something that would require Verovkin to move on again. Perhaps there were deaths of unknown travellers, of vagrants, but maybe not. Maybe instead, I decided, he had created a different kind of route to blood.

I had witnessed it myself, their ceremony; a sacrament of their own blood, provided freely and presumably frequently. How many of them were involved? I wondered. The thirteen of them I had seen that night? Or others too? I thought about how much blood a man or woman could give, regularly, and not feel any ill effects. Each of them had given not so very much. Their actions could certainly be repeated on a weekly basis without any trouble for a healthy individual.

What horror! I thought. What disgust I felt. There was something so sickeningly primitive and yet so cold about this calm, considered, reverent imbibing of our most vital fluid.

And the carving? The female, bloodstained figure? What was the purpose of that? What was the symbolism? Was she supposed to represent fertility? True, the menstruating woman represents a girl who has become old enough to bear children, but there,

there lay a paradox, for the flow of monthly blood also demonstrates that the woman is not pregnant, not for another month at least.

Whatever mythology he had created, Verovkin seemed to have drawn in more acolytes than he'd had in Paris, although once again much of this was guesswork.

And there they were, drinking the blood of their lord, worshipping some idol smeared in blood from millennia before. I thought about that, and the words of Leclerc. *No crime has been committed here.* No, no crime; drinking the literal blood of their blood-smeared idol.

Revolting, hideous. And then a thought hit me. Wasn't that just what happened in a Catholic Mass, wasn't that the message of transubstantiation? That the wine literally becomes Christ's blood? The wine in the cup, which the Lord passes to his disciples, saying this is my blood. Do this in remembrance of me. And whenever it was in the Middle Ages that the Catholic Church declared that the wine of the Eucharist is literally Christ's blood, since that time, surely every Catholic has done just what Verovkin was doing. Drunk the blood of their Lord underneath an image of Christ hanging on the cross, which now I stopped to think about it for one minute I found to be an undeniably horrific and brutal one. Blood flowing from the wound in his side from the spear, blood from the wounds to his head where the crown of thorns cut him. His mouth hangs open, his head lolls on one side, his eyes roll back. The nails through his hands and feet only cause more bleeding, more horror.

Whatever perverted blood-cult Verovkin had created in Avignon, their actions were no more illegal than those of a billion or more Catholics, during each and every Mass in their Church.

I thought of Catherine of Siena, of her lust for blood; I thought of Verovkin; and I thought of Marian, all alone in the ground in Montmartre.

Over the next few days I argued long and hard with Hunter. I asked him what he thought was happening, who this man was, but Hunter wasn't himself, or rather, he didn't talk as freely as before. I saw him watching me carefully as I spoke, and he seemed always to hesitate before answering. When I pushed him, he said he supposed that such lunatics might exist, but that I would be better off asking a psychologist about such matters.

'Come on, Hunter,' I said. 'Humour me. Just play along with me. I can't be the first person ever to think about this.'

Hunter raised an eyebrow.

'I'm sure you're not,' he said, 'but that doesn't mean it's a healthy direction in which to keep thinking.'

'You know something.'

'I do not. Not really. I was reminded of a film. *M*. You know it?'

I shook my head.

'A Fritz Lang film, about a serial killer. Made in thirty-one, I think. Although Lang always denied it, it was assumed he'd been inspired by a killer known as the Vampire of Düsseldorf.'

I found that my heart was beating fast. I didn't say anything, because I felt that Hunter was on the verge of going silent on me. One wrong word and he'd clam up, and yet here, for the first time, someone seemed to be giving me reason to believe that Verovkin could really be what I thought he was.

Hunter seemed to be hesitating.

'Go on,' I almost whispered.

'I forget the details.'

'You remember his name?'

Hunter shook his head.

'But this murderer, he drank blood?'

'Not as far as anyone knows. But they say that the mere sight of the blood of his victims was what he was after.'

'The sight? Why?'

'Oh work it out for yourself, man,' said Hunter, and there was more than an edge to his voice. 'He was some kind of pervert, obviously.'

The penny dropped into place in my mind and I felt myself blush for being so slow.

'If you want to know any more, I'd find a shrink.'

'To help me with my research?' I laughed. 'Or to cure me?'

Hunter didn't respond to my joke, but I thanked him for what he knew, and left soon after. I think it was the first time I ever saw Hunter defer the opportunity of giving his opinion, and pass the chance to someone else.

I could see he was reluctant to talk about the matter any more. He had tried, he said, and we had our answer – the case, far from being closed, was never to be opened.

So I did ask a psychologist: Donald. I wrote to him, explaining what I was after, and we met in a pub in London one evening in September.

'My God,' he said. 'What happened to your face?'

'You should see the rest of me,' I said, smiling weakly. It had been weeks since my double assault, and yet I still bore the scars. My nose had been put straight, but was still swollen, a few cuts had yet to heal.

'What happened?'

'I was hit by a car,' I said. 'Nothing serious. Look, what do you know? Did you find anything out?'

Donald looked at me oddly.

'What's all this about anyway? Something to do with your research? Got a screwy patient?'

I decided that was the easiest angle.

'Yes,' I said. 'Something like that. So, what do you have?'

'Not much. There have been a few papers written, no books. It appears that there are cases of certain people who have been found to . . . well, drink blood.'

'Go on,' I said.

'Listen here, Charles, what is this about? If you have a patient with some disorder you ought to pass them on to the psychiatric unit. It's not your—'

'I know, I know. I just want to know what I might be dealing with before I decide what to do. What do you have?'

Donald seemed placated by that. He sipped at his drink, then sighed.

'As I said, not much. Essentially, we have two types of blood drinkers. There are those with the desire to drink others' blood. And there are those who drink their own. In this latter camp are some cases of patients who display factitious disorders; who want to maintain the fiction that they are ill, in order to seek attention. There's some French guy, I'd have to look the name up again, who's writing about cases of self-induced anaemia in young girls. The doctors were mystified until it was found how they did it. These girls were biting the backs of their own tongues and swallowing the blood in massive quantities. Very often they'd be sick, but the resulting anaemia was all too real.'

I listened to everything that Donald had to say, and felt sure that he was telling me everything he himself knew.

'Do you think it's possible,' I asked, 'that someone could become obsessed with drinking blood? Other people's blood? Maybe thinking they are a vampire, or that they gain some power or strength that way?'

'Yes, of course. Anything's possible. And our mental institutions have plenty of cases of people who've done terrible things, without any idea that what they were doing was wrong.'

'But could such a person seem normal otherwise? I mean, aren't they all just raving lunatics? Climbing the walls, literally?'

'Not at all,' Donald said. 'Many cases of psychosis go undetected for long periods of time for the simple reason that the sufferer appears, to all external appearance, to be utterly normal and rational.'

Donald told me the rest of what he knew. He'd asked around his colleagues and found that there were a couple of Americans who were about to publish on the subject of what they termed clinical vampirism.

'It's not exactly been a popular field of study,' he said. 'For obvious reasons. No one even seems to have agreed on a name for the thing. For the will to drink blood, and the wider, underlying cause, a desire for blood in general. It ought to be called haemophilia, but your chaps bagged that one, didn't they?'

I nodded, smiling wryly. 'I've always said it was a stupid name.'

'A blood drinker would be a haematophage, I suppose.'

'And what about someone who derived pleasure from blood? Sexual pleasure.'

'Christ, Charles, I really think you ought to—'

'Please, Donald. I can handle it. I'm just trying to know a little more.'

I had nearly said 'know my enemy', but managed to swerve the sentence elsewhere.

He blinked. Looked at me hard for a while.

'Well,' he said, finally. 'A sexual obsession, or deriving sexual pleasure from blood, that would be haemolagnia, I suppose, or haematolagnia. We use the suffix in relation to various perversions and lusts.'

So there, finally, I had a name for Verovkin. There really were such people in the world.

'Actually, now I think about it,' said Donald, 'I read an account of a case like this during my training. There was a man called Peter – oh what was it? Peter Kürten, I think. A serial killer. He murdered a whole string of people, young children, for their blood. Not to drink it. Just for the sight of it, which made him orgasm. This was in Germany, in the twenties.'

The hair stood up on the back of my neck as I realised Donald was talking about the man that had inspired Fritz Lang's movie.

'He had a name, a nickname,' Donald was saying, though I wasn't really listening too closely any more.

'Yes,' I said, 'the Vampire of Düsseldorf.'

'You've heard of him?'

'Not really,' I said. 'Thank you, Donald. You've been a great help.'

I meant it, for above everything else, he had shown me that I wasn't going crazy, that it was entirely possible Verovkin was a madman acting out some deeply perverted desires.

So, I knew he was out there, and we had met. He had an advantage over me in that I didn't know his real name, but I had one advantage over him: he hadn't connected me with Marian, and presumably thought that I had been sufficiently scared off in Avignon to leave him alone.

But my bruises healed, and my fear left with them. Instead, in its place came the determination once more that having turned to the law for help, and the law having failed me, I would find him myself, and bring him to some kind of justice.

Just what that meant, I don't think I had decided then. It was more a feeling, an intention, a determination not to let go, not to let Marian's memory go.

I wouldn't be able to act, not for a very long time, but somehow I didn't care. I didn't forget what I wanted to do; if anything, I had a chance to think about what I would do, and how I could do it, in a calm manner. And I knew that was important. I'd been stupid before, blundering into the South of France without a clue what I was up against, but then I hadn't had any reason to suppose that I was fighting an army.

Now I knew differently, and I decided to be better prepared when I went back. I thought about arming myself. I'd barely used a gun in the war, once my training was over. I had been a doctor, not a soldier, not really. It would be a little tricky to get one, but I thought I could, and decided to look out for the chance to get hold of a pistol of some kind, as soon as it came my way.

In the meantime I threw myself into my work, which needed attention. That group in Oxford had left behind snake venom and was instead starting to make serious progress on identifying clotting factors, or so we'd heard. The goal of a cure for haemophilia was becoming a reality, and meanwhile, the lives of sufferers would be helped enormously through the production of these factors. We were being left behind, and the pressure was on me to catch up.

So work got in the way. I worked hard, and when an invitation came to speak to an Italian research group at the university in Rome, I knew I should accept.

THREE

Rome

October, 1961

The question is not what we think about when we're not having sex, the question is what we think about when we are.

Zlatan Miličević, *The Symmetry of the Soul*

I

The morning I left for Rome, I had another strange letter. I took it with me on the train to London, reading it on the plane a dozen times or more.

It was from Captain Leclerc. There was no return address.

Mr Jackson,

I got your address from the department; I was aware that you did not take my advice, to leave this business well alone. I am also aware that you made enquiries into the man you met in Avignon. You called him by some Russian name, but that was not how we knew him.

I knew something of his affairs; we turned a blind eye to many things, but I was not about to sanction murder in my city. Fortunately for you, the owner of a photographic shop thought better of his involvement with this man, and informed me of your situation.

After I intervened in your case, the man you hunted used his influence to have me dismissed. That is what I believe. I also fear for my life now. I heard that the owner of the photographic shop was beaten to death one night, without apparent motive. So I am going to retire to my mother's country, and hide in the mountains, where I trust he will not bother me.

But I want to tell you three things. First, I urge you to do nothing more. He is rich and has power. Secondly, since something tells me you are going to ignore this first thing, I should tell you that even your clumsy work has had some effect. You upset a precarious balance here and he came under more scrutiny than he liked. He has left Avignon; my best sources tell me he is still in France, though I do not know where. And thirdly, I will tell you his name, then I ask you to burn this letter in return for the favour I once did you. His name is Lippe, and to all outward appearances he is a rich German business tycoon, though I do not know what type of business he is in.

François Leclerc

2

The office of Professor Enzio Mazzarino at La Sapienza had written to me in September asking for my help. They were trying to improve their research methods into various blood disorders, and had heard of our work in Cambridge. The professor, they explained, craved my advice. I had to admit that this was very flattering; Mazzarino's had been one of the few papers I had seen given at the Paris conference, all those years before, and that this enormously respected man should *crave my advice* was enough to get my interest. The offer of a hotel, my plane fare and a generous 'consideration' was enough to seal the matter, and I exchanged a couple of letters arranging things.

I arrived at lunchtime and checked into the hotel that had been booked for me by Mazzarino's secretary, but was disappointed to find it a squalid little place near Termini Station. Perhaps Mazzarino had not been as impressed with my Paris paper as he claimed, but I soon found the hotel to be close enough to the sights, the Spanish Steps, the Trevi Fountain and so on, and my spirits lifted. Having never been to Rome before I was naturally eager to see these things.

That afternoon, I found myself wandering to the Vatican, for everyone has heard of the Sistine Chapel, and I was keen to see it too. I knew very little about it apart from the image of God creating Adam with a languid touch of a fingertip. I had been expecting it to be a light and uplifting place, like the Lady Chapel at Ely, but with paintings. I found I was wrong.

An interminable series of gaudy hallways finally led to a small set of steps that led down into the chapel: a dark box of horrors. The windows were way above head height, the light was poor. There in the centre of the ceiling were God and Adam, but this was just one part of a mismatched and hideously coloured series of frescoes.

This was not what disturbed me the most. The entire end wall of the chapel was given over to a massive depiction of the Last Judgement, I assumed, depicted with pornographic horror and morbid excitation. Hell and the devils and souls in torment, skins being pulled off, bodies rising from the grave, crucifixions, punishments and terrors of all kind, and all of that could be understood to be shocking. The glabrous flesh of even the good figures in the painting was equally repulsive.

Very soon I was desperate for sunlight, desperate for something less horrific, and though I found my way outside again, I did so only after passing a series of exhibits of reliquaries and chalices, with which, I assumed, the faithful would worship pieces of saints' bodies and drink Christ's blood.

Even though it was October, it was a powerfully hot evening.

By the time I wandered back across the river I was starting to feel exhausted from the sun. I was supposed to be meeting Mazzarino and two colleagues of his for dinner, but suddenly my head swam and I knew I needed to sleep early, so I took a taxi back to my hotel and had the receptionist phone the restaurant I'd been told to meet them at. I asked them to give sincere apologies but that I had a migraine. That wasn't strictly true, but I didn't want to offend them.

Instead, I wandered down a quiet, narrow alley, looking for somewhere to eat, and finally I staggered into a small pizzeria in some backstreet and had an early supper, drinking lots of water and only a little wine.

It took me a while to sleep, and as I waited to get drowsy, I found myself thinking about Michelangelo's masterwork. Impressive, undeniably. But also undeniably grotesque, hideous, and to my mind, of dubious intention.

3

I woke early and prepared for my ten o'clock meeting with the professor. I thought back to '51 and the Paris conference. Even ten years later the shame of my failure burned, yet Mazzarino had been impressed, according to the letters from his office. And he'd been reading about our progress with haemophilia with interest. I tried to picture the man but wasn't sure I had him right; I could see a fifty-something, grey hair and bushy beard, but then wondered if that was Doure of Heidelberg.

I'd know soon enough.

I found my way to the campus easily, and arrived early, but made my way to Mazzarino's offices anyway, hoping to brush away any offence I might have caused by my no-show at dinner.

What happened next took me by surprise, and threw me so much that I know I didn't think clearly.

I knocked on a door and let myself in to find a secretary for the Department of Medicine looking at me expectantly.

'*Lei parla Inglese?*' I asked and was relieved when the woman smiled.

'Yes, of course,' she said.

'Good,' I said, 'because that's the total of my Italian.'

She politely ignored my apology.

'How may I help you?'

I explained who I was and that Professor Mazzarino was expecting me.

'There must be some mistake,' she said.

'No, no mistake. I'm sure. I have a letter here which . . .'

I trailed off as I fumbled in my briefcase for my papers, but she wasn't listening.

'No, sir. No mistake. The professor is away today, he has no appointments. Perhaps you have the wrong day?'

I was surprised enough not to be angry, not then, anyway.

'Well, I suppose . . .'

'Why don't you come back tomorrow? The professor is here tomorrow. Leave me your name, please, and I'll inform him as soon as he arrives in the morning.'

And with that, leaving my name and the name of my hotel, I stumbled back out into the streets, without even thinking to check my letter with her, or to see if she was the one who was meant to have invited me.

Trying to work out if I'd got the day wrong, or even the month, I wandered through the backstreets and finally came into a beautiful square, the Campo de' Fiori, I think. I was by now getting angry at being stood up by the professor after flying to Italy to meet him, and cursing the lackadaisical nature of the Mediterranean in general, when suddenly I laughed. I was being foolish, for here was a chance for a pleasant holiday, and at someone else's expense.

I sauntered into the square in a much better mood.

The campo was long and surrounded by elegant buildings, but what attracted me was the market in full swing in the centre. There were flowers, of course, but also fruit and meats and cheeses. There were stalls selling clothes and others selling trinkets of various kinds, some of them aimed at tourists, for sure, but much sold by locals, for other local people.

I slowed myself down and crawled around the market, taking in all the wonderful smells and colourful sights, and then, I saw a girl.

I should correct that; I mean I saw a young woman, with long, light brown hair, cross in front of me. One second she was not there, a moment later I could not take my eyes off her. She was fingering the material on a skirt hanging from a stall, idly, her head on one side, and then she drifted on.

I could do nothing but follow her.

What had happened to me? I have thought about it a lot, and though I would like to claim it was love at first sight, I have to confess that it was lust.

Something inside me just switched on, switched on again, having been asleep for a long, long time. I hadn't been with a woman since Sarah died, and even when married I think I can guess that our physical life was no better than adequate. We did not have sex very often; she did not seem very interested in it, and once she became ill, not at all, and at that point nor was I any more. I just wanted her to be better. But she died.

I've often wondered why I married Sarah. We met at a college ball one summer; we dated for a little while. I think we got married because she wanted to, and because I thought I was supposed to. Then it became simply what we were doing, but I don't think I ever stopped to wonder if I was getting married because it was the right thing to do, and certainly not if it was what I wanted.

She and I were close enough, I suppose, and I thought I had loved her, but when the girl in Rome walked past me, I think what had actually been stirred up in me was the memory of Marian.

I watched the girl in the market furtively, developing a sudden interest in oranges as she stood nearby in front of a high pile of aubergines and artichokes. I tried not to make it obvious I was trailing her, and at the time I don't think I even realised that that was what I was doing. I was so taken with her that I was just pulled after her, magnetically. She stood still once more, her body adopting that curving stoop common to tall people, but which in her gave off powerfully sexual signals.

People passed by me, passing between the woman and me, locals, tourists, but they were no more than shapes and colours; suddenly the only living person in that whole square was the woman.

I saw that I was not the only one appraising her. Two stall-holders, young men, stared at her blatantly, their Italian masculinity putting my furtiveness to shame. They were open about what they were thinking, and whistled at the girl. She appeared not to notice, or certainly did not react. One of the two men turned and caught me looking at her too, and winked, grinning from ear to ear. He turned back to stare at her some more as she moved away.

I followed.

She was barely dressed. She wore a light white blouse, open at the neck, with two or three buttons undone. It was clear she wore nothing underneath, and pathetically I found myself manoeuvring opposite her as she bent over to smell some flowers, in order to catch a glimpse of her. I did so and was rewarded with the glimpse of one dark nipple on a small pointed breast.

She straightened, and she caught me looking. For a brief moment our eyes met, and I knew she knew what I had seen. She showed no reaction, maybe just the slightest smile before she looked away. I, of course, turned and picked up a dreadful souvenir of cheap rosary beads, waiting for her to move on.

She did.

She was tall and slim, and if not beautiful, she was very pretty, with a delicate face, and an elegant neck. She moved gracefully and slowly, and I walked after her, trying to make my progress appear random. I didn't know what I wanted. The stallholders did, for one of them made a rude gesture with his fist as I passed, leering, his eyes popping.

His friend laughed, and I followed the girl more directly as she left the square and headed down a small street heading east. The street was busy enough for me not to be noticed, and I ambled along, pausing when she did, taking her in some more.

She wore tiny denim shorts, torn from an old pair of light blue jeans, and had bare legs down to her knees. She had knee-length socks in light sandals, making her look younger than she probably was.

She stopped by a shop window and peered in, and I saw that her shorts were so brief that the curve of one buttock peeked out below. The skin was golden brown. She lifted a strand of hair out of her eyes and tucked it behind her ear.

In that moment I knew I was seriously affected. I turned away from her, staring blindly into a shop window of my own, waiting for my heart to stop beating so wildly. I turned back and looked at her thighs again, and suddenly the image of Marian in her guest room at Caius came back to me. I remembered wanting to kneel in front of her and kiss her naked stomach, and now I had similar feelings towards this strange girl. I saw myself stroking her whole long naked body. I saw other things.

Turning away again, I waited once more, and this time, when I turned back, she was gone.

A desperate feeling of loss suddenly swept into me and I hunted for her. I ducked into shops and down alleys, retracing my steps, turning this way and that, but in the end I had to concede she had gone.

I cursed myself. Why hadn't I just told her what I wanted, like the stallholders had? And then I knew why. Because she was half my age, because she almost certainly was married or had a boyfriend, because I would be unattractive to her, because a million reasons.

I slunk away and by twelve o'clock I found myself in a bar, sipping a long cool drink. And then she walked in, sat down at the next table, and looked straight at me.

She ordered a drink, knowing my eyes were all over her as she spoke to a young and handsome waiter. She fingered the topmost of the closed buttons on her blouse as she spoke, as if suggesting she was about to undo that one too. The waiter went away and soon came back with her Campari, but she this time ignored him, and he went away, scowling.

She fumbled in her bag, fishing for a pack of cigarettes. She found them, and dropped them. On the floor, right by my feet.

She bent over quickly to pick them up, and this time, as she straightened, she kept her eyes on mine as I gazed at the beautiful sight of both her breasts, realising she had somewhere along the line undone that button.

She smiled, and I smiled back, and that was how we met.

4

Her name was Arianna. She was Italian, but spoke perfect English, and explained that her mother was English, and she had spent many summers in England, though her father was from Sicily.

I asked her what she was doing in Rome.

'I'm studying art,' she said, and lit a cigarette, offering one to me.

'You shouldn't smoke,' I said.

'Oh, and why's that?'

'It's bad for you. I'm a doctor.'

'But you're not *my* doctor, are you?'

Even I, as old and out of practice as I was, could see that she was flirting, very openly. I found that I liked it. There was no pretence of what was happening, no games. For some reason she wanted to flirt with me and I was enjoying it.

I didn't even care that I felt I was spouting awful clichés as I did my best to flirt back. I was pretty clumsy; it had never been, how to put it, my line . . .

She began to suck on the cigarette, blatantly teasing me.

'What kind of doctor are you?'

I thought about telling her I was a haematologist. It didn't seem like a great chat-up line.

'The usual kind,' I said, instead.

'And what's that? Kind? Caring? Or brutal and cold?'

She held my eyes again.

'That depends,' I said.

'On?'

'On what's called for. A good doctor knows that every patient needs to be handled differently.'

I was more pleased with that one.

'Oh. I see. And if I were your patient, how should I be handled?'

She had moved a little closer to me, and sat with her legs slightly apart, allowing a slight view disappearing up inside her thigh.

Then I wanted her. Quickly, soon. As hard as possible.

'Well,' I said, 'I'd have to give you a full examination first.'

It was corny and clumsy, but I didn't care, because it seemed to be working.

She looked me in the eyes again. Long and deep. Although she was young, I was impressed with her. If I'd noticed her to start with from pure sexuality, she wasn't the young giggly type. She seemed mature, thoughtful. Intelligent even. I knew she could be dangerous too, though I couldn't have explained how. But I didn't care. All I wanted then was to be naked with her, in a more powerful way than I think I had ever felt before, with anyone else.

'Do I . . . make an appointment?' she said, her eyes twinkling.

'Tonight?' I suggested. Then more decisively, 'Tonight. Nine o'clock?'

She smiled, downed her drink in one.

'Via Farini. There's a bar. La Bianca. *Ciao*.'

She stood, and left.

I was paying for both our drinks, no more than a minute later, when she came back in.

She grabbed my wrist with her delicate hand and winked at the barman.

'We have places to go,' she said, and laughing, I let her drag me outside.

It was lunch, and suddenly the streets had emptied as they always do in France and Italy at the stroke of noon.

'Where are we going?' I asked, but I wasn't really interested. I was more interested in the fact that she was taking me down a quiet street, and then turning into a tiny alley, at the end of which was a little yard behind the back doors of some restaurant or other.

She pushed me against a wall and began kissing me hard.

I kissed her back and then pulled away.

'What's going on?'

'You want me to draw you a diagram? You're the doctor.'

Then there was no more talking.

We did it standing up, but before we did she took my hand and pushed it down the front of her shorts. She flicked the button open and pushed my hand further in, and up, tilting her head back as I did so.

She opened my trousers and turned around, dropping her shorts to her ankles, and as she did so, I saw that my fingers had blood on them, from her.

I said something, nothing really, I can't remember. Maybe I just said 'Oh', but she looked at the blood as I showed her my fingers, and she gave me a look that was neither a smile nor a sneer.

'So?' she said. 'You can't have sex without a little blood, can you? We wouldn't have this, for a start.'

She took my erection in her hand and tugged it.

'No blood,' she said, 'no sex,' and putting me inside her, turned her face to the wall and the rest . . . well, the rest is obvious enough.

I went back to my hotel where I lay on the bed while the shower ran.

I washed myself, washing the dark, red-brown blood from me, and thought about nothing but Arianna.

No blood, no sex.

I didn't know if I was disgusted or aroused by what she'd done. What I'd done. Disgusted or aroused, or maybe both.

She'd told me to meet her later, as we'd arranged before the two minutes in the alleyway.

At seven thirty I ate in the restaurant for speed, after which I felt sweaty and went upstairs to shower again and change.

My head was full of her. Of her long brown hair, her legs. The sight of her breasts, the intensity of the way in which she'd set out to catch me, and had. That was what excited me the most. Maybe she had a thing for older men. I really didn't care, I'm not sure I even thought about it. I just wanted her again.

At half-past eight, I left my room, dropped my key in at reception, and as I was walking away, the receptionist called me back.

'Signor Jackson?'

I turned. 'Yes?'

The receptionist, an older woman, was holding out something towards me. 'You have a telegram. And a message.'

'Yes?'

'A lady calls from the university.'

She was reading carefully from a note.

'She says that the professor phoned this afternoon. She says to say he does not know of your visit and cannot help you. She is sorry for your trouble.'

I stared at the woman for a long time, but there was nothing to say. She had no idea why I was so confused, what the mystery was.

'And the telegram?'

She handed it to me, and even before I read it, I knew it was something serious. No one would send me a telegram otherwise, but I knew more than that. I knew immediately what it was.

It was from my sister, and that was how I learned that my father was dying.

All thoughts of the Roman girl vanished, and within two hours I was catching the last flight home to London, to wait with my father while he died.

5

I didn't go home.

I went straight from the airport to Richmond and met my sister at the hospital.

'You look bloody awful,' she said.

'Hello, Susan,' I said. 'How is he?'

'He's dying, you idiot. How do you think he is?'

I kissed her cheek and she filled me in on our father's approaching end.

It's fair to say that we were not a close family. Mother was the one who held the rest of us together, and when she died, Father became a recluse, and he and Susan and I all saw very little of each other.

We could have tried to treat Father's leukaemia. If we'd known about it. But he kept it to himself until it was well beyond that time.

Leukaemia. The irony was not lost on me, nor on Susan.

'Can't you lot fix this stuff by now?' she said, as we walked away from my first visit to see him.

Father looked worse than I'd guessed he might. But then, as Susan said, he was dying.

Already he didn't know who I was, what time of day it was, or even what was happening to him. He was no longer there, because of the morphine they were giving him. Pain control was all there was to do. That and wait, and it turned out there was a lot of waiting to be done.

I waited for another day or two, finding a cheap guesthouse in the same road as the hospital. Susan lived a half-hour drive away.

There was no suggestion I stay with her and Roger. That was fine by me.

After another day had passed, however, Susan put her foot down.

'Charles, go home and wash, will you? Get some clean clothes, for God's sake.'

I wrinkled my nose.

'Right.'

So I headed for Cambridge, making sure not to sit next to anyone on the trains and walking from the station to Hills Road.

The last thing I was expecting to see when I got back was a police car in my drive.

6

I knew things were serious when I saw a detective in plain clothes standing by my front door. A cop in uniform hung at his shoulder with an unpleasant look on his face.

They were talking to Mrs Sully, my cleaner. She hadn't let them in, but maybe they'd only just arrived.

The detective turned as Mrs Sully saw me coming, and I saw from the look on her face that I was in trouble. She wouldn't meet my eye.

'These gentlemen—' she began, but the plain-clothes man cut her off.

'That's fine, ma'am, we'll handle it from here. Mr Jackson? Mr Charles Jackson?'

I nodded.

'May we come in?'

'Look, this isn't the best . . .'

I saw there was little point in protesting.

'Be my guest,' I said, and followed them in, shutting the door behind me.

I waved them into my study, Mrs Sully hovering in the doorway still with a duster in her hand, probably wondering if she should offer us tea.

A sick feeling had started to crawl up from inside me, and as I listened to the detective it did nothing but get worse.

'Detective Lovering,' he said, then nodded at the cop. 'Sergeant Francis.'

He stopped.

'Yes?'

'We have received certain information that we are sufficiently concerned about that, well . . .'

He hesitated and pulled out an official-looking sheet of paper. He handed it to me and though I looked at it, I didn't notice a single word.

'This is a warrant we have obtained in order that we might search your house. I trust you have no objection to that.'

I had all sorts of objections to that, but we both knew that didn't really matter.

'Why?' I asked. 'What am I supposed to have here? Who gave you . . . Look, you can't just go looking in—'

'Yes, we can,' said the sergeant, who had already begun to pull drawers open in my desk. He rifled through a few things and then seemed to freeze.

'Sir?' he said, looking up, and handed a plain Manila envelope to the detective.

I had no memory of having such an envelope in that drawer, though I might have been mistaken.

'I see,' said the detective, and then he read me my rights.

An hour later, I sat in an interview room in the station in St Andrew's Street.

Detective Lovering sat across from me at a table on which were spread a sordid little array of photographs of naked girls. Young girls. The sergeant, and another come to gawp, stood behind him.

I repeated again, and again, that I had no knowledge of the photos, of how they came to be in my possession, in my drawer, in my desk, in my study, and while I spoke, and while I felt sick, and while I was fully aware of everything going on, another terrible idea was screaming at me in my head.

They have been in my house. They know where I live.

Why? I thought. They came for me, but why? I felt cold; I almost wanted to appeal to these mindless policemen for help, have them protect me. Get them to help me understand what he wanted with me. It was a stupid desire, and I repressed it; these men wanted to do nothing but humiliate me.

'So you deny these photos belong to you?'

'I told you that.'

'And you claim someone broke into your house while you were abroad and put them there?'

'I don't claim that,' I said, 'I *deduce* that, because there is no other explanation.'

'Unless Mrs Sully, your cleaner, put them there?'

'Don't be ridiculous.'

That wasn't a smart thing to say.

'Listen,' I said, 'I'm not saying anything else till my solicitor arrives.'

'What gets me about guys like you is how arrogant you are.'

I knew he was trying to wind me up, and it was working. Despite my firm intention to shut up till I had representation, I couldn't help myself.

'You have absolutely no proof whatsoever that these photos are anything to do with me,' I said.

'Apart from the fact that they were in your house.'

'Someone broke in!'

'A proposition that we are looking into at this very moment,' Detective Lovering said, unsmiling. 'And in the meantime, you say you have never bought or otherwise obtained photographs of this nature.'

'I have not.'

He shoved the photos towards me again.

'Nothing to do with you?'

'Nothing,' I said, and I knew they were struggling then, because, to be honest, even if they could prove the photos were mine, it was far from clear how old the girls in the photos were. There were three of them in all, in about ten pictures, and they might have been fifteen, or they might have been eighteen.

'Nothing to do with you?' he repeated.

'I just said that, I—'

'And this one is nothing to do with you either?'

The bastard. Holding his trump card till the nicest time to play it. He pulled a new photograph out from inside his jacket pocket, and flicked it over to me.

It was me, and the girl. In the alleyway, in Rome.

7

It was many hours later that I staggered home again.

I replayed the moment when I saw the photo of me and the Italian girl, again and again, and each time I felt more and more sick.

There was no point in denying it. It was clearly me behind her. The photo was taken from somewhere slightly above us, to one side. From a window of that restaurant, the kitchens, maybe.

She had her face up to the camera, mine was just behind, less distinct, but it was me, holding a bunch of her hair in my clutching fingers.

Am I so stupid, I thought, as to have actually believed that girl really wanted me?

Am I so stupid, I thought, that only then did I wonder how old she was? Twenty, is what I would have said if I'd been thinking, but I wasn't thinking. But maybe she was younger than that.

But not illegal. Then it occurred to me that I didn't know the age of consent in Italy, and it further occurred to me to shut my mouth until my solicitor arrived, which I did.

John Hulme had sorted a few things for me in the past. Things like buying houses and arranging a will. Not things like defending a client from accusations of paedophilia. But he did a good job, and gave as good as we got.

We debated all afternoon, and I must have looked pretty guilty, but what I was wondering was this. How much do I tell them? Do I tell them about Verovkin? Or Lippe, should I say? Should I tell them about Marian? Hunter could vouch for me that I had been attacked in Avignon. Couldn't he? Wouldn't he?

John kept a straight bat. That's how my father would have described it, before he was senseless with morphine.

The sum of it was this:

They had been sent a photo, anonymously, of me having sex with a young woman. I had photos of naked girls in my house. They may or may not have been teenaged. I claimed the house must have been broken into, and the photos left there, as an attempt to incriminate me, and my God, how I breathed a sigh of relief when they admitted, much later that day, that there were signs of a forced entry to the kitchen window.

I was let out of the station, eventually. They charged me with nothing, but said they would be making further investigations. Whether they meant into me, or into the break-in at my house, I didn't ask, and they didn't say.

The police kept the photos. Even the one of me. Perverts.

And they also kept something else: my passport.

'You won't need to be travelling anywhere for a while, will you?' the detective said, with a leering smile that made me want to punch him. I fought that desire and instead hurried out of the station house before they changed they minds.

But my anger subsided into fear as I walked home. And as I reached the doorstep, and read the note that Mrs Sully had left, saying she was a bit too busy to be my cleaner any more, and as I slumped into an armchair with a very stiff drink in one hand, the one thought I had was one of terror.

They had been in my house. Someone, one of them, I didn't know who. Now I knew why a very attractive girl maybe twenty years younger than me had had sex with me in an alleyway. Because she'd been paid to. To have my photo taken.

When Verovkin saw my passport that night in Avignon, he must have seen my profession. *Doctor.* My place of residence. *Cambridge.* That would be enough to know how to find me.

And they'd been here.

In my house.

The phone rang and I dropped my whisky on the carpet.

I stared at the phone for ever before picking it up.

'What?' I barked.

'Oh, Charles,' said Susan. She was crying. 'Daddy's dead.'

8

Rome.

The girl. That hot day in Campo de' Fiori. Two minutes in a foetid alleyway. These things grew; they took on a greater significance. In my mind the phrase *what happened in Rome* repeated itself often, when it would have been more honest to say *what I did in Rome*.

No one made me follow that girl. Arianna. No one, and yet I fell for that trap, for trap it almost certainly had been, easily. Not just the girl, but the whole trip. The real Mazzarino had never written to me. I marvelled at the trouble Verovkin had taken to set me up, fly me there, invite me to a dinner that only my rudeness had prevented me from attending. I marvelled and was terrified in equal measure.

What had been his plan? For me to meet Arianna there and then? Even though I'd cancelled, they'd found me anyway, lured me in, got the photos they wanted.

How pathetic I felt, and never did I stop to wonder how many other men would have behaved differently from me, given such a direct approach from a young, attractive girl. The stuff of male fantasy.

From all the impressions and memories that returned from those fleeting moments in the bar and the alley, the one that always succeeded in rising to the top of the pile was the one of the blood on my fingertips.

No blood, no sex.

She'd pushed my hand on to her breasts too, making me feel her nipples. Made me? I had fumbled them eagerly, and again knew their arousal to be a thing of blood, of the blood inside them.

I said that the sex in the alley was obvious enough, and yes, the details of it were, but for one thing. One thing: this had been my first taste of sex in a very long time, and it would be natural to assume that it overwhelmed me and for a short time at least I thought of nothing else. But even during the act, some part of my mind was elsewhere, making other connections. From nowhere, as I pushed my fingers into the hair on the back of Arianna's head, an image surfaced in my mind, the image I'd seen in the museum in Saint-Germain in 1944, of the decapitated woman supposed to be a vampire.

We cremated my father in Guildford, and had drinks at his golf club. Susan and I made small talk with his few friends and colleagues who'd shown up. Hunter was there, for which I was very grateful, but he was always a loyal friend, and had loved my father deeply, something I found mysterious to say the least, as two more different men I could not imagine

I watched Susan forcing smiles at people neither of us knew, nodding frequently to compensate. She seemed smaller to me, younger even.

'Roger didn't make it,' I said, rescuing her from another such conversation and steering her to the bar.

Where before she would have withered me with a taut rebuke, she turned her face to me, looking lost.

'He's on a business trip,' she said, failing to find the lightness she was after.

'Important?'

'Yes, very,' she said. 'Couldn't be helped. Of course.'

I got her another Scotch and water and we turned and looked at the handful of mourners.

'Don't say it,' she said.

'What?'

'That awful thing everyone says at funerals. "I wonder how many people will turn up for me when it's my turn." It's such a cliché.'

'Hadn't crossed my mind.'

'Liar,' she said, and I smiled, because she looked a little more herself then.

'What do we do now?' she asked.

'Do?'

'Now . . .'

'It's just us?'

'Us,' she said. 'There isn't really an "us", is there? Not these days.'

'No, maybe not, but you have Roger, and . . .'

'Yes. Roger. And you . . . have your work.'

'You make it sound so awful. Yes, you do. That's OK. It is pretty awful. I was just never very lucky with the love thing.'

'I feel I was never there. When Sarah died.'

'You came to the funeral.'

'You know that's not what I mean.'

'What's up with you?' I asked. 'Don't tell me Dad going has made you all philosophical.'

She didn't answer, just sipped her Scotch and tried to avoid eye contact with an old couple who clearly wanted to chat. She won and they passed slowly by.

'Just don't end up alone, Charles,' Susan said. 'That's all.'

I offered Hunter a lift back to Cambridge but he was staying on in London, he said. So I drove home by myself that night and sat like a stranger in my own house.

I couldn't shift the feeling that Verovkin, or, more likely, some thug in his employ, had been there, and that very night I determined to sell up and take a little flat somewhere. By the Cam if I could find the right thing.

Susan might not want me to be alone, but I was, and there seemed little point knocking around in the house that Sarah and I had meant to fill with children.

I went through the post that had come since I'd gone down to Surrey, and my hand slowed as I pulled out a handwritten letter from Dr Downey, asking me to pop in and see him at my convenience.

I knew what it was. Despite the informal tone, I knew the way he worked. This meant a dressing-down, an 'interview without coffee' is how we described it in the army when an officer was in hot water. I'd been away too much, neglecting my work, and now had no explanation for my absence in Rome, because I dared not admit to the trap I'd fallen into.

Deciding I had better not dilly-dally, the next morning I found myself sitting in front of Dr Downey.

I was wrong.

He didn't want to give me a talking-to. He wanted to give me the sack.

Of course, that was not how he put it. He mumbled various things about how I must be wanting to look elsewhere for employment, that it was time for me to move on, that references would be written.

'Are you firing me?' I said, bluntly, because I was incredulous.

Downey mumbled some more, and then mumbled something about unprofessional conduct, and about the moral integrity of a Cambridge institution, and then I went cold as I realised he knew about the photographs.

Essentially he was asking me to leave before they had to do anything as grotesque as hold an enquiry.

I flushed red in the face and stumbled out of the door as fast as I could, assuring Downey I had no intention of staying any longer than was necessary.

I hurried through the streets, and realised that Verovkin, as I still thought of him, had not wanted to kill me. That he could probably already have done that. That what he wanted to do was destroy me, totally. To humiliate and ruin me, utterly.

In a daze I ended up at Hunter's, where I was received with a bellow of welcome as usual, but one that faltered a little.

I unburdened my fears to Hunter, and admitted to the Roman affair, and I suppose I thought our friendship was indefatigable, but though the conversation began badly enough, it ended worse.

Hunter seemed not to be listening. Not to what I was saying, not properly. I tried to tell him about Verovkin and that my house had been invaded but he seemed to want to avoid talking about it. He kept returning to the issue of my father's death.

'Maybe a holiday would do you good. It's been a trying time for you.'

I found him patronising and told him so.

He held up his hands, but refused to listen to the stories I had to tell him.

'It's just not . . .' he said, and stopped as I turned the subject back to Marian's murder.

'Not what?' I snapped.

His face clouded.

'It's not credible, Charles. I'm sorry but there it is. You're simply—'

I don't know what he would have said, because I didn't stay to listen. I flung some words at him; in fact, I shouted something idiotic about betrayal, and then I left.

9

It's a foolish thing to say that life is anything other than a river. It flows in one direction only and to try and swim upstream is nigh impossible. And I was already far downstream.

I never reported for work again.

The day after I'd met Downey and rowed with Hunter, I returned to Surrey. I drove down in a foul mood, one that was lifted slightly by seeing Susan smiling faintly as she saw me pull in to her drive to collect her.

'Has something happened?' she asked after five minutes of one-way conversation.

'I'm sorry,' I said.

'Do you want to tell me? I know how important work is to you.'

Grimly I smiled back.

'Nothing worth mentioning.'

We drove on and had the devil of a job finding the office of Father's solicitor, which was tucked away at the very top of the High Street.

All the while my mind was sinking further and further into a depression. I'd lost my job, and my reputation was probably going to take some time to repair, if that was at all possible. I knew I wanted to sell my house and move but that would take weeks. I had some small savings I could live off for a time, so maybe I should just disappear while I found a way to go on.

The reading of the will changed all that. In fact, it determined the rest of my life, pushed me on, led me to where I have ended, because as the two of us, the entire remaining branch of the

Jackson clan, sat in the solicitor's cramped and dark office, it transpired that my father had not only been a rich man, he had been a very rich man indeed.

He had left it all to the two of us, divided exactly in half. That was the way Father worked; everything was always very, very precise.

We stepped out on to the pavement, a little shell-shocked I think.

'Did you have any idea . . . ?'

I shook my head.

'Mother always said he was so tight,' Susan went on. 'I see what she means now.'

I nodded, speechless.

'Why was he living in that house?' Susan said. 'He could have lived in a palace and had servants waiting on him, ministering to his every need.'

'But that wouldn't have been Father,' I said. 'Would it?'

Half an hour later, I drove Susan back to her house. Neither of us said a word the whole way.

As we pulled up, I glanced at the windows.

'Is Roger . . . ?'

'Munich. Very important.'

'Yes, of course,' I said.

'Do you want to come in?' Susan asked.

'Why break the habit of a lifetime?' I said, easily, and we both laughed.

She opened the door and got out, and was about to shut it when she leaned back in.

'I'm going to leave him,' she said.

I wasn't sure if she was joking.

'Find a young lover and travel the world. Book a cruise.'

'Susan,' I said, 'think big. You could *buy* a cruise ship if you wanted to.'

'Good idea, Charles. Listen, thanks for the lift. And for . . .'

'What?'

She smiled briefly.

'Nothing. Everything. Listen, whatever it is. Whatever it is that you're dealing with. Good luck. Be kind on yourself.'

'Thanks,' I said. 'I might disappear for a while. Lay low. So don't worry if you don't hear from me.'

'I never hear from you anyway.'

'That's a very good point,' I said. 'Well, good luck to you too. Have fun on your cruise.'

'I was only joking.'

'Were you?'

'Maybe.'

I drove off, heading back to Cambridge, but I never got there, and neither did I ever see my sister again.

On the way, it began to dawn on me what had just happened. I began to see and feel things more clearly than I had in a very long while. I could see what my life would now be, and I knew what I was going to do, and how I was going to do it.

I grew excited. I felt as if I was alive again after a lifetime of death, and as I drove, I felt a lightness surge inside me, happiness even, and I laughed.

FOUR

Lausanne

May, 1963

On the continent, the disease is universally called haemophilia. In Germany, haemophilia is also called Bluterkrankheit, *and individual patients* Bluter, *a translation of the word bleeder, used by the American physicians who first described cases of this disease. In France the disease is now always called* hémophilie. *I am unable to say from my own observation by what writer the name was first used. The word is so barbarous and senseless that it is not wonderful that no one should be proud of it.*

One very important social point is the question of marriage. Should a bleeder be allowed to marry? I think the question of marriage ought not to be entertained – it seems only necessary for the facts to be known to prevent such marriages among the better classes. I say in the better classes, for the artizan class are so ruled by their passions, that no moral restraints would ever be allowed to interfere with the gratification of a lust: the law must stop such contracts.

John Wickham Legg, *A Treatise on Haemophilia*, 1872

I

Slowly, time passed.

It had taken some weeks for probate to go through, and for my inheritance to appear in my bank account. By this time I was in Scotland, living in an old crofter's cottage at the head of Loch Nevis.

Driving back from the reading of the will, it seemed pointless to do anything about my house in Cambridge. It could wait, I decided. In fact, it could burn to the ground and I would be no worse off. What couldn't wait, was me. I found myself desperate to start again, to start afresh, to find a new life, and to plan my future. But the very first thing I wanted to do was make myself safe. Safe from Verovkin, yes, but from the police, too, in case they decided to make things hard for me.

It hadn't worked for Richard Hannay, but I knew I could make it work for me, and I headed north that very day. I drove into London and abandoned my old car in Rufford Street, part of the slums behind King's Cross. It occurred to me to drive it into the Regent's Canal, or even the Thames, and maybe someone would think I had drowned, suicidal after the death of my father. But I decided against it. It was too dramatic, too complicated. It would lead to investigations into my life, it would lead to Cambridge and it would create more fuss about me, not less. What I wanted to do was to slip away into obscurity, to hide from just one man, and that, I believed, was easy enough to do.

I bought a ticket for the sleeper to Edinburgh, using a false name at the ticket office. I paid in cash, having visited a branch of my bank in Bloomsbury and taken out almost all of my existing savings.

I spoke to no one; I didn't emerge from my carriage until we reached Waverley, where I changed trains for Glasgow and headed for the west coast, simply because it was somewhere I knew nothing about, where I'd never been and, as far as I could be sure, had absolutely no connections with.

I spent a few days catching local buses here and there, and, after making casual enquiries in the various pubs I stayed in, found a cottage to let on a local estate.

The tourist season was over, and I was usually a lone figure in the bars, eating my evening meal early. I worried that I would draw attention to myself, but the landlords I met were a wonderful breed, who turned a hair at little, I guessed, and all it took was me to mention bird-spotting and they would leave me in peace for the most part.

Once a month, I made the trip to Glasgow, staying overnight, to visit the bank.

My first two visits were fruitless; on the third, as I asked the teller to produce a statement for me, I nearly passed out.

'Is anything the matter, sir?' the teller asked, tilting his head in a slight show of concern. I flicked my eyes back up at him, managing to pull them away from the paper for a brief moment.

'No, no,' I mumbled. 'Everything is quite all right.'

It was hard to believe the figure before me was correct, but it more or less matched what the solicitor had told Susan and me, minus sundry expenses and his fees of course.

We, Susan and I, hadn't even decided whether to sell the house or not, which alone must have been worth £20,000, an unbelievable sum. The number before me on the paper put my current wealth at close to one and a half million pounds.

'No,' I said, 'everything is fine. Thank you. I think I would like to speak to the manager. Please.'

The teller almost gave me a smile.

'Yes, sir. Very good.'

I doubted the manager thought it so good, though, as I stayed in Glasgow for a few more days, making some new arrangements for my finances. Something told me to be careful. Something made me scared, protective of my wealth, because it was all I had now. I had no job, no friends, no security, and no weapons, apart from that of a ridiculously large sum of money in my bank, and I wanted to keep it. Safe.

So I organised the transfer of sums, each of them vast, into various offshore bank accounts. I had them open accounts in the Isle of Man, and Jersey. I put the bulk of the money into long-term bonds, and still had plenty to transfer to a numbered account in Geneva, enough for me to live on for two lifetimes, I conservatively calculated.

That done, I returned to Loch Nevis, to my croft, and I hid.

2

I did not spend my time in Glasgow idly. While waiting for various formalities to be completed, for telexes to be sent to and received from Geneva, I had two other occupations.

Firstly, I engaged the services of a private detective based in London. His name was Hayes and I found his meagre advert in the small listings in *The Times*. He said he would not accept any assignment unless we met face to face at least once. I told him it was not possible and that I would double his fee, which convinced him to reappraise his methods. When I told him the work would be abroad, he again refused me, but another doubling of his daily rate allowed us to reach an agreement.

I was cautious. Someone, probably my father, told me never to get involved with such people. That they are all dishonest and will sell you down the river to the people you want them to investigate if the terms are favourable. This seemed entirely possible to me, so I gave a false name, and a Glasgow post office box as the only means of communication.

I deposited what amounted to a month's wages for him in his bank, and let him get to it. I didn't give him much to go on. I had little, and what little I had I felt protective over. I didn't mention Marian, or in fact anything to do with my suspicions of the man I had first known as Verovkin. I merely gave the two names I knew he had used, and the places and years in which he had used them, and said nothing of why it was I wanted to find him.

Meanwhile, I devoted myself to some form of education. I wanted to know my enemy better, so I phoned Donald one evening, and had him point me in the direction of the best writing on the subject. I could remember a little of what he'd told me before, about the psychologically disturbed and their relationship to blood, but I wanted to read in more depth, and after some delay while he checked his notebook, he gave me a list of the names he'd mentioned that evening in London.

'Look, where are you, anyway?' he said after I'd taken notes for five minutes.

'On the moon.'

'Fancy a drink sometime? Catch up?'

'Absolutely. Next time I'm in town.'

'When will that be?'

'Haven't the faintest idea. Thanks, Donald. Look after yourself.'

I looked at the list of doctors Donald had given me, and knew the bookshops of Glasgow would be of little use. But I made a day trip to Edinburgh, where my supposed status as a research specialist from Cambridge was enough to get me access to the university's fine medical library.

There I made notes from the small amount of work that had been done on what might be termed clinical vampirism.

Some writers postulated that the manic desire to drink blood was of modern origin; a perversion adopted by the already insane having been exposed to the numerous vampire novels of the nineteenth century and, more importantly, the lurid and sexually charged films of the twentieth. Films like the one Hunter had mentioned, I supposed, and other, later ones.

Something about this explanation immediately struck me as wrong. Something made me believe this was an older story, and one with roots in our deepest, oldest selves.

For example, there was the case of Antoine Léger, who in 1824 not only murdered his victim, a young girl, but drank her blood. However, although Stoker's monster did not exist at that point, Polidori's did. So perhaps that was enough to set these fiends in action. But there were other, even earlier cases of such horrors; another French case, for example, from the Mayenne, of a man who murdered or attempted to murder several people, biting them in the attacks, and who killed a cow by bleeding it to death. This was 1791.

One or two commentators attempted to define vampirism as a recognisable though rare mania, characterised by blood-drinking, an affinity with the dead, and a weak sense of personal identity.

I read more, and I hunted for deeper psychological explanations of such things, but already I felt vindicated. Vampires are not real, of course, I told myself, but that does not mean that there are not certain lunatics in the world who perceive themselves to be just that.

Various Freudians elaborated on intense oral-sadistic-libidinal needs. The ingestion of blood, I read, served as an attempt to restore some kind of energy or sense of self to the drinker that had been lost or perverted in childhood.

Maybe, I thought.

I read Freud, and his *Totem and Taboo*, and I read the sources Freud had read, most notably *The Living and the Dead in Folk Belief, Religion and Saga*, by Kleinpaul.

If Kleinpaul believed that originally *all* the dead were vampires who bore ill-will towards the living, Freud was moved to wonder how our beloved dead, for most deaths we encounter are of our loved ones, become demons.

The answer, as so often with Freud, seemed to be one of ambivalence. That although we still love our dead, we fear them too, hate them, even. These ambivalent feelings of hate are inverted and projected on to the dead, so that it becomes they who hate *us*. And wish to do us harm.

But this was getting me away from the idea that a real, though disturbed, person would come to associate with the notion of vampirism so greatly that they would begin to kill, to drink blood, in order to satiate themselves. Here my reading took me towards an understanding of the sadistic nature of such patients, how love became symbolised during infancy by the act of sucking, and hate by biting, which then became fused and combined in these individuals.

But it was the work of Freud's pupil Ernest Jones that interested me the most. In a brilliant paper of 1924 he showed how death is a reversal of birth. Rather than emerging from the womb, we are placed in the tomb. This 'tomb = womb' equation thus explains the vampire's need to emerge each night from the ground. He is born anew, and begins anew his search for life-sustaining blood to be sucked from its donor.

Thus, according to some, the origin of the word itself: vampire. The *pi-* stem, from the Greek verb meaning to drink, for the drinking of blood is the sine qua non of the beast.

I returned to Glasgow with my head in strange places, and I shunned the company of people. I ducked along the streets, unwilling to make contact with anyone, even the merest look, and I spoke as little as I could in my hotel, or to the people in the bank.

I felt exposed. The readings I had done had touched something inside me that was frightened, and all the horror of Marian's final moments assaulted me whenever I even so much as glanced at the female forms I saw around me, in the hotel or out in the city.

I looked at a woman walking towards me in Sauchiehall Street. She had no resemblance to Marian, except for her hair, which was almost identical. She made eye contact with me briefly as she passed, but looked away immediately, scowling, as if she'd seen what I was seeing in my mind: not her, but Marian. Marian hurt, being hurt, being attacked; the knife breaking her skin, the horrible wounds emerging all over her body in some supernatural way. Verovkin was not there, I didn't see him at all, just the results of his work, messy and red.

There were other visions, repeatedly; something would trigger a memory of Marian and similar horrific images would play through my mind. I began to feel I was being haunted by living ghosts, these people all around me in the city, the women whose forms would remind me of Marian, again and again.

I began to fail to see people as people. They were bodies, in which the blood was contained in veins; the existence of their minds inside their heads seemed to have disappeared for me; they were not people, but merely walking flesh and blood, and I feared for them all, as I knew how easily Verovkin could make their blood flow for his pleasure, were he here. I thought I saw the way he saw; what a terrible temptation the world must have presented to him, with frail, delicate victims around him continually, each and every one with the potential to excite his desire, and satisfy it.

After each excursion to the city I felt sick, and time and time again I hurried back to my bed, and I wept.

3

The exclusion and isolation of my lochside home seemed to help. I didn't feel lonely at all, though I rarely spoke to anyone beyond buying food and other provisions. Somehow it seemed to be healing me, to have taken myself away from everyone and everything, and I let the landscape and the weather into me, replacing the horrors that had been there before.

Finally, feeling much stronger, I returned to Glasgow, taking the train down the coast on a bitter winter's morning in order to check my post-office box for any communication from Hayes, the detective.

There was nothing.

I had been brooding over the way things had been with Hunter. I wrote him a short note, giving him the assumed name I was using, and the box number, and asking him to tell it to no one else, not even Susan. Since he had a key to my house, I asked if he'd forward any important post that came for me. I asked him if he'd mind checking once a week or so. And I told him I was sorry for our disagreement, and sorry that I'd been angry with him.

I was disappointed over Hayes' lack of progress, and had nothing to go on, nothing at all. I wondered if I was wasting my time, hiding away in the wilds of Scotland like a frightened lamb, sending this flatfoot out to do my work for me, because I was too afraid.

Just as I was about to leave Glasgow, I paid one more call to the post office, and found a letter that had arrived that day.

He said he had reached the end of his investigations, that he had been unable to find out anything about the man called

Verovkin or Lippe, and that he therefore resigned from the case. His wording was strange, the note unusually brief.

I wrote back immediately, doubling his fee for a third time, and sent it off to London.

I went back to Glasgow for the next two weeks, but there was nothing from Hayes. He had simply stopped replying to me.

There was nothing from Hunter either.

4

On my final trip to Glasgow, a more sinister interpretation occurred to me. The idea was triggered as I stepped aboard my train back to Loch Nevis, because as I did so, I saw, two carriages along, a man climbing on, a man whom I was sure I'd seen at the post office.

That in itself proved little, but I was worried. I stumbled into an empty compartment and put myself by the outside window, glancing at the corridor. Supposing Hayes had strayed outside his brief? If he'd made contact, he might have been rumbled. If so, Verovkin might have extracted Hayes' purpose from him. Of course he only knew my false name, but to a man used to using aliases of his own, it wouldn't take long to work out that it was probably I who'd hired a detective.

I thought about Hayes' last note, and wondered if he'd actually written it, and as I remembered that it had been typed, I felt the urge to be sick. All his other letters had been handwritten.

They'd got to him.

They'd got to him and most likely he was dead now, but not before he'd told them the little information he had on me. My false name, my post-office box number. They wouldn't have known he'd written by hand before, and had typed his resignation letter to allay my suspicions.

I sat, breathing hard, still staring at the corridor, and was about to leave the train when it began to slide out of the station.

An elderly couple came into the compartment and smiled at me as they settled themselves in, carrying such a quantity of shopping baskets that it made me think they were going a long way. Just as they sat down, the man from the post office came past.

He didn't stop, he didn't even glance round, but I knew it was him. He looked hard, and strong, possibly Eastern European. He stole along the corridor, and there was something of an animal in the way he walked. I grew afraid.

'Christmas shopping,' said the lady across from me.

Startled, I looked over and saw her shaking her head at their baskets.

'We've left it too late, as always.'

She laughed and I nodded, trying to smile. Her husband's eyes twinkled as she patted his hand, and they settled down to some sandwiches that she produced from some wax paper.

The train began its long steady journey up the west coast, and with every stop I grew more and more alarmed. At each halt I leaned from the window cautiously to see if the man got off, but he did not.

It was dusk now, but the train was not busy and it was easy enough to see the few faces walking briskly along the little platforms, hurrying into the dark.

'Are you not local?' said the old lady.

I sat down, wondering what to say.

'Are you afraid you'll miss your stop? Where are you going, dear? We can tell you when to get off.'

'Unless he's voyaging beyond Arisaig,' said her husband, holding a forefinger up theatrically. 'That's where we alight.'

He twinkled at me and I didn't know if he was deliberately being quaint or if this was how he really spoke.

'You'll be for the island, mebbe?' he added.

I was still too confused to answer, unsure what to say, as the man who I was now sure was following me passed the compartment again.

This time he walked slowly, and this time he did look at me. Deliberately, I could see. He half smiled as he saw the old couple, and walked on, and as he went out of sight, I grew more afraid.

'Where do you need to get off, dear?' said the old lady again.

'Mallaig,' I stumbled out.

'So! He's for the island.'

'That's two after us, dear,' the lady said, addressing me again. 'But it's the end of the line, so you can't miss it. Where's your bags? You'll be on Skye for the holidays? A schoolteacher, I'm guessing. Yes? Well, we have everyone coming this year. So much shopping . . .'

She spoke on, and on, and I was glad of it, because it meant I had to say very little. Her husband sat with his eyes twinkling, rocking gently as the train sped along into the night, the stops fewer and fewer.

Before I could think further, we had reached Arisaig, and the old couple gathered all their things together and made a great display of leaving the train.

As the door closed, the man nodded at me.

'The compliments of the season to you!' he announced, and they left.

I tried to calm myself, but as the train rolled on, I knew I had less and less time to make a decision. There were two stops left; Morar, and mine: Mallaig, the end of the line.

The man had not reappeared, and I wondered if he'd got out at Arisaig when I'd been occupied helping the old couple with their Christmas shopping.

I made a decision, and as the train pulled into Morar, I readied myself. I waited for a few seconds, and heard one or two doors slam further along the train. I opened my door and stepped out, looking first up and then down the platform. A second later, the man got off, just a carriage away.

He looked at me.

Still, there was the possibility that this was coincidence.

Then the guard's whistle blew, and just as it did, I stepped back on to the train, and even in the dark of the poorly lit platform, I could see the eyes of the man as he climbed swiftly aboard.

It began to move, and now there was no doubt.

It was only a few minutes from Morar to Mallaig, and yet it was an agonising wait as I sat by the door to the outside, my eyes on the corridor in the direction he would come.

As the train rumbled on, I started to doubt that he was going to make his move, and as we pulled into Mallaig I could see he didn't want to draw attention to himself, and I knew he was going to follow me out of the station.

It was around ten, a late December night. Mallaig was deserted.

The cottage I was renting was a good walk away, a couple of twisting miles along the southern shore of Loch Nevis, which usually took me at least forty minutes.

I was afraid. I had formed no plan, beyond calling at the police station and banging on the door and demanding to be let in until the murderer following me got bored and left. The idea was ludicrous, and I knew I was on my own. I'd thought about what I had in the cottage, and knew I could leave it all without returning. I had bought a few clothes, some books. I had some money there. I had much more elsewhere, and the few thousand pounds in cash in the cottage could be lost easily enough. There was nothing I could not leave behind, just as I had left more precious, more valuable things in my house in Hills Road without a second moment's thought.

It was time to move on again, I could see, but first I had to get away from the man behind me.

It was a cold night, and as I leaped from the train and began to walk briskly out of the station a bitter wet wind welcomed me. I tried to glance behind me as I walked around the side of the station and was pleased to see I had a good head start on him.

Walking several miles a day had made me fit, and I used my speed to put more space between us. I turned from Station Road, not heading down the bay road as usual, but up on to Annie's Brae.

Beyond the town it was always pitch-black at night and so I took a torch, but I didn't use it this time. Instead, as I passed the last few houses, I saw a chance. I looked behind me. I couldn't see him, but I knew that didn't necessarily mean he couldn't see me. There was nothing else to do, so I slipped around a small outcrop of rock that the road to the headland cut through, and waited.

Above the noise of the wind, I only heard his footsteps at the last moment. For a second I thought my plan had worked and he had walked on, but somehow he seemed to know what I'd done, and was turning to me in the darkness before I realised what was happening.

I saw his arm out in front of him as if he was holding a knife in his hand. He was right on top of me and I flung myself out of the dark crevice I was hiding in, and wrestled with him.

I wasn't even thinking as I pushed him away, and he stumbled back over the short drop to the beach.

It wasn't far, maybe just ten feet, but he landed on rocks. I heard the air come out of him as he fell and I heard something crack.

I began to run back to Mallaig, but I stopped. There was no sound from behind me. Cautiously I picked my way back up the short steep slope and peered over. I could see nothing. There was no sound but the wind, and the waves on the shore.

I stared long into the darkness and then saw the headlights of a car climbing out of Mallaig.

Scrambling down, I hid as the car passed, and then felt my way in the dark to where I thought the man had fallen.

I stepped on something soft and, recoiling, I crouched.

It was him. His neck was broken, and he had died instantly.

Something made me want to search him; I suppose I wanted to know my enemy. In the darkness I fumbled through his pockets and found a wallet, a bunch of keys, and nothing else.

I felt wetness on my hands.

The wetness was warm. I pulled the torch from my pocket and dared to flash it on briefly, and saw that his blood was all over me. My hands, my clothes. I saw the back of his head, and the hole in it, and with morbid horror, I knew where the blood had come from.

I stared at him for a moment more, but I cannot really say I was thinking what to do. I just did it.

I switched off the torch, then felt down and fumbled for his wrists, and began to haul him backwards across the rocks. I had to lift his body at times; at others I was able to let it roll a foot or two, when it would smash into more stones.

It took me for ever to get him to the sea, and then I pulled him as far out as I could wade, until I was so frozen and in danger of being swept away myself that I abandoned his body.

As I staggered from the sea I tried to wash the blood from my hands, but in the dark had no way of knowing if I was successful.

I was just climbing away from the site of the fall when I kicked something and heard the clink of metal on stone.

He'd had that knife in his hands.

I risked the torch once more and it didn't take me long to find the thing, but it wasn't a knife, it was a gun. A revolver.

I put it in my pocket, and then headed back to my cottage, half walking, half running through the town, only slowing when I reached the end of the bay road and climbed out past the last houses.

My place slowed, and I began to shiver. I was soaked through to the skin as high as my waist, the night was cold and then the rain came down, hard.

I think I was on the verge of hypothermia as I finally made it into my cottage around 11 o'clock.

I pulled off my wet clothes, and wrapped a blanket around me until I felt warmer. I struggled to light the fire I'd laid before I'd set out, using almost half a box of matches in my clumsiness. I drank a glass of whisky and then took another long swig from the bottle, which I clutched as I rocked backwards and forwards on a chair in front of the fire, waiting to get warm.

I stared into the flames for a long time as it slowly dawned on me that I'd just killed someone, something I'd never done as a soldier.

Then I remembered that I'd taken his wallet and, still wound up tight in the blanket, I reached for my coat and pulled the fat fold of leather from the pocket.

Along with twenty pounds in cash there were a few slips of paper, and a small bunch of business cards. In fact, five copies of the same business card. *His* business card.

The name on it read Douglas M. Hayes, and only then did I realise that I'd killed my private detective.

I dropped the cards on the floor, staring at them in horror, motionless for a minute.

Then I picked them all up, and the wallet and the money, and dropped the lot into the fire, where I watched them smoulder and burn till they were just a foul black crisp.

5

Was it my father who'd warned me about private detectives?

Whoever it was, they had been right.

There was nothing to suggest that Hayes' intentions towards me had been anything other than bad. He had not introduced himself, but had followed me to the wild Scottish coast with a gun in his hand. It was an old service revolver, and I guessed that maybe he'd been a young officer in the war, or that he'd snaffled the weapon when he'd demobbed, as many people had. Whatever, he must have decided that I was worth blackmailing, or robbing; somehow he had found out something about me, about who I really was, and decided I was a softer target than Verovkin. Or perhaps it was simply the carefree way I'd doubled and redoubled his fee that had made him think I was a fat target.

He'd hung about in Glasgow till he saw me collect my mail from the post-office box, and trailed me.

All these thoughts, however, were secondary to something much more shocking: I had killed someone.

For a day or two I wondered over my emotional state, which surprised me at first, because I felt nothing. I felt no remorse for what had happened. I decided there was more to it than that; I'd seen enough in the war to know that the way people react to death can vary enormously. Sometimes there is rage, sometimes there is grief, sometimes a terrible weakness, from fear, and sometimes, very often, there is simply an emptiness, a false kind of emptiness, which belies the fact that emotions are present but just lie hidden, very deep down.

So I told myself that it was normal to feel this nothingness, and anyway, I also instinctively felt that what had happened to Hayes he'd brought on himself. Yet there remained an empty, aching depression inside me, which rose to the surface from time to time, whenever I thought about his blood by the torchlight.

Suddenly I craved crowds, and noise. In Scotland I was exposed; there were so few people around that anyone looking for a stranger would have no trouble locating me sooner or later.

It was time to leave.

I'd paid my rent till the end of the following month, and I told my landlord I was moving to Ireland for a while.

Then I took the train south and decided to lose myself in London instead, because though Verovkin had not had me followed to Mallaig, he could have been very close to doing so. Hayes hadn't needed to know my real name in order to find me. The mere idea that my hideaway had been discovered by anyone was enough to scare me into running again.

Another thought occurred to me then: supposing Hayes *had* found Verovkin? It was possible that he'd found him, and approached him, and then my enemy had put two and two together and realised that I was the one who'd sent a detective to find him. Instead of killing him, he'd turned him against me. I already knew that he was a very persuasive man, whether through money, or less obvious means.

And if Hayes had traded sides, and had been working for Verovkin, then presumably he had passed on details of my whereabouts. The detail of why Hayes' last letter had been typed bothered me; it had made me think Hayes had been killed by Verovkin, yet that had not been the case. Maybe it was all part of Verovkin's manipulative game. Or maybe I'd been reading too much into what had been a chance decision on Hayes' part, and it merely showed what a paranoid state of mind I had developed.

Yet I knew one thing for a fact: Verovkin hadn't killed Hayes, *I* had.

I stopped a night in Glasgow and bought a smart suitcase and two sets of clothes, and then I boarded the London train, feeling jumpy all the time, thinking that Verovkin's men were everywhere. Every man I passed seemed for a moment to be Jean, or his brother; I sought their faces everywhere but of course never found them, and only when my train arrived in London did I start to relax a little.

London was wet and I was glad of it. The light was poor, the rain fell incessantly in sheets that made everyone keep their heads down as they hurried on, making no eye contact as they went. It suited me well.

It was a few days before Christmas, and no time to be finding lodgings. I made a trip to the bank and withdrew a few thousand pounds, a vast fortune to some but which barely made a dent in my inheritance, and then I found a small but expensive hotel in Mayfair. I gave a false name and address on the register, a different name from the one I'd been using in Scotland, asked for a quiet room and hid myself away.

The days ticked by. Christmas came and went and I moved hotels so as not to arouse any suspicion, and finally I decided I had to find cheap lodgings in a rough part of town, somewhere where people didn't know each other and didn't want to.

At random I headed out into the city with my suitcase. The New Year had come and gone and it was still miserable weather. I found myself wandering the length of the Mile End Road and saw a card in a newsagent's window offering a bedsit nearby.

I went to see it immediately. It was on the third floor of a block overlooking the railway line and it was awful, but I took it, deciding I could move again whenever I wanted to.

The landlord lived on the first floor, an original East End boy I guessed. He made no pretence of welcome or kindness, but I was glad of that. I discreetly peeled off a few weeks' rent from one of the bundles of notes in my pocket, and counted them into his hand. He counted them again, then slunk away downstairs.

What happened later that afternoon is for ever left in my memory when so much else has gone. I can see everything so clearly, without struggling to remember. I was hungry, and I had seen a café next to the newsagent's back on the Mile End Road.

I didn't yet trust my landlord, or the lock on my door, so I hid as much money as I could, and the revolver, in the various pockets of my overcoat. This was before they brought back the £10 note, and carrying thousands of pounds in fivers was inconvenient; they filled a quarter of my suitcase, which I locked and shoved under the bed.

I checked myself in the grimy mirror in the bathroom along the hallway from my room, and decided I didn't look like I was a wealthy man, or even one worth pickpocketing, then headed back out into the rain.

I ducked into the newsagent's first and bought a copy of the *Herald* since anything else might be out of place and headed into the greasy spoon. I ordered tea and pie and mash and sat down to read my paper, and then I saw it.

The headline said MURDER IN ACADEMIA. I didn't even need to read more to know that somehow it was something to do with me, but I read. I read that Cambridge academic Hunter Wilson had been found murdered in his rooms in college on 2 January, but that his death was believed to have occurred some days, possibly even weeks, before that. With the university down for Christmas, it said, no one had been near Professor Wilson's rooms until finally a cleaner had reported a bad smell in the stairway.

I read how the murder was particularly brutal, and that a motive for the crime was unknown. I read that a bungled break-in was being considered as a possibility, as was the idea of a feud. Hunter Wilson, the paper said, was a *well-known homosexual*. It left those two unconnected ideas somehow connected, without justification or any shame at such blatant supposition.

I read more. I read how police were eager to speak to a close friend of Professor Wilson's, a doctor named Charles Jackson, who had not been seen for some time. It was thought that Dr Jackson and Professor Wilson had had a kind of falling-out, and that the former was now in either the Glasgow or London areas. A manhunt was in operation, taking in both those locations, and Cambridge too.

I stood, or tried to, but my legs collapsed, and I made the other people in the café jerk their hawkish eyes towards me. The waitress was bringing my food, and I mumbled something about being sick and staggered out into the rain, but not before sending my tea flying across the dirty lino floor.

There were shouts and I ignored them and pressed on, clutching the paper in my hand, walking faster and faster until I found myself running back to the bedsit, where I locked myself into my room and read the article again.

Cambridge. And Glasgow and London.

As I read all of the article for the first time, I knew why. They had my false name. The police must have seen my note to Hunter, and had published in the newspapers the false name I'd been using in Glasgow, though I'd been using a different one in Loch Nevis.

And London? I had withdrawn enough money from my bank to buy a house just before Christmas. They would know that.

A manhunt. A manhunt for *me*. The police were hunting me, and I knew Verovkin was pursuing me too, that he would be reading everything in the papers about me that I was.

I knew immediately that I would not be able to touch my British bank accounts again, and possibly not those offshore either.

I had the money in Geneva, which would be safe, but I would have to . . .

Suddenly, my thoughts stopped, and the paper fell out of my hands. I stared at the dirty wall opposite me.

Hunter was dead.

6

It was no way to lose a friend, and no way to mourn him.

I had dragged him into this. Not intentionally, but the result was the same. He was dead because I had been unable to let go, as he'd urged me to.

Every day the papers produced more details of the crime, of the investigation. It lived briefly as a story that people gossiped about on the trains and the tubes, in cafés and at bus stops. Whenever I overheard such talk, I grew angry, but always managed to force myself to walk away, even to leave a meal untouched if need be, because if I accosted those people, I knew my rage would lead me into trouble.

The police, said the papers, were hoping the errant Dr Jackson would be able to help them with their enquiries, and might be able to shed further light on a possible motive, as well as clear up the possibility that there had been an argument between the two men. One day I read that nothing had been taken from Professor Wilson's rooms, the next that papers, valuable books and personal letters had been stolen.

Had he read my note? He must have done.

Why hadn't he written back? I had no answer to that, save the obvious one. That he hadn't wished to speak to me. But Hunter was not the type to bear a grudge, and once I'd stopped sulking with him, I couldn't believe he would have stayed that way with me. More than anything else, it hurt that I didn't know for sure if he had been angry with me, if he had no longer been my friend.

One day, buying milk, I saw that they'd printed a photograph of me in the press. It was on the front of every national paper, and in fear I hurried home, convinced that everyone was staring at me, whispering and pointing.

I didn't come out of my room for three days, until hunger forced me out. In a café I saw a photo of a man in an old newspaper, and stared at it.

Then I knew I was safe.

I knew the man was me, but I no longer recognised him. The photograph they had of me was from some years ago, when I had not long graduated. I was clean-shaven, and had an eager look in my eyes. I was wearing a doctor's white lab coat, and my hair was neatly parted. I looked as if I knew I was about to cure cancer. Smiling into the lens, smugly. Secure, confident. It didn't look like me at all.

Back in the bedsit, I stared at myself in the bathroom mirror. My hair was getting long, almost at my shoulders. I had a thick beard that I'd started to grow in Scotland, and now saw no need to remove. Even my face seemed to have changed shape and colour. My skin was sallow and greasy, and I had lost weight. I had been eating badly, neither often nor well, and had been drinking more than was good for me.

I stared closely at my skin and saw grime in the lines around my eyes, and wondered when I had stopped washing myself properly.

I gazed out of the window, across the railway tracks. It was the line that led to Cambridge, I knew, and my thoughts went back to better days, when I had sat at Hunter's elbow over good food and cheap enough wine, and we'd been friends.

Then I began to cry for Hunter, and I could not stop, did not stop until I knew I was crying for me too, and then anger welled up in me and I hated myself, but then my hate turned outwards and I knew where it had gone.

The details of Hunter's death were slowly emerging, and it got worse with every reading. There was always talk of the quantity of blood found around the body and in the room. One day, *The Times* reported how inside sources had revealed that the missing Dr Jackson had interestingly been questioned over some pornographic photographs of children shortly before his disappearance. Interestingly. The same turn of phrase that the French had used about Marian's murder, the word that had made my blood burn with rage. Yes, it was interesting. Interesting that Marian had been ripped to pieces and her genitals mutilated. Interesting that Hunter was a homosexual. Interesting that his missing friend was a paedophile. Once again I was furious at the unspoken connection between these things. The deep insinuations. Yes, they were saying, all perverts are perverts of every kind, of the most sordid nature. They are all worshipping the devil and eating babies and fucking your children, and it's very, *very* interesting.

And finally, one day, I read that interestingly some words in Latin had been written on the wall of Hunter's room, using his own blood.

Mors mihi vita est.

Death is life to me.

Of course, I was scared to start with.

I was a wanted man. Maybe not for Hunter's murder, though I couldn't be sure of that. But at the very least, I would be in difficult waters. There was too much to explain, and I feared every day that Hayes' death would be discovered, and linked to me.

And I was scared of Lippe, or Verovkin, or whoever he was this month. His name no longer mattered to me. I could still see his face in that hole in the park in Saint-Germain. The look on that face, that mocking look. I had seen him again, in both Paris and Avignon, and he had looked the same, a little older maybe, but only a little. And all I saw was the same thing: some hint in his eyes of a distorted mind, a mocking disdain for others. Every day I feared pursuit down the street, the sound of footsteps in an alley, the shape of his face rising before me in nightmares.

So I stayed in hiding. I had enough cash to see me survive in a meagre way for a year or two, if need be. I just had to be careful not to be mugged or robbed, but with every day that passed, I felt with ever-growing certainty that the danger had passed. No one knew where I was, no one knew how I looked. I had changed my name, and I moved my lodgings every month, always to a new part of London, which I discovered had an inexhaustible supply of cheap and filthy rooms to rent by the day, if that was what was required.

I spent the rest of the year brooding, slipping away into deeper and deeper places, and my thoughts became darker with each passing week.

As Christmas rolled into my view again, I knew I was safe. It seemed very certain that neither the police nor Verovkin had any idea where I was, or indeed who I was. But if I was safe from outside forces, I was not safe from myself.

If I looked in the mirror, which was a rare thing, I barely knew who I was seeing. I watched my eyes looking back, uncomprehending.

I stared at Charles Jackson, hard, and for a long time, because I wanted to be sure I knew what I had become, or rather, what I would become when I had done what I wanted to do.

I was going to kill him.

I spent some time in the London Library most weeks, and I found that the Latin scrawled on the wall in Hunter's blood was a family motto. Of a British family in fact: Wolseley. I made a few faint attempts to investigate the modern branches of this family, hunting for a man of the right generation, of the right age, who might be Verovkin, but in the end I concluded that this was a dead end, that he was merely using the Latin to taunt me.

And I began to read about blood again, of perversions and taboos associated with it, and I began to wonder what his mind was really like, whether he really had been drinking the blood of that girl in the bunker, and Marian's too.

Certainly I had seen blood drunk in that blasphemous ritual in Avignon, and when I recalled that, and pictured the scene of that terrible night again, I wondered what the taste of blood would be like.

The London Library held another book that I wanted to read, namely *The Golden Bough* by Sir James Frazer. Referenced frequently in Freud's work, I'd seen it mentioned from time to time in the reading I'd done in Edinburgh. I wanted to see for myself a few pertinent passages from the eleven volumes that comprise the third edition of the book, a book so wide-ranging that the index and references alone constitute a twelfth volume.

Here, then, in *The Magic Art*, I read of the use of blood by various peoples around the world, of its use in magical systems, sometimes as a substance of power, or life-giving energies, or conversely sometimes as a thing of taboo. How the men of the Wimbaio cut their penises and let the blood spurt across their thighs before warfare, for unity and strength, and how if one of their men harmed his wife, he would be cut and his blood allowed to flow over her until he fainted.

I read about the drinking of blood.

In many places, this appears to have been taboo. Some of the old tribes of Esthonia would not take blood since it contained the animal's soul, but there were many more examples to the contrary.

I read how the priestesses of Aegira in Ancient Greece would drink the blood of the bull to assist in making their prophesies. How various tribes in central Australia would use human blood to fortify their sick and aged. How the Takhas of Kashmir would drink the blood of decapitated captives.

In *Spirits of the Corn and the Wild*, I read how the flesh and blood of dead men were commonly eaten and drunk to inspire bravery, or wisdom. Or so said Frazer, citing the Basutos as eating the hearts of their enemies. I read how Sir Charles McCarthy had his heart eaten by the Ashantee so that they could imbibe his courage.

I read how the Sioux Indians, the Yoruba of the Slave Coast and the Indians of the Orinoco all dried and powdered their enemies' hearts to gain their valiance. How the young men of the Esquimaux of the Bering Strait would drink the blood of their first enemy killed.

I read how the Masai drink fresh blood and milk from their cattle, and the thought that black pudding, or blood sausage, or something similar to it, is a dish eaten in many, many countries did little to make me feel less uneasy.

I felt sick, but I read on nonetheless.

I read about taboo, about taboos of menstrual blood, how it was considered unclean, even destructive to men. And though Frazer did not mention it, I had already read about one of the laws of the Catholic Church contained in the *Corpus iuris canonici*, which made the assumption that since women bleed they were therefore unclean and threatened the holiness of the church.

I had read enough. I wanted to know no more.

Whatever my enemy was, whatever had made him, it made no difference to me. It was what he'd done that mattered to me, not why, and it was that that I was motivated by.

It was then, as the dark December days closed around me even tighter, and my thoughts grew even wilder, that I sat at the little table in my latest fleapit of a rented room, with a knife and a cup in front of me.

I stared at the things.

I had been careful. I had bought a small, sharp penknife and a bottle of neat alcohol, with which I had made both the blade and the skin of my forearm antiseptic. I had a simple tourniquet ready, in the form of my belt, and dressings and sticking plaster with which to stop the wound as soon as possible.

I was, I had been, a doctor, after all, and I only wished to know what blood tasted like, not to hurt myself in the process.

I picked up the knife and, carefully selecting a vein, pushed it into my skin till it bent deep under the pressure, but I still needed to push harder to make the cut.

I stared again at my forearm, I stared at the blade of the knife, and I looked at the grey-blue line of the vein under my skin, and still I hesitated.

Then I yelled in frustration and with a giant sweep of my arm sent the whole lot flying on to the threadbare carpet of my room.

I had determined that I would find Verovkin, and hunt him, and stop him from being. That was how I said it to myself. Not kill, or murder, but just stop him. I wanted him not to be any more, I couldn't bear that he lived on in his hideous way while Hunter and Marian were dead, and who knew, maybe many more young women besides.

So I wanted to put an end to him, but as the months moved on, and spring came, I had not found him, nor even tried, in truth. I sat in the many hovels I lived in during that time feeling as if I was a monster in a lair, but I did nothing. I *was* nothing.

I was powerless and slowly rotting away, and then, one day, I picked up the newspaper, and I knew I had found him again.

7

Of course, there was every possibility that it was a trap. I knew that from the start, but I didn't mind if it was. I understood completely that he might be waiting for me, but if he was, so be it.

Overnight, I changed. I had been running, running and hiding, and now I was no longer scared, and it was time to pursue him, not have him pursue me.

If I had been afraid of him, I was now ready to face him. I saw myself as his equal at last. He had always had money on his side. It meant he could move at will, create new personas and new lives for himself wherever he went, and I had been unable to find him, but now we were the same. I had money. Lots of it, maybe even more than he had, and I could use it.

Once I got to Geneva, I would be safe taking my money out, and just as I didn't know his name, he no longer knew mine.

I felt as if the months of dirty torpor I had suffered had fallen away in a stroke, I felt as if I'd stored up every bit of energy I might have been using during that time, and that it had all rushed to the surface of my skin that morning.

And all this because of the article I read in *The Times*.

The headline: MIRACLE CURE FOR 'BLASPHEMOUS' GIRL. The subject: the bizarre story of an apparent impossibility, a female haemophiliac.

The journalist, since he was writing for *The Times*, should have known better, or done a little research, or phoned up one of the country's experts on haemophilia, which, until what happened in Rome, would have included me.

A ten-year-old girl from the Alban Hills had made international headlines. She was bleeding, and the priest of the tiny village where she lived declared that she was a stigmatic. This was news that spread within Italy, for it made good reading for the Catholic buyers of newspapers. What sent the story worldwide was this. The priest was making big claims for little Giovanna Scozzo, but if he was delighted with his potential saint-in-waiting, her parents were not. Despite being devout Catholics, they had shamed themselves and the little village of Chiesa di Sasso by wanting to see if their daughter could be cured, and had taken her, eventually, to a doctor in Rome.

The doctor had declared that she was a haemophiliac, and had immediately been condemned by the world's media and even many of his colleagues, since everyone knows that only male haemophiliacs exhibit the disease, females being mere carriers of the defective gene.

This information was pounced upon by the credulous, who gave it as prima facie evidence that Giovanna was in fact a miracle child, and should be revered as such.

The Times's correspondent did little to clear up the matter, since in fact we had known for almost ten years about the varieties of clotting-factor abnormalities that cause the various types of the disease. And while haemophilia A and B are sex-linked, haemophilia C is not, and can appear in either sex, albeit in a milder form than the other types.

There was, of course, another possibility. The girl herself could actually be type A or B. An extremely rare, though not impossible, event, occurring only where the girl is the child of a haemophiliac father and a haemophilia-carrying mother. Yes, an extremely rare event, but one made much more common in areas of heavy inbreeding. Such as in small villages in the Lazio hills, such as in Chiesa di Sasso, where, I read, an incredible ninety per cent of the population shared the same surname: Scozzo. I could find no mention of whether the girl's father was a haemophiliac, but equally, I found no word that he was not, so my hypothesis was not yet disproven.

So far, it was just an *interesting* piece of gossip from the Mediterranean. What made me sit bolt upright on the bus as I read to the conclusion of the piece was this. A clinic on the shores of Lake Geneva had heard about Giovanna's case, and was ready and willing to see what could be done for the girl, though it would be at a cost only the likes of a Swiss clinic could command. The girl's parents were desperate to accept. The unwritten yet clear implication in the story was horrific. So far, the girl's bleeding had been profuse and prolonged, yet she had always pulled through in the end. But she was prepubescent, and what happened for her at menarche would be more than the trauma common for most girls. Because when Giovanna had her first period, she would die.

Her parents could not begin to afford the trip, let alone the cost of treatment, and a kind Swiss philanthropist, who wished to remain anonymous, had stepped forward to aid the girl's plight. He was prepared to bring the girl to Lausanne, where some of the world's leading clinicians might be able to help her.

I knew who the philanthropist was. It was him, and I knew it was almost certainly a trap for me. At the very least he would be expecting me, waiting for me, but I gave that no thought at all. Within a week I was crossing the Channel, bound for Lake Geneva.

8

Of course, that turned out to be harder than it should have been. I was still wanted for questioning. My passport was in Cambridge, in the police station, and even if I'd had it, I couldn't have used it to travel, because I was still a wanted man.

I had to find another way to cross the Channel.

I took a train to Dover where I hung out in some of its roughest pubs. I took my time, I waited a couple of days, visiting drinking haunts in Folkestone and Deal, until I got to know the kind of place I was in. One evening, dressed as poorly as I could manage, I struck up conversation with a fisherman in a pub called the Falstaff, a short walk from the harbour.

I asked him if it was possible to get across the water.

He didn't reply, so I added that I meant without using the regular ferry service.

Still he didn't reply, but finished his pint, and then nodded at a rough man sitting in the corner. I watched him for a while, and then, when the landlord called last orders, I wandered over and offered to buy him a drink.

He swore at me and called me queer, and I was reminded of that private who'd thought I was after the same thing. It made me angry; I wondered why these stupid men had to be so coarse, or if there was something about me that gave off such signals.

I held up my hand and said I wasn't offering the drink for free, but in return for some information, and that was how I found a man crazy enough to sail me across the Channel in the middle of the night in a small fishing boat for fifty pounds.

His name was Dyer and I didn't trust him in the slightest.

I'd offered him twenty-five pounds to begin with, and he'd easily haggled me up to fifty. He knew I was desperate, and I also guessed he knew I had more money on me than fifty pounds.

He told me to meet him, the following evening, outside the Falstaff.

He arrived on a pushbike very late, and told me it was off for the night. The weather was rough and he didn't fancy it. He told me to meet him again the following night, which I did, and the one after that, until finally he was ready to chance it.

'Get on,' he said, and I must have stared at him.

'We're not moored here,' he said, and so I climbed on the parcel rack of the bike as if we were two kids mucking about, and he set off grimly out of Dover, wordlessly pushing the pedals and hauling both our weights down the coast, to Folkestone.

Just outside the harbour was a headland known, appropriately enough, as Little Switzerland, and he'd beached his boat, the *Margareta*, on the shore there.

He explained it was far too risky to put out from Dover, which was crawling with customs men and the harbour patrol. He'd sailed the boat round earlier that afternoon and borrowed the bike from a mate of his.

We both had to work hard to shove the *Margareta* back out into the shallows, soaking ourselves, then I clambered aboard as he got the diesel motor chugging into life.

'Where are we going to put ashore?' I asked.

He shrugged.

'Depends.'

'On what?'

'A lot of things.'

I was getting more and more suspicious the more time I spent with Dyer. I knew he knew I had a bit of money in that little suitcase of mine. Maybe he had no intention of putting a few hundred yards out to sea and then ditching me, and heading home with the easiest catch he'd ever make, and the most lucrative.

He'd get a surprise when he opened that case. Not just a few more quid; I still had enough money left for Dyer to buy himself a new boat.

I pictured the events in my mind, and worked out where to put myself to be safest, and I grew afraid.

But then, he didn't know I had a revolver.

'Get below,' he said, nodding at the hatch in the wheelhouse. It would mean passing him, and turning my back on him.

'I'm fine here,' I said.

'Dry clothes in there,' he said. 'You'll freeze.'

'What about you?'

'I'm fine.'

'So am I,' I said, and leaned back, across the tiny wheelhouse from him, my hands in my pockets, my right clutched around the handle of Hayes' Webley.

Dyer gave me a look that saved him the bother of telling me to suit myself, and he pointed the nose of the *Margareta* out to sea.

The journey was slow, and Dyer was tense. I think only then did I start to realise that what we were doing was dangerous, not just illegal. We were crossing the busiest shipping lane in the world. It was a dark night, though we could see a few stars, which was how Dyer was navigating, I supposed, along with the compass in front of him.

Where we ended up on the French coast was likely to be as much by chance as by design.

But it was a calm night, the sea was smooth and black and the only sound was the constant drumming of the *Margareta*'s engine below, and the shush of water on the prow.

An hour had passed, and we could still see the lights of the English coast, and nothing as yet from France.

'Fog,' Dyer grunted, a little while later, and we headed into a bank that seemed to roll on to us without warning. The stars went, and we were alone in the sea, with only the hope that we'd hear a big ship in time to steer clear of it. Dyer now watched the compass in the binnacle more than ever, and I wondered how good a sailor he really was.

Another half-hour passed, maybe more, and we heard the sound of foghorns in front of us, and away to one side.

'Gris Nez,' he said.

'What?'

'We've come too far south. Cap Gris Nez.'

He turned the wheel and corrected our course.

Then he began to talk to me.

'You in trouble then?'

My lips tightened, my fingers reached for the trigger of the revolver in my pocket.

'Eh? You must be. Crossing the Channel at night. What did you do?'

'Nothing . . . I've lost my passport.'

It was a terrible lie, and he laughed so suddenly then, I nearly pulled the trigger.

'And you didn't want to go to the post office and get another,' he said, with heavy sarcasm.

'Is it much further?' I asked.

'Depends.'

'So you said.'

'Kill someone, did you?'

I started to get angry. I was paying him a small fortune for a few hours' work. Why couldn't he just mind his own business?

I said nothing.

'Or maybe there's something in that suitcase? Something you don't want seen, eh?'

'Just shut up and drive the bus,' I snapped.

Then he turned away from the wheel, and let it go, and stood looking squarely at me.

'Don't fucking tell me what to do,' he growled.

I was terrified. I tried not to show it. I pulled the gun from my pocket and levelled it at him, at waist height.

'I'll tell you whatever I want,' I whispered, my voice stuck in my throat. I think it sounded tough, but I felt the trickle of urine warmly down my wet leg, and I wanted to cry.

As he saw the gun, he stiffened. I thought he was going to jump at me, but he stared at it, and put one hand back on the wheel.

But he didn't take his eyes off me, and I knew I needed to do something more, so I lifted the gun, and carefully keeping my distance, I pointed it straight at his eyes.

'Get us to shore,' I said. 'And don't talk to me again.'

He did as he was told, but kept himself half turned towards me the rest of the way.

Another half-hour, and we heard the sound of the waves on a shingle beach somewhere ahead.

'Where are we?' I asked.

He said nothing.

'Where are we?' I shouted, and he actually flinched.

'France,' he muttered under his breath.

The boat skimmed the shallows and he spun the wheel, pointing the nose out to sea again, but as he did so a wave breaking for the shore caught the side of the boat and sent me staggering off my feet. I put one hand down to get myself up but before I could Dyer was on me.

He pounded me backwards into the rear of the boat, and brought his knee up into my chest, wrapping his arms around me.

The breath had gone from me, but I acted instinctively, somehow knowing I had just one moment to make this all right, or I would be dead. He was feeling for my wrist, for the gun, and I held on to it tightly, more tightly than I had ever held anything before. My fingers locked like a vice around the handle, even as he swung a fist twice into the side of my head, and then I managed to twist the gun, just enough, and put the tip of it against his stomach.

It was point-blank range; there was no way for me to miss.

The bang of the gun was muffled by his body, so it was strange the way he flew backwards, almost silent in the roar of the noise from the sea.

I hadn't killed him. But there was a very large hole from which blood was flowing rapidly. His eyes bulged with fear as he tried to press his hands over the wound, and his feet scrabbled against the deck. I stumbled as the boat tossed free in the waves, and fell to my knees. He watched me, stared at me, and tried to speak but couldn't. His eyes turned back to the blood pouring out around him, and I knew he didn't have long.

I looked at the shore.

I looked at the little ship's wheel turning wildly.

I looked at Dyer.

I put the revolver in my pocket, stepped forward and knelt by him.

He was trying to speak again and as I reached for him his hands pawed me, but gently. I undid his belt buckle, slipped the belt from out of his waistband, and stepped back to the wheel-house, where I used it to fix the wheel straight, just as the boat was pointing out to sea.

Then I opened the throttle a little further, grabbed my case, and threw myself overboard. As I went, I took one last look at Dyer, whose eyes were dull now, though fixed on me. There was no anger from him. No rage, nothing. Just the loneliest look on the face of a man that I have ever seen.

Touching the bottom with my toe tips, I half swam, half waded to the beach, where I pulled myself above the tideline, and then crawled for the cover of the dunes.

There were no lights, and though dawn was coming soon, I was freezing, and I shook violently from the cold.

I lay wretched on the French sand.

As the sun came up, the fog was quickly burned away. It was now a clear May morning and the temperature rose. I lay still till I felt alive again, letting the sunshine bring me back. When I shut my eyes, all I could see was Dyer. I was aware at last that he had hurt me before I'd pulled the trigger, and then I was thinking that I had killed someone again. Unlike Hayes, this wasn't an accident, though as I lay on the beach, I knew I had had no choice. It *was* an accident in a way, because he had forced it on me. He would have killed me for what he guessed was in my case, that was certain, and I'd had no choice but to pull the trigger. He was stronger than me and in a few seconds more would have finished me, easily. All that was true, and yet it left a bad taste in my mouth.

A long while later, feeling warmer and stronger, I stripped to my vest and trousers and swung my shirt and jacket over my shoulder as I climbed up the beach and headed inland, swinging my suitcase as I went.

There was a short stand of trees just behind the beach, which I pushed through to find some fields, and then a small coastal road. I didn't know which way to go, but I knew I was heading east in the long run, so that's the way I went.

9

I didn't know it was him, the philanthropist who was going to help poor Giovanna. I didn't know, but I felt it was. I was starting to understand the way his mind worked, feeling the way *it* felt, and the prospect of a girl who bled spontaneously would be too much for him to ignore.

But why come out into the public eye? There were only two reasons, as far as I could see. The first, he had to. I didn't know what he was planning, but I could guess. He meant to abduct her, presumably once she arrived in Lausanne, though he might try it before. Either way, my only hope was to make it to Switzerland before she did, and hope that I could track him down.

And the second reason was the one that gave me fear, because this was the thought that it was all part of an elaborate trap, to lure me out of hiding, and it had worked.

I didn't know any of this, but I felt it. I felt that I knew him. I saw inside him and knew what he meant to do, and why.

I saw what he had in mind for Giovanna too, and what excitement it would cause him, in the time that she had before her own blood killed her.

What a prospect.

I had been following the case as closely as possible while struggling to leave England, gleaning what I could from amongst the garbled and extravagant reports in the press.

The girl's bleedings were under control, I assumed, or she'd be dead already. Where her priest took the bleeds to be the miraculous stigmata of Christ's sufferings, I read signs of the disease I'd been trying to cure. While some papers loosely spoke about bleeding palms, I noticed that there was no categoric statement that that had been happening to Giovanna. The only thing that was clear was that her wounds would not heal, and while there was nothing to suggest this in what I read, it was also possible that some form of purpura, or bleeding into the skin, was present as well as her rare form of haemophilia. Such bleeding often accompanies various coagulation disorders of the blood, and it would take little to set off a pronounced bleed through the skin.

There was of course the possibility that the girl was now initiating her own bleeds. She was a tiny girl from a tiny Italian village; now she had priests and doctors and the rich of the world interested in her. It would not be the first time an impressionable youth had created a mystery to attract attention. I was reminded of the girls who started the Salem witch trials, and the Fox sisters, those girls who heard mysterious rapping sounds and so founded the Spiritualist Church, despite the fact they later admitted they'd made it all up. In Giovanna's case, all it would take would be a small scratch, something that could be done secretly in a moment, and she would have the whole world at a buzz around her.

I wondered if anyone had told her what was approaching her, so very soon, when she reached the point of menarche. And if anyone had, could she understand what she was being told? That she would start to bleed, and while this was a normal thing for every other girl in the world, for her it would mean death.

I doubted that anyone had told her; she was from a small, rural, Catholic community, and I knew that it was unlikely that anything had been done to help her understand. But maybe that was a kindness.

I remembered my childhood, and I remembered Susan, how it had happened for her. I don't know if she knew anything until the day she bled for the first time, and it took me years to work out what had been going on one mysterious summer day when I had found my big sister crying in the garden, and she had run inside and shut herself in her room.

Our mother, not the most sensitive of creatures, had spent the rest of the day with Susan, while I was left sitting at the top of the stairs, wondering what was wrong.

Eventually my father had come home and did a very rare thing. He played cricket with me until it got too dark to see the ball, and still we had not had supper, and still Susan had not emerged.

When I asked if something was wrong with Susan it was even more mystifying to be told she was fine. We ate very late, and a very quiet Susan joined us briefly. I wondered why everyone was telling me she was fine when I could see she was anything but.

She disappeared up to bed, but next morning she seemed well enough. Am I imagining it now, or had something changed in her already? Maybe I'm just projecting a cliché back on to her: *she became a woman.* But I know that she no longer went camping with me in the woods behind the house, or played with me all day in the valley beyond, as we had for as long as I could remember.

She just stopped doing those things, and I was an adult before I pieced together enough hints and implications to work out that she had been told to stop doing those things, she had not wanted to stop doing them.

If that was the experience of an upper-middle-class girl of educated and wealthy parents in Britain, I couldn't imagine that Giovanna had had more consideration, albeit a few years had passed in between.

So Verovkin had played a card, and now it was my turn to play one back. He had put the girl down before me as bait and, that being the case, I knew he would want me to get to Lausanne before making his move, or I would have no trail to follow, and there would be no trap to close around me.

I knew of the Swiss Haemophilia Clinic. It was a genuine establishment, and though I had never corresponded with the doctors there, it was a respected institution, founded on the groundbreaking work that Feissly had done in the twenties. Obviously, Verovkin was using them unwittingly, but how and when he intended to take the girl I was left to guess. For now, there were more pressing problems to solve. I was hungry. I needed to travel fast. I had money but it was English.

It took me most of the morning to walk into the nearest town, a fishing village called Wissant. I was dry by then, but must still have looked a little out of place. I hitched a lift from there into Calais, and as in Dover, I found that ports are a good place to engage in activities that border on illegality. I managed to change a good deal of money in a little office near the quay. The lady asked for my passport. It didn't take much to convince her that I had left it in my hotel and was in a hurry: a couple of pounds extra for her were enough.

I found a down-at-heel café along the street and ate a big meal, and then waited to feel my hunger drain from me. As it did, I prayed that the night's fog had allowed Dyer and his boat to travel far before being found. Maybe I would be lucky and the thing would have been dragged out to the Atlantic. Even if it was found, there was nothing to connect it to me, and that thought gave me some satisfaction.

Leaving the café, I stretched my arms out in the strong morning sun, and started to feel better. I walked to the outskirts of the town and found the shabbiest garage I could, where the owner was happy to allow me to rent a battered old Peugeot 403 without adhering to the formalities of paperwork. It was important to me to avoid the trains, for there was always the possibility that the ticket inspector would want to see my passport too. Being unable to produce one would lead to an unravelling of events that I could not afford.

I left the garage owner clutching a large sum in francs and set out to drive as far as I could before the light went. He must have known there was a chance I'd not be coming back, but I'd given him more than the car was worth, and I knew he'd be perfectly happy with that arrangement.

I made my way across France. The first night I stopped on the outskirts of Amiens, the next Dijon. Both nights I was forced, despite the sums at my disposal, to choose the cheapest guest houses I could find, places where they would not demand the production of a passport at a polished walnut reception desk.

I didn't mind; it suited me well enough. There was a greater problem on my mind, and that was crossing the border into Switzerland. I knew I would have to make the trip cross-country, in the dark, to avoid border formalities.

In Amiens I had bought a few road maps, which I now pored over every time I made a stop for food or to rest, or to buy petrol. Finally, by driving the roads near the frontier, I made my choice. I fixed on an insignificant village called Chappelle-en-Bois, in the Jura. The woods after which the village was named gave out at the top of the hill, and from there on, I would be in Switzerland. The only problem was the Peugeot, and I knew I would have to abandon it and get hold of another. But that was a matter of inconvenience to me, no more, and I understood again how money makes all the difference. It was how he, Verovkin, had made his life so free, and how he had been able to get away with the terrible things he'd done, and it was how I was going to track him down. And when I had, I would put a stop to him, for good.

IO

God bless the Swiss, I thought.

It had taken quite a lot of work in Glasgow to set up the bank accounts in Geneva, as they had been reluctant to do so without my physical presence there. Once again, I'd learned that money opens every door. When they'd heard the sums I was speaking of investing with them, things had changed, and to make matters even better for me, the beauty of a numbered account was that all I needed to access my money was that number, and a password.

The Peugeot had taken a big chunk of the money I had left England with, and I needed a new car and money to live on. I armed myself with Swiss francs on top of the dwindling French ones I had left, and also lire and marks, because I wanted to be prepared.

I assumed they were used to eccentric foreigners in the bank in Geneva, because they didn't even blink at the long-haired, bearded and battered man wearing a suit that might once have been expensive but was now clearly showing the miles it had travelled. Nevertheless I felt very conspicuous, and decided I needed to clean myself up a little. I found a barber and had my hair cut a little shorter, and my beard trimmed, enough to smarten myself up, but still enough, I hoped, to make me appear very different from my old persona.

If money was easy to arrange in Switzerland, it took me a while longer to find a car. Geneva was not Calais. It was a mild, sedate kind of place, a place that stuck to the rules, and the one car dealer I spoke to on the outskirts of town was so horrified at my suggestion of a 'simple' purchase, in cash, that I could see him practically calling the police on the spot.

I wanted a car, but time was running out. According to the last news I'd seen, Giovanna was due to arrive in Lausanne at the end of the month. I could find nothing more specific than that but it didn't matter; May was almost over and so I took a risk and caught the train the short distance to Lausanne.

When I arrived, I found I was too late.

I knew something was wrong as soon as I stepped from the train, because I saw packs of men, obviously journalists and photographers, standing around the station – on the platforms, in the ticket hall, on the pavement outside. There was even a TV camera crew.

There were raised voices and passers-by were stopping and staring. Something had happened and it didn't take me long to find out what it was.

Giovanna had gone missing.

11

She'd been collected from Rome by two clinicians from Lausanne, a man and a woman. They were to bring her to Switzerland for her treatment to begin.

The train travelled overnight, the girl sharing a sleeping car with the lady from the clinic.

In the early morning, as the train climbed through the Alps and stopped for Swiss border checks at Brig, the woman had woken to find the girl not in the bunk beneath her.

She'd woken her male colleague, and they'd alerted the conductors, who were fully aware of the precious passenger they had on board. A search ensued. She was not found. Finally, massively delayed, the train had rolled on to Lausanne, minus three passengers: the staff of the clinic, who were being held for questioning by the Swiss police, and little, fragile Giovanna herself, who had vanished into the night, as if some supernatural force had simply spirited her away into the mysterious mountains that towered on each side. But I dismissed these ideas as soon as they came to me. He was clever, very clever. I knew that. He'd found a way to take the girl, that was all.

That was all there was to know, for the time being. The journalists at the station were sending the news of the abduction worldwide, and by now there was probably no one in the West who had not heard about it. The whole town seemed to be in uproar over the news. Lausanne, I soon started to feel, was a very different place from Avignon, or Paris, or even London. This was Switzerland. Nothing bad happens here, that was the message. Nothing bad happens. In fact, nothing happens at all, and certainly not the abduction of a young, sick girl. Lausanne was an elegant place of large, austere buildings set on steep hills and the occasional long flat street parallel to the lakeshore.

Aside from the station, it was obvious that there was one other place where some news might be had, and that was at the clinic itself. It turned out to be only a short walk down from the station, in the Boulevard de Grancy, one of those long quiet level streets with shops at ground level and flats above, and altogether an unlikely place for a world-leading research clinic. But there, at the end of a row of old apartments, was a modern block of straight lines and wide windows. The steps were thronging with another gaggle of journalists. The doors were firmly shut, and it was clear that they had been camped out on the street for some time.

It was twenty-four hours since Giovanna's disappearance. The clinic had had nothing to say. I began chatting to one of the reporters, a stooping young man standing by himself having a cigarette. I played the innocent but nosy tourist, and found out what I could. The police were due to make a statement to members of the press that afternoon. Knowing I would not be able to get into that announcement, I was at a loss as to what to do.

I thought about staking out the clinic, but I could see it would be hard. It was a well-to-do residential street; I couldn't get into the flats either opposite or above. There were one or two shops at street level that faced the steps to the clinic, a dry-cleaner's and an insurance office. Neither offered me the chance to hang around for long. The only hope was to loiter with the reporters, but first I needed to find somewhere to stay, somewhere to dump my case.

And that was what I was about to do when the door to the clinic opened and a stern-looking man in a dark suit emerged. He held a sheet of paper in his hand.

He was immediately surrounded by the journalists, who began shouting questions at him and taking his photo, while he held up his hand for quiet.

He stood waiting for a long time, saying nothing, and finally the reporters fell quiet as he made his announcement. He introduced himself as Dr Sforza and said he was the director of the clinic. He read a short statement regretting the situation and the extreme distress that he personally felt at the disappearance of Giovanna, and explained that they, the clinic, were as short on information as everyone else. They were in constant contact with both the Swiss and Italian police, and would do everything that was in their power to help find Giovanna. They were at a loss to explain what had happened, and then, in a rather sour end to the statement, he defended the role of the two staff from the clinic, asserting that the door to the train compartment had been locked from the inside by the female clinician, and that there had been no signs of damage to, or tampering with, the lock from the outside.

There were shouts and further demands from the journalists then, but Sforza merely turned his paper over and waited for the silence to descend again.

He would also like, he said, to read a statement from the 'deeply saddened' and 'kind benefactor' who had paid for Giovanna to be brought to Lausanne, a man who still wished to remain anonymous, but who was likewise helping the police with their investigation.

Dr Sforza read, and I listened hard. My French not being perfect, I didn't understand everything, but I understood enough.

'*My heart is heavy,*' he said. '*I only wished to bring comfort to poor little Giovanna, and now this terrible event has descended on us all. I shall not rest again until she is found, and I shall blame myself for ever if she is not.*'

There was some more after that, but I didn't hear it.

I don't know what made me look up, up into the window on the second floor of the clinic, way above my head. Maybe I saw something, a slight twitch of the net curtain that shrouded the windows. Or maybe it was just the sudden realisation that if Sforza had just prepared his own statement, inside the clinic, then there was every possibility that he was in there too. Verovkin.

And as I looked up, while everyone else's eyes were firmly on the beleaguered Swiss doctor, I saw him through a crack in the curtain, half his face and no more, standing sideways, looking down on the scene in the street below. That hard face, the long nose and wide mouth. His eyes.

I looked down at the pavement, tried to slide myself out of sight behind the young journalist I'd spoken to before, tried to make myself invisible.

Had he seen me? I wasn't sure, but in the briefest moment that I'd seen his face, I'd seen his eyes again, and terror welled up inside me like never before.

Sforza was finishing, turning, and going inside.

I was frantic, unable to decide what to do. The journalists were pressing in on the doctor, who was even now pulling the door shut behind him, aided by some staff.

Should I try and hide myself in their crowd, or should I slink away? Unable to decide, I did neither, and was left frozen to the bottom step, suddenly feeling cold and desperately scared.

My head jerked up, and I found I was looking at the second-floor window again. He had gone. The curtain was redrawn, and he was gone, and still I didn't know if he'd seen me. And if he had, would he have even recognised me?

The journalists were banging on the door of the clinic, shouting questions that stayed unanswered, and finally I decided to move.

Still clutching my case, I walked off down the boulevard, until finally I found a café at a street corner, and ordered black coffee and brandy. I sank the brandy, and then began to sip my coffee, my eyes staring at nothing through the window.

I lost track of time as I sat there, but not much could have passed, for I was still sipping my coffee when a police car came down the street, its lights flashing. I was not the only one in the café to get up and watch it, and I headed out on to the street to see it stop by the crowd of journalists.

Even at a distance it was clear what was happening. The clinic had called for help, and a few scuffles broke out as the police forced the reporters to move off the steps.

I shook myself.

The shock of seeing him again had been too much for me, even though I had been hunting him. I hadn't expected to see him so soon, even if it was for a split second and no more.

But I had found him and this was my chance. I cursed myself because even sitting in the café I had wasted precious time, time in which he might already have let himself out of the back door to the clinic and away into the city.

I paid for my drinks and asked to use the lavatory. Inside I quickly took the rest of my money from my case, and the revolver. I stashed both in my jacket pockets and then closed the case again, which now contained nothing but a change of clothes. There was nothing in it that could identify me, and I knew already there was a chance I might not be coming back for it.

I asked the waitress if I could leave the case behind the counter for a short while. She seemed a little puzzled but I smiled at her, explaining I wanted to go for a walk and didn't want to carry it. I bought a pack of cigarettes from her, and some matches.

Things were already calmer at the clinic, and this time I was being more professional about my work. I walked past slowly, being careful not to stare but checking the building as I did.

The block stood on its own, and it was not big. I walked past the front steps and turned down the side. Here a small access road led to a large garage door, large enough for ambulance cars to enter, but currently firmly closed. I turned the corner again at the back of the block and found no other door. Completing my circuit, I emerged on Grancy once more, knowing that there were only two ways out of the building.

As I came around I saw something I hadn't noticed before. There was a steep, narrow street that led up to the back of the station, and on the corner the building opposite the clinic made a kind of dog-leg back from the pavement. I could tuck myself in there, unseen, and be able to keep a close enough eye on both the front door and the access road.

I stood there, as nonchalantly as I could, pretending to smoke cigarette after cigarette, nodding as people passed by, and trying to look as if I was perfectly happy, enjoying the late evening sunshine.

From time to time I would take a peek around the corner of the building and check on the clinic, but it was just the same scene as before: the journalists staking it out, the odd local stopping and staring for a while before moving on. The police car had vanished, but I now saw there was one gendarme left, preventing any further unwelcome attentions to the clinic's front door.

I cursed under my breath, and leaned back against the wall, and wondered what I was doing, what I was intending to do.

Was I really waiting for him to emerge from the building? Would I walk across the street, calmly, and levelling the Webley in front of me, put a bullet straight into his head?

No, I wasn't. I knew I wouldn't do that, couldn't do that, for then I still had some idea of returning to life. Of getting my old life back, or something like it. Of getting back to England, and waiting for my name to be cleared in relation to Hunter's death. I would confess to living as a recluse, scared of implication in the Hunter Wilson case, and I might be fined for not aiding the police with their enquiries. Maybe even a short custodial sentence. I doubted it would be bad; I had done nothing seriously wrong, assuming, that is, that no one ever found Hayes' body, or Dyer's, and made any connection to me. It was a risk I was prepared to take, but one that would be lost to me entirely if I shot an apparently innocent philanthropist in the usually peaceful streets of Lausanne.

I couldn't shoot him. I could follow him if he left on foot, but with the journalists outside I thought the only likely way out for him would be by car, from the garage door on the side of the building. Then I would be stuck.

So I stood, letting the cigarette ash pile up at my feet, trying to work out what to do, until, without warning, all the reporters began to leave, almost as one, and it was then that I saw my chance, and without even thinking, I took it.

12

First blood. Bad blood. Hot-blooded. Cold blood. My blood ran cold. Fresh blood, young blood, new blood. Royal blood, blue blood, true blood. Blood on your hands, blood is thicker than water. Blood ties, blood money.

Blood. An old word, one of the very oldest. Like the man I followed, I had become an expert in it. It was a word that stalked through my mind all the time, day and even at night, in my dreams, which would sometimes become horrific, saturated as a bloodbath. A bloodletting.

Blood, from an old word, from the first words spoken on the Continent, in a language that never was, the Proto-Indo-European assumed to be the mother of us all. Blood, in that assumed language, meant something that gushes. Something that spurts and wells, and that was how it always appeared in my nightmares, not as something still and calm, but something hot and rushing, something frightful and fearsome, something violent and virulent, too, something that possesses, infects, and commands. Something that controls us, unseen, from inside, carrying our life force through our bodies, carrying the chemicals within it that cause us to become afraid, or to feel excitement or sexual desire, to swell inside our lips and our genitals, to pound through the chambers of the heart, causing our pupils to dilate, our skin to break sweat, our libido to be unleashed.

Blood is our master.

It was undeniable, and all these blood-soaked thoughts ran through my head as I watched the reporters hurrying away, plus one more thought: that if blood was controlling his life, it was now also controlling mine, because my sole intention and desire in that moment was to be alone with him for one short second, and shoot him. Just as blood was his unseen master, it had become mine too, and I hated him for that, for making me part of his perversion, of his hideousness. If Hayes' death was an accident, and Dyer's unfortunate, I knew I would be happy to pull the trigger on Verovkin, and it would provide me with satisfaction.

As the journalists moved away, I guessed what was happening. It was ten to seven; probably the police were about to issue a statement, on the hour, somewhere else in town, maybe at the police station, somewhere I had overlooked till that point.

Some of the reporters were hurrying off on foot, one or two on scooters, but I noticed the stooping one from before heading for a beaten-up Renault parked across the street from the clinic.

The policeman looked relaxed, paying little attention, relieved that the siege of the place seemed to be over.

I headed towards the young reporter, meeting him just as he reached his car. Everyone else had gone; the policeman was looking the other way down the street; and I struck up conversation with the journalist.

'You speak English, I assume?' I said.

He turned and stared at me, but I could see he was paying me little regard, which angered me for some reason.

He opened the door to his car and began to get in.

I stepped smartly forward into the space of the door, so he couldn't close it.

'Can I help you?' he said.

'You want a really big story?' I asked.

That straightened him out a little, but his eyes narrowed nonetheless.

'What do you mean?'

'The big story is in that building,' I said. 'Not at the police station.'

He stared at me for a moment.

'Get out of my car,' he said. 'I'm going to be late.'

Then in a single motion I showed him my gun, and showed that I was pointing it at him, and swiftly pulled the rear door of the car open and got in behind him.

'Shut your door and do nothing,' I said, briskly, and he did just as I said. I touched his back with the tip of the barrel, so he knew not to be stupid.

'What do you want?' he asked, and I could hear the fear in his voice.

'You're all right,' I said. 'Just sit still and quiet and do what I tell you.'

'Yes,' he said. 'Yes, I will.'

'It's very simple. All you have to do is wait. And then, if I'm right, you will need to drive a little. Can you do that?'

'Yes.'

His voice was even quieter and for a moment I thought I might have scared him so much he would be unable to act when the moment arrived.

'There's nothing to be worried about,' I said. 'Just do what I say.'

I glanced over his shoulder, towards the clinic. The policeman was speaking to someone through a crack in the door, nodding as he did so. He turned and came down the steps as the door closed again, and set off along the street.

I shoved the revolver a bit harder into the young reporter's back, just above the top of the driver's seat. I pressed hard enough to feel his spine against the muzzle of the gun. I wanted to remind him to be careful.

Then the policeman was gone, and we were left, waiting, and there was not long to wait.

Maybe half an hour later, a car pulled out from the access road and turned into the boulevard. I slid down as far as I could behind the driver's seat, but I had seen enough to know it was him inside.

It was a large dark grey Mercedes. There was a thickset man at the wheel, and a tall shape in the rear seat. The car turned away from us and set off down the street, and I pushed the gun into the reporter's back once more.

'Follow him,' I said.

13

We drove along the lake road, heading east.

I told the reporter to keep his distance, but that he should on no account lose sight of the Mercedes, and at first that was easy enough.

Our way took us along roads that were flat for the most part, along to the corniches of Lake Geneva. We passed through a few small villages, surrounded by long narrow strips of vineyards that rose in terraces from the lakeshore up to the mountains on our left.

The views grew more and more magnificent, though I saw nothing but the car ahead of us, and the reporter's hands on the wheel. Every time he moved even to change gear I nudged him a little with the revolver, but I began to realise he was terrified and would do anything I said.

I hoped that was the case. As we drove I pictured him making some effort to attack me, or get away, and I saw myself pulling the trigger of the revolver, sending him crashing into the dashboard in a mess of blood and glass that would appear in an instantaneous flash.

We passed through one small town, and then as dusk fell we came into Montreux and out the other side, and the Mercedes showed no sign of stopping. The town had a few cars on the streets, of which I was glad. I told the reporter to hang back a little, so we would not always be immediately behind Verovkin's car.

As we left Montreux, the Mercedes turned and headed south.

'Where's he going?' I asked the reporter.

'This is the road to Martigny,' he replied, desperate to help, to please me.

'Where does it go then?'

'That depends. To France. Over the pass to Italy maybe. Or you can take the road by the river. That's east.'

'The river?'

'The Rhône.'

I stared out through the windshield ahead of me. The Mercedes was in the distance on the narrow but straight road. It had its lights on now and that was almost all that could be seen of it. I began to worry. I was worried it would get away, I was worried that I had the young reporter on my hands; he was nervous and making me nervous too.

Suddenly I told him to stop and get out of the car.

He stopped quickly enough, but wouldn't get out at first. I think he thought I was going to shoot him, and was paralysed with fear.

I shouted at him, told him to get out, told him to start walking home, and then he moved.

I matched his movements as he got out from the Renault, and when he was a few paces away I slid in behind the wheel and sped off to catch the Mercedes, which was now out of sight. The young reporter would take at least an hour to walk to the last village we'd passed. Even if he could call the police from there immediately, it would be a long time before they got themselves sorted out sufficiently to radio all across Switzerland and stop my car.

But there was the problem. Suppose he left Switzerland? The reporter had told me that both France and Italy were close by, and I had no passport.

I had to catch him before he made it to either frontier, force him to a stop and then do what I wanted to do.

I pushed the accelerator and moved a little faster, and was soon rewarded with the shape of the Mercedes' tail lights ahead.

There was no one else on the road, nothing to slow him down. Nothing to stop me getting closer, except that I couldn't catch him.

The grey car swept on ahead of me, and I was struggling to keep up with it. As we came into Martigny, it slowed a little but I was still a way behind it as it approached the fork where it could turn for France or Italy. If it made either of those turns, I would be lost.

I held my breath as the big car slowed a fraction more, and thought about trying to pull alongside in the narrow streets and shoot through the window, but there were people on the pavement, cars coming the other way. Instead, I hung back a little and watched with relief as they passed the French and Italian turns, and took the road east instead, the Rue du Simplon, whose name I picked out in my headlights as I swung round the corner.

Martigny was small, and very soon we left it behind. A long straight road opened out in front of us, as flat as the wide river that lay somewhere to our left.

I put my foot to the floor.

The road was empty, it was darker by the minute, and it seemed my best chance.

For a moment or two I began to close in on the Mercedes, but then I wondered if he knew I was behind him, because suddenly the car pulled away from me easily, until I lost its lights around a slight bend half a mile or more in front of me.

I didn't give up. The road was mostly straight, with few turnings, and I had a feeling that they were making a long journey somewhere east. There was still time for me to catch them.

I drove faster and faster, as fast as the old Renault could manage, trying to remember the geography that lay ahead. I'd never been there before, but my days of poring over maps had not been entirely wasted, and I could remember a little of it. There was at least one other pass south, over the Alps, to Italy, and if not, then the road must lead east, to Austria, perhaps. I wasn't sure, but I knew I had only one hope: that they were held up, delayed, that their powerful car was slowed by bad roads and we would be on a more even footing. So I kept on, glancing at the petrol gauge from time to time, the speedometer, the tail lights ahead of me when I managed to get them into range once more.

I lost track of the time, but just beyond Brig we began to climb a little. Not much at first, but then without warning, round the next bend, the road tilted up steeply into the mountains. Tight bends wound through sections of dark forest, and then the road would open up again for stretches before taking another twisting series of curves, rapidly gaining more height.

I had the car in low gear more than once. The engine whined pathetically as I pushed it on and on, and every time I did, I saw the lights ahead of me, always disappearing into the gloom around the next bend.

The temperature gauge on the car began to climb, and I could smell the heat of the engine from behind the wheel. Then the road levelled off again, and even in the dark I could sense the wide-open space that had just unfolded around me. We had climbed up into a high mountain pass, flat and wide, and though the road ducked and wove over slight rises and falls, there was nothing to trouble the Renault. The needle began to fall back to normal again, but still I was not gaining on the Mercedes.

We drove on, now in some German-speaking region; the signs had changed language at some invisible barrier, though it mattered little to me unless we reached a national border.

But if I thought we were done with climbing, I was wrong. At Gletsch we crossed the Rhône and then in three loops the road ascended steeply once more. At the head of the valley we crossed a narrow-gauge railway, and then a tiny bridge. Furkastrasse, I read on a small road sign. And in English too, the Furka Pass, and a spot height of over 2000 metres.

Night had fallen, and the weak beams of the Renault's head-lights picked out little ahead. I thought I was dreaming, because I caught a glimpse of the Mercedes' lights, but impossibly far above me, as if they were flying.

I watched, craning my head sideways as their lights seemed to cut back on themselves, and then vanish, but as I turned into a crazy hairpin bend, I knew they were ahead of me on a terrifying climb up the side of a mountain.

I dared not force the speed of the car higher, because the second hairpin was on me without warning, and I nearly put myself over the edge. The Mercedes was out of sight now, its lights only a memory, and I urged my car to go faster, ignoring the needle creeping higher again, the needle that showed the engine was overheating.

A third hairpin and the car began to complain terribly, the clutch sticky and the smell sickening, but then from the darkness a huge building loomed up on my right, a massive hotel over-looking the valley.

The hairpin looped around the end of the building, and then rose more gently, and before I knew what I was seeing I drove past the Mercedes, which had pulled into a parking space right on the road, at the back of the hotel.

Its lights were off, it was empty, and I knew they were inside already, out of a night that was cold, from the altitude if not the season.

I let the Renault recover by pulling over just a hundred yards past the hotel, where a slim parking bay hung over cold vertigin-ous space.

Turning the engine off, I waited a few moments and then climbed out of the car. There was no one around.

I pulled the revolver from my pocket and stole as quietly and as swiftly as I could back to his car.

The hotel towered above me in the cold air. Belvedere, I read on the side. Lights were on in some rooms, others were in darkness. There was a door to reception by the car park, on the side of the building that faced the mountain, and it suddenly spilled light as someone came out into the darkness.

I turned to the Mercedes as if it was mine, and pretended to fiddle with the boot lock, listening to the sounds of whoever it was receding, heading in the other direction.

Then there was a voice beside me.

'Mein Herr?'

I didn't even have time to turn.

That was the last thing I can remember.

FIVE

Unknown

1964

Pulling the key from the forbidden door, she let it fall to the ground, and when she took it up again, she saw that it was covered in blood. She tried to wipe it away, but no matter how hard she tried, some trace of it still remained.

Now, Bluebeard, his affairs having been resolved well, returned to his castle, and though she tried to hide the blood-stained key from him, she could not do so forever.

He took it in his hands.

'How comes this blood upon my key?' he roared.

after Charles Perrault, *Bluebeard*

I

I woke in darkness, in some dark, moving space, and as I tried to sit up, and failed, and then to stretch my legs out, and failed again, I knew I was shut in the boot of a car.

From the powerful hum of the engine I guessed it was the Mercedes. I had no idea how long I'd been out for, but my head throbbed, and feeling in the dark through my hair I touched a wound on my head, swollen and sticky.

I was sick immediately and sank back on to the thin carpet, feeling wretched.

The car was moving steadily, but it was hard to tell how fast; only when we took a corner did I get any sense of speed, but by then I no longer cared. I just wanted it to stop.

The air was thick and vile now. I could smell my own stink, and I began to bang on the wall of the boot, just beyond which would be the back seat of the car, where he would be sitting.

I begged them to stop.

We drove on.

2

I lost all sense of time.

We drove on and on, and still it stayed dark inside the boot of the car. Perhaps it was day outside now, perhaps still night, I had no way of knowing. I was ill again, and lay still, shut up in that tiny space, coming and going from consciousness.

I was hungry and my head pounded from thirst; we might have been travelling for a day or more.

Only once was I aware that the car had stopped, and I banged on the lid of the boot, hoping that someone might hear me, and might investigate and set me free, but no one came, and I grew weak. It was getting harder to breathe, and there were slight exhaust fumes creeping in from somewhere. I tried to turn myself around, to place my feet against the seat backs and kick my way through, but I only succeeded in wrenching my ankle.

We drove on, and then, finally, there was a change.

The road had been getting worse for a while, for a long while in fact. It had become bumpy where before it had been relatively even, and even the soft suspension of the big car wasn't enough to smooth out the potholes we were driving over. This had made my ordeal even more intolerable, but then it changed again.

There was the sound of gravel crunching underneath the tyres, and this went on for only a few minutes, and then we stopped.

The engine was turned off, and I heard doors open, and at least one shut again.

I braced myself, and I didn't have long to wait.

The boot flew open, and rough hands pawed in at me. I tried to struggle, but it was dark and I could see little. A torch flashed in my face and then as I reached out, someone hit me on the jaw, and I fell limply back into the boot, my head pounding.

The hands reached in and pulled me bodily from the car, where they were joined by another pair of strong arms.

I was dragged across gravel, my feet scrabbling to stand but not managing it, and I saw the dim outline of a vast house appear from the gloom, a light here and there.

There was the faint smell of water, and I heard a bird call in the darkness, the sound of wingtips beating.

Then someone hit me on the wound on my head again, and I nearly passed out. I managed to stay awake as I was hauled down some stone steps, along a short passageway, and thrown on to a dirt floor.

I heard the rattle of a chain, and my arm was tugged to one side and a metal bracelet closed around my wrist.

I had the sense there were at least two men holding me, two men who had pulled me from the car, but what unnerved me more was the sense of a third man, standing at a distance, walking behind, watching it all.

As the two who'd manhandled me turned and left, the third man lingered. He stood in the doorway, watching me for a time.

It was him. I couldn't even see him, but I knew, and when he spoke to me, I knew I'd been right.

'There is no one to help you now,' he said, then the door closed, and a key turned in the lock.

3

The cellar was dark, save for a dim, bare bulb hanging from a beam across the centre of the ceiling.

It cast a weak light, showing the limits of my space. I lay on a loose earth floor, here and there made more uncomfortable by the presence of small lumps of coal, from a time when the cellar had been used to store fuel. There were a few dilapidated wooden wine racks set into the far wall, and there seemed to be a cramped brick funnel of a skylight sloping up to ground level outside.

I could reach none of these things, however, because my left arm was bound at the wrist by an iron manacle, and from there a short chain held me to a metal hoop in the wall.

The two men who'd pulled me from the car and put me in the cellar came back. I recognised one of them as the driver I'd followed out of Lausanne, a heavy man whose shoulders hunched over. I didn't know the other. They walked up to me. The driver was holding a knife.

'Please,' I begged, 'please. Don't.'

They showed no sign that they'd heard me, and then they knelt down, pulled my shoes from me, and cut my clothes off, leaving me in my underwear and vest.

They left, and I lay in the dirt, too scared to feel the cold, or the ache where my arm was held awkwardly by the chain, or the rough floor beneath me.

I began to cry, curling up into a ball, and then, somehow, I slept.

4

I don't know how long he'd been standing in the doorway, looking at me, but when I woke he was there.

Behind him, through the open door, I saw a dirty corridor, filled with a weak daylight, and a little more spilled through the narrow brick vent that allowed a small amount of fresh air to filter down to me.

As I stirred, he tilted his head to one side, and then walked into the room. He didn't close the door, but walked over till he was directly underneath the bare bulb, which cast a faint orange glow over his skin.

I saw he was holding something out towards me, but it took me a while to see what it was. My sight was bad, maybe from the blow to my head, or the dust in the room, or from hunger, but things were fuzzy, and it was still almost dark.

Then I saw that he had my gun, the revolver I'd taken from Hayes, and he was pointing it out towards me.

At first I cowered, waiting for him to fire, but something told me he wasn't going to pull the trigger. Why drag me across what felt like half of Europe in the boot of a car if all he wanted to do was put a bullet in me? There must have been a hundred lonely spots on forest roads where he could have done that. So I stopped shaking and stared back at him, saying nothing, yet almost daring him to do it.

Finally, after a long, long pause, he lowered the gun and put it in his pocket.

He didn't say anything.

He left.

5

What was it that had led me from one hole in the ground in Paris to another, to this cellar?

It was him, and it was what he'd done to Marian. It was my desire to set things right, to punish him.

Over the years I had probed and pushed and wondered and sought to find out who he was and what made him behave the way he did, and now that he had me, trapped, I shouldn't have cared about any of that any more. Yet I did. Even as I lay on the earth in the cellar there was still room enough in my mind to be fascinated, to wonder at his terrible ways.

There was huge anger in me, yet I couldn't feel it. It lurked, somehow trapped inside me. I should have been able to let it out, but it would not come, and I felt unsure of my feelings as a result, uncertain about many things.

I wasn't even sure that I wanted to live, but I did know one thing clearly: that I wanted him dead.

And so it was he came before me again, later that day, for the daylight had stolen away from the vent, and I had only the weak bulb for illumination.

The door opened and he came in.

Once again he left it standing open, for there was no chance of escape for me. I had been pulling at the manacle closed around my wrist, but it was tight, there was no way of loosening it, and the metal loop that was set into the wall was heavy and solid.

Then he spoke. Aside from a few words he'd muttered in the church, and then under the bridge in Avignon, I had not heard his voice. And now he spoke as if he was making up for all the years that had been lost between us. He spoke, and he spoke, and the strange thing was that I did not reply. Not once. Not even when he told me things that made me churn and rage inside. Something made me hold my tongue, and merely watch him, unblinking, as he told me the story of my life, of *our* life.

'Charles Jackson. Dr Charles Jackson. I confess it took me some time to understand. At first, I did not know you. But now I do. I met you in Paris. There was that girl . . . The American. Marian. Marian Fisher. You knew her. She spoke about you. She told me your name, as well as, I might add, a few other things that were useful to know.

'But I did not then connect you with the war. You were the one who saw me in Saint-Germain, were you not? You saw me there, and ran away! Coward! You saw me at that French girl in the hole, and you could have stopped me then, but you ran away. Why? Why did you run? You could have fired upon me, you were an officer, I could see. You must have had a weapon? Yet you fled the bunker and gave me time to push the girl over the wall of the park and into the brush below. Gave me time to get away.

'Was it just chance that brought you back to Paris? It must have been, because you cannot possibly have guessed that I was still there, making a comfortable living from certain items and enjoying certain girls. You came and made my life awkward. I was starting to educate Marian. Showing her the pleasure that can be had from blood. I had moved her to a place where she let me cut her, willingly, but then she began to pull away.

'Because of you. You said something, I know it. You scared her, made her frightened, and she began to pull away. So that finally, one night, she tried to resist me, and I had to kill her.

'You forced me to move, and you forced me to kill the American girl before she said something that would put me in danger. Were you in love with her? Were you? I think that's true. You loved her. Then you should know that you killed her. By trying to warn her about me, you are the one responsible for her death. You.

'I think it was then that I began to hate you, as you seemed to hate me. You had interrupted me twice, taken what I wanted from me, and I would have had you killed in Avignon, but for that captain. I had my comfortable life disturbed once more, by you. Things were easy in Avignon. It is a dirty town, and there were many willing to join me. I told them it was a religion, a true religion; a more honest form of that ridiculous play-acting the Catholics do, and it was easy to find men and women eager to join me. Yet you spoiled it for me.'

All this while he stood in front of me, above me. He was tall, I'd forgotten that. And strong, despite his age. He stood with his feet slightly apart, his weight evenly balanced, showing total command of the situation, of everything around him. Of me. And yet I noticed one thing: he had chosen a spot to stand, and that stand was outside my reach. Even broken and feeble as I was, it gave me a little courage to see he kept his distance from me.

But he wasn't done speaking, not by a long way.

'So, all this time, I have been wondering about you, Charles Jackson. From that moment, the first moment, in Saint-Germain, when I saw the look in your eyes.

'There was fear, I saw it. Fear, of course, but there was something else. Curiosity. Is that how I should put it? Curiosity, wonder? You wondered what I was at, even though you knew it well enough. I was drinking the warm blood of the girl I had just killed when you found me, and in the same moment that you turned away, you wanted to stay, too, and watch what I was doing.

'So what does that mean? What does that make you, Dr Jackson? Are you guilty? You should be. You could have saved that girl, but you merely let yourself become guilty.

'What were you doing, coming back to Paris? Why did you come to Avignon? Why did you come here? I understand, since you followed me with a gun in your hand, that you intended to kill me. You think I should be killed, because of what I've done. Maybe I should, but I don't care to think about that. I do what I do because I like it, and because I can.

'Do you think I am evil? Is that why you wish to kill me? Do you wonder why I do what I do? Why? Because it excites me. I worship it. I crave it. I do it because I can. You think it's evil? To feel human blood pass across my lips? Have you never wondered what it would be like? Did you never kiss a woman, and think about the blood in her lips? Did you not push your mouth on to her neck, and feel the pulsing there? Did she never stretch back her head and offer you her neck, and beg you to kiss her there? To bite her? Gently, yes! She wants you to bite her, and you do, but you both know what is really happening. You are playing the monster, and you nip her skin with your teeth to excite yourself. And her.

'You think I must have used violence on the women. You think I tricked them and captured them and used violence against them to get what I wanted, but you are wrong. There was always violence in the end, but in the beginning, there was no violence. I met them, I took them, I spoke to them, I told them what I wanted, and I led them to a point where they came to me willingly. Every one of them gave me their blood willingly. At least, they did at first. And the blood rushes, the blood rushes.

'All down the years, there is the rushing of blood inside us. It spills out of us so easily, so feeble are we. You must have seen much of that in the war. I saw much of it. I saw so many things. I saw how men looked without heads. How much blood there is inside a man. How long it can take to die, and how fast. How a shell could go off beside you and leave you untouched but coat you in the body of the man you had been whispering to but a moment before.

'Blood. We are born in blood as we slide from the mother, covered in it, and it never leaves us, it rules us and we should worship it. All of us. Some of us do.

'You remember, I'm sure, what happened in Rome? I set you a trap, and you dutifully flew into it, and you took that girl without even wondering how old she was. I'm right. I forget her name now, but she was an interesting one, for sure. She relished what she did to you, I barely had to pay her. She told me she was bleeding when she took you. She told me how you reacted.

'Blood! You were excited by her, and you made my life so very easy, until . . . Did something scare you? You returned to London that evening, when you were supposed to see the girl again. Then I didn't know what to do about you. I thought often about killing you, but I had those photographs taken of you with her to offer me a more interesting idea. The chance to destroy you, completely.

'So I had your house watched. We saw that man come and go. Collecting your letters. We followed him. We killed him. We found your false name. Your address in Scotland. But by the time we got there, you had moved on again. What made you move on? You can have had no idea, no warning, that we were coming.

'So I still needed some way to get to you, to find you. Then along came the Italian girl, and I knew you wouldn't let me down. So now I will do it.

'I will reduce you to nothing. And if you beg me hard enough, one day I might walk in here and shoot you. But not yet.

'First of all, I am going to find out what it is about you. What is inside you. I believe you have a connection to blood, just as I do, and I am going to make you find it. I don't know what it is, but I know it's there. You are as fascinated by blood as you are scared by it.

'I'm going to leave you now. We will begin tomorrow. But it's important you know one more thing before I start. I have the girl upstairs. The young Italian girl. Remember that.'

6

He left, and then the anger came. I pulled and pulled at my chain until my wrist began to bleed, but I didn't care. I kept struggling, screaming soundlessly, and I could almost feel the hot blood in my brain driving me to madness, but it was a madness that wouldn't come, no matter how much I prayed for it to come and take me away.

Eventually I stopped struggling, and kicking out at the air, and I collapsed on the ground, panting hard, gasping. But despite everything, I remained lucid, and I knew, as much as I hated it, that I was still logical enough, still alert enough, to have focused on the most terrible thing he'd revealed to me.

He'd killed Marian because I'd tried to warn her. He was right. It *was* my fault. It was so long ago, so many years ago, but I wanted to scream at my younger self for my lack of control. I'd made the wrong decision, after all, and that weakness had led him to kill her, as she'd tried to resist him. I saw it all; I imagined his luxurious apartment in Saint-Germain; how he'd kneel before her, holding a small surgical knife in his fingertips, or maybe some authentically oriental knife, and make a small cut in her wrist. I saw it, I saw it all, and I saw Marian refusing. One night, she refuses, and he grows angry, and then she knows I'm right. That she is in danger. But it's too late, because he's already locked the door and hidden the key. He's already turning towards her from the table where he keeps larger knives. No, he's picking up something less subtle, something that will be worse for her, and more innocuous for him; a table knife, as to be found in any brasserie on any street in Paris.

She goes down, now he towers over her, and when it's done, and his anger goes, he stares, looking around him at the mass of blood that's spreading over the varnished floorboards of his consulting room, and his head hangs, because he knows there will be much work to do before the night is over.

I killed Marian. And I killed Hunter, therefore, too.

They'd tracked him down in Cambridge, found that note I'd written to him with my address, and only the fact that Hayes had been so clumsy had, by chance, made me move on again before Verovkin and his men arrived in Scotland. Hayes had nothing to do with it; nothing to do with Hunter, or Verovkin. In fact, his greed had saved me, but poor Hunter, I thought. Poor Hunter.

I knew then that Verovkin had beaten me. It was hopeless. I didn't know what he meant by *We will begin tomorrow*, and I didn't want to.

I hated him, and in the night I found out why.

I no longer cared who he was, or where he was from or what he'd done before the war, or how he came to be who he came to be. I didn't care that I couldn't understand how his English was perfect, as good as mine, and yet he had some strange mix of accents that I couldn't untangle. I didn't want to shout at him or argue with him. I just wanted him to be dead.

I already knew that I hated him for what he'd done to Marian. I knew that there had been many girls. The girl in the bunker whom he referred to only as French, and Marian, and presumably Arianna, and who knew how many others he had lured into some twisted mess of sex and blood until he'd had enough of them and moved on. And now he had the Italian girl, somewhere in the house, and presumably meant to do her harm too.

I hated him for all those reasons, but I hated him most of all for starting my mind working, and working, until it made a connection that it had been trying to keep hidden from me for years.

I have said that my marriage to Sarah was loveless and functional, but there was something else. There was a little more to it than that, and that, I now realised, had everything to do with blood.

Sarah didn't love me, not in the end, but I think she loved me once, and I her. And I think she married me because I was what people used to call *a good catch*. I was a young doctor, I had become a specialist at a very tender age, and my prospects were good. Yet if Sarah loved me, she did not desire me. But that is not to say that she did not want to have sex. She just didn't want to have it with me.

In the early days of our marriage, we made love, infrequently, and though I did all I could do make her excited I never got the feeling I was succeeding. I never once gave her an orgasm. The details of how I found out she was having an affair are as mundane as they are irrelevant, but when I discovered she was sleeping with a young student I was devastated. I accused her one evening, and she did not deny it. She almost seemed proud of it, and I grew angry, I made her tell me all the details, every nasty and sordid little fact. And here was the thing: on the last night I had tried to have sex with her, and was refused, she'd used the excuse that she was bleeding. That same night, I forced her to confess, was the night when she'd come home late, from a party, she said, but it was in fact the first night she'd taken her student to his student bed. Despite her blood, which was presumably left behind, smeared on him, like the blood on Bluebeard's key.

I, a doctor, knew as well as anyone that there is no medical reason to avoid sex during menstruation. It is a matter of taste, of taboo, and the idea has been spread that it is, in some very unspoken way, wrong. Certainly Sarah would never let me near her for a week either side of those few days, and yet she stood before me in our new house on Hills Road and defiantly told me that was just what she'd done with her lover.

Damn him, and damn the man who had locked me in a cellar to rot with my hate, for it was he who had shown me why Arianna had excited me so much; she had relished the blood from inside her and let me relish it too, in a way that Sarah never had. I wanted from my wife what that student had had.

He, Lippe, Verovkin, couldn't possibly have known any of that, of course. It didn't matter; the effect on me was the same, and I lay on the cold earth of the cellar as if a worm was chewing slowly but steadily through my brain, eating away what little peace I had left.

Somewhere in the night, I slept. My dreams cannot bear repeating, but they were as nothing to what began the following morning. Because when I woke, on the floor in front of me, within my reach, was a cup of blood, and I knew from where it had come.

7

I was hungry, and desperately thirsty. I think at least two days had passed since I had drunk anything, longer since I had eaten.

Already I felt weak and nauseous, and I knew at once what he was trying to do. He wanted me to drink the blood of the girl, and he was going to starve me to make me do it.

But I wasn't going to.

I had a little freedom of movement from the chain. I could either sit up against the wall and let my arm hang down by my side, or I could lie down and stretch my legs out. If I did that, I could move my right arm out into the room a short way, and the cup, a white enamel mug, was within my reach.

I took one look at it, and kicked out as hard as I could.

The day passed. I lay still, moving only when I felt a need to urinate, which I was trying to do as far to one side of me as possible. Nevertheless, I was already aware of the smell I was creating, and the smell of the girl's blood was lost amongst the other odours already present.

Evening had come by the time the driver came back into the room. He picked up the enamel mug from where I had sent it sprawling, and placed another identical one down, again within my reach.

I glowered at him from where I lay weakly on the floor, and he didn't say a word.

He left me, locking the door behind him, and I stared at the mug as I lay on my side, stared at it long and hard.

I edged over, and my fingers closed around it. I picked it up, and dragged myself back to the wall, where I sat upright, breathing hard.

Then I lifted the mug and with all the strength I had I threw it at the bare light bulb hanging from the ceiling, trying to smash it.

I missed, and the cup hit the far wall. A trail of blood led across the room from me to the impact there, and the light bulb hung, still intact, but once the idea was in my head, I couldn't stop. I felt around on the floor and found three lumps of the coal in the dirt. With my second throw I hit the bulb neatly and with a fizz the room was thrown into darkness.

I lay back in the dirt, closed my eyes, and let the weakness take over.

8

When I woke it was still dark, but before me, in the centre of the room, was a candle in a tin candlestick, and also on the floor, and once more within my reach, a white enamel mug.

I hung my head.

9

I think I managed to push the mug away from me twice more, and twice more it reappeared at some point whilst I slept. It was unnerving and eerie the way it appeared. I had only once seen the driver bring it in and set it on the floor; every other time they must have waited for me to pass out, and then brought it back, so that it appeared like some evil magic, as in a nightmare where you cannot escape your demon, as in a fairy tale where the guilty blood cannot be washed away. The mug kept appearing and reappearing, and each time it did, there was fresh blood inside it.

I couldn't do it. Somewhere in the house was that girl, Giovanna, and somewhere they were taking her blood and feeding it to me. I knew I was dying. I knew the blood could save me, but I knew he would have destroyed me if I drank it.

But the day crawled by, so slowly, and I grew so weak I no longer thought, could no longer function, could barely even breathe. My head was pounding, my eyesight was feeble, my stomach screamed at me, and so it was that my fingers closed around the mug, and I drank.

I drank it all, desperately, horribly, greedily, and when I had, I sat still for the length of a heartbeat, and then, retching, I vomited it all back up.

I howled in anger and shame and threw the mug across the room again.

This time I was awake as the door opened, and the driver returned with another mug, which he set carefully down within my reach. He collected the other, empty one, and left. I glared at

him as if I was a beast, and just as he turned to close the door
behind him, I saw him smiling with satisfaction.

Even the tiny amount of blood that was left inside me after I'd
been sick must have done me some good. Very slowly I felt a
little energy creep back into me, and I stared at the mug in front
of me again.

I would like to be able to say I hated myself then, but I didn't.
I was too weak, too feeble of mind to even know what I was
doing. The hunger pawed at my brain, and I was more animal
than human; I had little control. Or so I tell myself now.

I stared at the cup of blood, and I pulled it towards me again,
and this time, I took small mouthfuls. I held my breath as I swallowed, and I waited a long time between each sip.

With what little control I had left, I tried not to think about
what I was doing, but I knew it was the only way I was going to
survive, and so it was that I finally tasted blood, salty and thick.

I would also like to be able to remember something else, by
which I mean I would like to misremember something else. I
would like to recall that it was only after I'd begun to see a way
out of the cellar that I drank the girl's blood; that it was only
then, with the possibility of escape, that I allowed myself the
shame of that. But that too would be a falsehood.

In fact, it was as I slowly drank, and very slowly felt a little
recovery, as I stared at the candle in the candlestick, that I realised there was a way out of the cellar. It was not a way I relished
much, but it was a possibility, though that's irrelevant here. The
point is that he had won. He had beaten me. He had lowered me
to the point where I drank the blood, and maybe even worse
than that was this: I didn't care.

10

There was a way out, perhaps, but in order for it to work, I needed some patience, and some luck. I also needed to keep taking the blood they brought me every day, and I began to justify to myself that that was why I allowed myself to drink it, but the truth is this: I cared more about myself than about Giovanna.

I told myself she was already dead. Not literally, but that nothing could have been done for her anyway, even before he caught her and took her. And now that he had, she was already dead, for he would never let her go. So if I could survive long enough on her blood to make my escape, then it would justify my actions. Maybe I could even find her and save her. That's what I told myself, but it was all lies. I just wanted to save myself.

I stared at the candlestick. Every day, when the sun went down, the driver would bring the enamel mug and put the candlestick on the floor. I stared at it closely. It was the traditional sort, made of tin, with a wide, flat base.

I only needed the driver to make one small mistake, and that was for him to leave it close enough for me to reach.

During the day, I had stretched out from the wall as far as I could. I had marked a small point in the dirt with my toe; the furthest I could reach. Then I sank back against the wall, making myself look as small and pathetic and immobile as I could.

Every time he brought the mug and the candle into the room, I watched, fixated on one thing only: where he would place the candlestick. I noticed that it varied, and finally, one day, he placed it just inside the limit of my reach.

That night I drank the blood, knowing it would be for the last time. If my attempt to escape failed, they would simply kill me, I was sure.

I waited a long time, counting away seconds and minutes to be certain I was not just imagining that time was passing, counting until I was sure the night was at its deepest, and then I stretched myself out, reaching with my bare toe to hook through the finger grip on the candlestick. I had misjudged it. It was not as close as I thought, and I pulled so hard that my hand started to be cut by the manacle again, stretching till I thought something would snap, and eventually I caught the candlestick with my toe, and eagerly hauled it back.

I sat up against the wall, and prepared for the operation. I knew I needed to do it fast. I was not a surgeon, but I had been a doctor, and I wanted to make the best of it.

I held my left hand with my right, and pulled it tight against the manacle. For what I was about to do, I needed to be sure. I needed to be sure what I was doing, and why, and so, although I had many times tried to squeeze the bones of my hand together and pull my hand out, I plainly saw what was stopping it: my thumb.

I stared at my left hand, at the thumb, and I tried to see it as not part of me, I tried to detach it mentally, because it was the only thing stopping me from getting away.

I tried not to think further after that.

I pulled the candle from the candlestick, and pushed it deep into the soil floor, then adjusted the chain so that a couple of the links were sitting directly in its small but steady flame.

Then I wedged my left hand, the bound one, up against the loop on the wall. It didn't take very long before it started to go numb, but I waited a long time, for the links of the chain to get hot, for my arm to go numb, and while I did, I took the metal base of the candlestick, and tested it against the brick wall.

It seemed strong, and yet thin enough to do the job. I wished it was sharper, but there was little I could about that. I tried to hone one side of the base against the brickwork, and I managed to put a little more edge on it, but then there came a moment where I knew I was just wasting time, putting off what I did not want to do.

Finally, I pulled off my vest with my right hand, and using my teeth I tore a big section from it, to protect myself as I worked.

I laid my left arm down, so numb and yet it screamed with pins and needles, and felt strange and alien, which was what I wanted. Then with my right hand I took the candlestick base in the strip of cloth, and lined it up across the joint at the base of my thumb.

With all my weight, and as much force as I could muster, I leaned down on my right hand, pushing the tin blade into my left hand, hard, then harder, and then, with horror, I realised I had severed the joint. Blood was flowing into the dirt but I had to work quickly to finish the cut through a tendon that would not break at first, and the flesh of my thumb, and then the skin.

When I was done I tried the manacle again. With horror I saw it was still tight, very tight, and my hand would still not pass through it. Appalled at what I'd done, I grew desperate and pulled my bleeding hand, harder now, until finally, with my own blood lubricating the metal, I yanked it free.

The pain was unbelievable. My head swam and I felt the urge to be sick. My heart was beating fiercely in my chest, pumping blood round my body in fear, which meant I was bleeding fast, and yet which helped me in a way, as that same blood would be carrying adrenalin through my body, the only reason I could survive this critical act. I had a small vision; of the adrenalin that the shock and pain had forced into my bloodstream. I saw the chemicals running around my veins, doing their work, and I knew that it was only that chemistry that got me through what I had to do.

Despite that, I started to feel I would pass out, and quickly, before I lost too much blood, I pushed the wound against the hot metal of the chain, trying to cauterise the main blood vessels. The chain lost its heat very quickly, but it just about did the work required of it. The smell was terrible but by then the pain was too much for me, and I blacked out, though not for long.

When I came round, I saw with relief that the candle was still burning, and I also saw that I had done the best job I could of stopping the bleeding, though the wound was a mess. I wrapped it in the strip of vest I'd used to protect my hand, tying a knot with the help of my teeth.

Then I took the rest of my ruined vest, and made a sling with it, a simple band to hold my left hand up and out of the way. It was useless to me now anyway.

I waited for a burst of pain to subside, and then, breathing as deeply as I could, I stood.

Standing up was hard in itself. I had not stood for days, and I was still very weak, but slowly I found my feet and staggered to the door. It would all end here if I had guessed wrong.

I had guessed that they wouldn't have left anyone to guard me. I had been making myself look as weak and as ill as possible, and I was chained to the wall. I had also judged that the door was actually quite flimsy, and though they were locking it, when I put my shoulder against it, I knew I was right.

It would make a noise, of course, but I couldn't help that, and if they found me and shot me, it might be a blessing after all. So I leaned back and then threw my shoulder at the thin panel of the cellar door, and a quarter of the door popped out of its frame, with a minimum of noise.

I waited, listening for sounds of an alarm being raised, but none came.

My hand screamed with pain as I climbed through, but I was scared and desperate and the adrenalin in my blood forced me on.

I was in a corridor, a dead end in one direction, the steps to the outside at the other. Halfway along the corridor was a flight of steps that I guessed ran up into the house itself. On either side of the corridor was a series of rooms, each like the one I'd been in. Mostly the doors were open, and as I stole along, I peered in.

One was full of junk; another had coal in it, looking like it was still in use. There were wooden boxes in a third, and wine in a fourth, and it was then that I had a further thought. I didn't want just to run away. I wanted to destroy him. I was weak, and there were at least three of them, and given the size of the house probably many more, but I was free, and I had one small weapon: the flame of the candle.

I began to hunt through the cellar rooms, looking for petrol or other highly inflammable spirits. I tried a fifth door, and then a sixth, and then there was the seventh room.

The door was shut, where all the others had been open.

I tested the handle, and the door opened, and there she was. Giovanna, dumped on top of a crate. I knew it had to be her. I had never seen her photograph, but I knew. She had obviously been dead for a long time. Days maybe. Perhaps she had been too fragile. Perhaps he had got sick of her crying. Perhaps a million things had happened to that poor girl, but the fact was simple. She was dead, she had been for some time, and so the very first thing I thought was that it hadn't been *her* blood I had been drinking.

Somehow this was enough to send me into a terrible rage, somehow it made me realise the full horror of what I'd done, what he'd made me do, how he'd tricked me into believing I was drinking the girl's blood. Did it matter? Did it matter what I had been doing, whose blood I had been drinking?

It mattered very much to me, and it was all I could do not to give myself away there and then with screaming, or by charging upstairs and blundering against the first person I ran into.

My anger gave me more strength. It rose up and hurtled around inside me like a hurricane, stopping me from thinking, forcing me into action, and so I went back to the wine cellar and found what I was hoping for: bottles of old cognac.

These I snatched at greedily, and then I headed for the steps to the house.

II

It hadn't taken much.

I sat in the woods, up behind the house, and then moved round in a wide circle, till I was looking at the facade from across the lake. It was dark, and though I could see everything that happened I felt safe enough.

They did not care about me. They did not, perhaps, even know I had escaped.

I had found the door to the cellars unlocked, and came up into the kitchens. All was quiet, not a single sound save the tick of a clock on the wall that showed it to be around three in the morning.

Outside the kitchen I came into a small hall, and then a dining room, the windows of which were covered in two layers of curtains, thin lace and then heavy velvet. I soaked the bottoms of them in the brandy and set them alight.

I could see the house was grand. Wherever it was, it was big, and though a little faded, it was a sumptuous place. The ceilings were carved plaster, the architraves ornate and old. There was plenty more wood besides; shutters to the windows, panels, floors, tables, chairs.

I knew if it was to work I needed to get several parts of the house alight before the fire was discovered, and I moved through room after room on the ground floor. There were two drawing rooms. A study. A library. And when I had something burning well in every one, I decided to let myself be free. I wanted to be free, whatever that freedom was. I would never lead a normal life now, I knew that. This thing had changed me for ever. Maybe there was only one freedom left for me, the kind that a desperate man inflicts upon himself in a darkened room when all other options are gone.

I headed back for the kitchen. As I did so, I passed the staircase to the upper floors, and knew I had to put them out of reach, so I emptied the last bottle over the carpet that lined them, and was almost scared by how quickly it began to burn.

By the time I crossed the dining room again it was already dangerous to do so, with flames licking across the ceiling. I knew it was already too late for them, even if they discovered the fire right then.

I found the back door from the kitchen, and I unlocked it with the key hanging on a hook on the door frame.

Behind the house there was an expanse of lawn, and then the trees soon started as a wooded hillside rose beyond. I worked my way around through the trees, watching the fire starting to really take hold.

The ground floor glowed, and I wondered how long it would be before anyone woke, before the flames roused them. I knew there was a chance they would be overcome by smoke before they even realised what was going on, but as I heard shouts come across the water, I knew that someone had woken in time.

I crept back a little farther into the trees, watching the flames. My hand gave me almost no pain at all. It was a warm night and though I was nearly naked, I felt no cold. I wondered where I was. The house was magnificent. The style could put it almost anywhere in Europe from the seventeenth to the eighteenth century, maybe a little later if pastiche. It was the house of a very wealthy man; a house that would have had servants, and hunting parties at the weekend, and where perhaps French or English would have been spoken as freely as the native tongue of wherever I was.

I saw the flames reaching higher into the house; the second floor was alight, and I could see that the third would follow soon.

There were desperate shouts from the upper reaches of the house. I heard a scream.

I felt nothing of what I'd done, save for one thing; I hoped the fire would engulf the whole house, even stretch down into the cellars, and that it would cremate poor Giovanna and give her soul rest where her body had known little. I sat clutching my left hand in my right, rocking slightly to try and somehow hypnotise myself out of the pain, and I thought of Marian, and of Hunter, and even of Arianna. I wished that they were all at peace, somehow, and I hoped they knew that I had done something for them at last.

Then there were people outside. I saw two men and a woman running around madly, and I heard dogs barking. I could do nothing more. I was unable to defend myself.

It was time to go.

SIX

Sextantio, Italy

1968

Blood didst thou thirst for, and with blood I glut thee!

Dante Alighieri, *The Divine Comedy, Purgatorio*, canto XII

I

I'm waiting.

The dogs are barking, as they have been barking throughout the long, hot night.

Opposite me, on the little isolated hilltop that sits like a ship sailing down the dry and barren valley, is the ruined village of Sextantio.

He's there, I know he is, though I have not seen him.

I have watched for three days and nights now. I have a small pair of binoculars in my hand, though they are useless now in the dark. I have scoured every visible spot, every narrow street and every window of the village from my latest hiding place, behind a stone hunting hut.

At dusk each day I have moved on, circumnavigating the hills, revolving around Sextantio like a planet around the sun, to gain a new vantage point on the village. Watching, waiting for him to come out, to show himself, just once, before I move.

It has taken me years to find him again.

When I left the burning house that night, near naked, wounded, starving, and near dead, I had no idea where I was.

I walked for a day through forest till I found a small path, my left hand throbbing unbearably at times, though I left it in the sling as much as I could.

At dusk I found a poor, pathetic, backward village, where I stole peasant clothes from a washing line. I drank water from a stream, and moved on, unseen, still with no idea of where I was.

It took me another day to discover I was much further east than I believed, but when I saw a sign reading Kranjska Gora, I guessed we had crossed into Yugoslavia, which only gave birth to yet more questions about the man I'd been pursuing. What right had he to be in Yugoslavia, behind the Iron Curtain? A softer place than other communist countries maybe, but still, I failed to see how he was able to come and go.

How had he managed to cross the border with me in the boot of his car? Was he known to the authorities? Was he someone powerful, above suspicion? Certainly, the palatial house I'd burned down suggested that he was someone from the elite; I had long ago learned how his money lifted him above the normal concerns of law.

I didn't know the details, but then all I was concerned about was getting away, and starting my life again, in whatever way I could that meant anything.

I tried.

It took me weeks to put myself back together, months. I travelled rough, I walked across the border into Austria, where I slept rough, stole food and begged on the streets of Klagenfurt, acting mute if anyone tried to bother me.

I stole enough money to buy some proper clothes from a cheap shop in a bad neighbourhood one day, and then went to the Turkish baths. I had my hair cut and my beard shaved.

I paid a local doctor to look at my wounded hand, and saw with some miserable satisfaction that I had done a decent job. There was no infection, the healing had started. I explained to the doctor in pidgin English that I had had an accident cutting wood. He didn't seem to care either way.

I needed access to my money, though, and it took me months to scrabble my way across central Europe, skipping across remote borders under cover of night, begging and thieving my way, until finally I reacquainted myself with my fortune in Geneva.

I knew I couldn't go on the way I had been.

I made one last illegal trip to Marseille, where I had heard I could get a fake passport. I called myself Jack Hunter, taking my father's name as my Christian name and my dead friend's name as my surname. Hunter, it now said on my passport, and I liked the private joke.

Because although I had told myself I was going to head home and quietly destroy my fortune for the rest of my days, and forget about pursuing the man who'd ruined my life, when I left Marseille I knew I was not done yet.

I still wanted him.

I had destroyed his big house in the woods, but I doubted very much that he had been killed in the fire. I'd seen people outside before I left; he would certainly have escaped too. I knew that house must have represented some of his fortune. Maybe it was insured, maybe not. But I knew he would still have money, somewhere, just as I had. And with that money, he could afford to start again, start taking people's lives again.

I began taking holidays in Yugoslavia, to Slovenia, where that house had been. Private tourism was opening up in the country; all that was needed was a tourist visa, and now, with my new, clean identity, and my fortune intact, that was easy enough.

I drove around the area I thought I'd been held captive in, and after a few excursions over many weeks, I finally found the ruins of the place.

I stared at it long and hard one dry evening as the sun set, and set myself to talking to the locals about it.

Yes, they knew the man who'd owned it.

No, he had gone away, after the fire.

So, he had survived it, news that did not surprise me greatly, but which renewed my determination. Did they know where he had gone? I asked.

No, they did not.

I was on the point of leaving when one of them, an old man but with a lover's eyes, referred to the man who'd owned the big house as the Italian.

Italian? I asked. *You're sure?*

Quite sure.

So began my years of wandering. I stumbled and stalked almost at random through Italy, following dead ends, asking strangers strange questions, digging here, hunting there, and always moving.

The months went by and I had nothing to go on, and before I knew it the months became the first year, much of which I spent coming to terms with losing the thumb on my dominant hand. I learned to do things differently, but even now I still sometimes reach out without thinking, expecting to clutch something with a thumb that is no longer there.

I travelled the length of Italy, and then I gave up on it. I hunted in Switzerland, Austria, back in Yugoslavia again, staying for one night here and several weeks there, always with one thing on my mind. The desire to possess him, to find him again and take possession of him, as he had done me.

Finally, in Slovenia, I did find out a little about who he was, or who he had been. It seemed he really was Italian, that he came from a vastly wealthy family, but that his wayward behaviour as a child and teenager had made him the family's black sheep. He had fought in the war, on both sides, and at some point in the fifties he had bought the mansion I had burned down, buying anonymity and protection from the local party official. Some even said that his bribery went as high as Tito himself, who frequently holidayed nearby, at Lake Bled.

I didn't know the truth, but truly, I did not care.

One year became two, and then three, and as I moved on, always hunting, I almost forgot what I was hunting for. But not quite.

Always, deep down, in the depths of whatever it was my mind had become, was the thought of him, of what he'd done to me, and of what I would do to him.

I reflected little on the past, if at all. My vision was always forward. My memories seemed to be no more than broken pieces, fragments that had skittered away to hide in the corner of my mind. If I thought of the past at all it was only with a peculiar sense of wonder over the passage of time, how endless our lives seem when we're young, how time flows faster and faster as we age, the way the sand in an hourglass appears to flow faster as it nears its end. That thought alone filled me with terror, that my time would run out before I had done what I wanted to do, what I *really* wanted to do.

I forgot everything else. I forgot Hunter, though I bore his name. I forgot Marian, and Giovanna. I forgot why I cared about how Arianna was linked to Sarah, I forgot my old name, but still I kept moving, moving. I saw nothing but the road, nothing but the suggestion of his presence in every bar in every town. I tasted nothing I drank, savoured no food I ate. Every part of me closed in, shut down, until I was little more than a machine in human form, a machine with one purpose.

And then, finally, I found myself in Italy, and I began snooping around the family of young Giovanna, something I should have done long before. What made me think about it was a small revelation in the news. Their tragedy had disappeared from the world's view a few weeks after Giovanna went missing, but one day I read in my improving Italian a small item in the paper: the deathbed confession of a woman who had once worked for a clinic in Lausanne; who had been sent to collect Giovanna from Italy; and who, she admitted in her final moments of cancer, had been paid a vast sum to smuggle the girl from the train that night. For whom she had been working, if she even knew, was not revealed.

The item caused a small stir, one that lasted no more than a week or two, but it reminded me of Giovanna's parents, who were said to be grief-stricken at this awful revelation. A few weeks later, having engineered my way into an interview with them, I could see her loss was as raw for them as it must always have been.

I pretended to be a journalist, following up on the possibility of Giovanna's sainthood, something else the newspaper article had briefly mentioned. Of course, I told them nothing. I didn't tell them how I'd found their girl's lifeless body in a cellar in Slovenia. I didn't tell them how I hoped to have burned it. I waited for them to speak, through the tears, waiting to pounce on the slightest hint, on any possible clue, to the man who'd paid for their daughter to travel to Switzerland.

But they gave me nothing. They knew nothing, and there was nothing to give. But it was when I left Rome that I found myself heading into the east, where, in a bar one night, I heard some wild stories about the foreigner who'd bought a ruined village, up in the hills.

They called him the Slav, and though no one knew who he was, or what he was really called, I knew it was him when they spoke about his disfigurement. He has terrible scars, they said, as if from a fire.

I smiled.

2

I'm close now, but I'm slow and dead. I am not fast any more. But I do not feel pain or fear; I am not scared. I am ready, that's all.

I watch for days, making my way up from the valley each morning, bringing enough food with me to see me to dusk, and I sit and watch, slowly dying in the awful Italian heat. And then, after three days of scouring the village through the binoculars, I see him.

The night of barking dogs has passed, and mutated into a brooding quiet as it does each morning. The early chill is burned quickly away, the dry heat rules everything again. I'm waiting, still waiting, and the hours pass easily, like flowing sand, until, sometime in the afternoon, the clatter of a door opening startles me.

It's hard to be sure at first. I see the door stagger open, and I see an old man hobble out into the fierce August sun, propping himself up with a stick. He holds his hand above his eyes, and even at this distance I can see the red scars on his face and his hands. He has shrunk, and he walks with a limp, but it's him.

Why he is living in this squalid ruin I have no idea. Maybe he has chosen this place, maybe somehow his money has finally run out. There could be many reasons, but I don't care. I don't care.

In all the time I've been watching, I have seen no one else. They said, down in the valley, that he bought the whole village from the last two families living there. I can see that most of the houses are falling down, their roofs caved in, their windows broken. Ivy is spreading over the broken tower of the church, and I know this area is prone to earthquakes. They said he lives there by himself, perhaps with the last of his fortune, but I wonder if he is completely alone.

I watch as he shouts at one of the dogs, the wild dogs that have made Sextantio their own. What they find to feed on, I do not know, but I suspect it's not much, whatever it is; they are mangy and thin curs that scamper away as he waves his stick at them.

I don't see him for long. He pulls a key from his pocket and opens another door. He seems to hesitate in the doorway for a moment, as if in anticipation, and then he goes inside.

That's when I'm sure he's not alone.

I crawl from my hiding place, and head down the hill in the heat. I'm sweating badly by the time I get to the narrow road that leads back up into his village, and I still have a steep climb before me. I don't want to use the road. It's too exposed and besides, I want to try and keep track of where I last saw him.

I can already see the village is a warren of alleys and leaning stone houses, of cobbled streets and cruel steps. I head up through an abandoned olive grove, and slowly climb up to a low broken wall, over which I slide, and then I lie, panting, trying to get some energy back.

The sun is burning my face, my hands, and I hate it, and I hate him for bringing me here, and then I stand, and realise I am lost.

A dog skips past me and I freeze at the sound, but I begin to explore. I realise I am on a small terrace almost underneath the one where I saw him disappear into the darkness of the doorway, but I cannot work out how to get from mine to his.

I set off through a small archway, but the steps beyond lead the wrong way, and all the while the stones of the houses, of the pavements, are throwing back the sun's heat at me, sucking my energy, draining me of what it is I've come to do. My feet seem far too loud on the dry cobbles, and I stop, and take my shoes off, and put them neatly out of sight on the top of a wall.

Then, I make another turn, and as I do so I see a short flight of steps leading up on to the higher terrace. I move up them, slowly, trying to be as silent as I can, and just as I reach the top, the door opens again, and as he steps into the sunlight, he sees me.

He does nothing.

He stares at me, like I once stared at him. And does nothing.

His skin is ruined by the fire, all down one side. I realise it has damaged his leg too, because he can't even stand straight.

His eyes meet mine, and I see that look on his face from so long ago, that look of curiosity.

There's a sound behind him, from the room, and a young woman, a thin and frail young woman, scrabbles for freedom, but she falls, landing on the doorstep. She is his last victim. She is, perhaps, some local peasant he has abducted, stolen, and secreted in his prison village. Her hands are tied behind her back, which, like a dog, is keeping her leashed to some unseen point inside the room. She lies on her side in the doorway, blinking, struggling, crying. A gag has fallen from her mouth and hangs around her neck. There is blood welling from her shoulder.

I look at her briefly, but he raises his stick, stepping towards me.

I pull the knife from my pocket and put it into the side of his neck, and he falls immediately.

He doesn't cry out, or make any sound at all, he just collapses with his hand to his neck.

There is no more. He twitches for a long time, trying to stop the blood coming out, looking up at me once or twice, trying to stop the blood, but he can't, because I have made a large hole in his neck, and the artery is pushing, hard.

The blood rushes, the blood spurts. It gushes, as it always does when allowed to burst free of the body.

I watch him for a good time.

Someone is speaking.

'Have you come to help me?' asks the girl, in Italian, and I step back.

I turn and am blinded by the sun.

Now there is nothing left but the sun. The sun and the blood; blood pouring out on the honey stone. The sun beats down, beats. That's what they say, the sun beats down, as if with violence, and I know it's why I was born English, that I need the rain, that this sun would drive a man to madness, driving up the heat of the blood, sending it faster and faster round the heart, and into the brain, spreading whatever lurks in the blood to the mind, and that lurking thing is evil.

What is it we should fear the most?

After Paris, I had decided that what Verovkin did to that girl in the bunker was no worse than many of the monstrous things war makes men do. But now I know differently. War doesn't make men do monstrous things. It *allows* them to.

What should we fear? It is ourselves, it is the monster inside us. That is what we should fear, and now there is nothing left in me but the sun. All through the long hot days it has been pounding at me, wearing me down, draining my energy, sucking me of life; a demanding god, one who demands that I make a sacrifice to replace the life lost from me. If I fill myself once more, I will be strong again, and then I can go on, go on another day, keep going, and going, until I find something worth finding, something that makes everything I have been through fall away. That something, I think, could be something like Verovkin had.

Everything does fall away, for there is only the sun now. Its heat burns its way into my heart, until I can bear it no more.

I drop to my knees in the hot dust, licking my lips.

Time passes.

A dog barks, just one this time, and I remember the dogs barking all night, all night every night.

I am tortured by a brief vision of Marian, silhouetted in the window at Caius. Then it's gone.

There is nothing left now but the sun, and the blood inside me.

I look down at Verovkin, just once more. He has stopped moving.

What had he seen on my face, in that tunnel in Paris? Fear, yes. Curiosity. Yes, that too. And now I knew he was right. He'd seen something more; he'd seen desire. So I had hated Verovkin. Yes. But it was only now that I finally understood the real reason why, because it was now that I knew that what had brought me to the cellar in Yugoslavia, and now to a hilltop in Italy, was indeed a desire; but it was not, as I'd thought, a desire to destroy him.

In the cellar, that night, I made the connection to Sarah, and her blood, and her betrayal of me. Then, I only knew that the connection hurt me, and that Verovkin had brought it back. But there was something else I had not been able to place, something that had remained unknown to me, and it was this: Sarah's affair did not *start* my fascination with blood. What happened with her merely poured fuel on a fire that was already burning, a fire for which I can see no original cause, other than that I may have been born with it inside me. And that fire is a desire. A desire; a love, like blood, that flows deep within us, guiding us, pushing us, controlling us, one from which we can never be free, because we can never be free of our own blood; except in death.

I have wondered, over the last few days, sitting on the hillside, I have wondered which of our emotions are actually real. When we fear, when we love, when we worry, when we hate; which of these are real, and which are merely performances that we put on for the benefit of those around us? Or for ourselves. Did I really love Marian? Did I really care so much for her that I threw my life away trying to avenge her? Did I really cry for Hunter, or were those tears simply meant to prove to the world, to myself, that I was kind, that I cared?

And when we claim to be repulsed by something, disgusted, horrified, is it possible that sometimes that object is what we secretly desire the most? That the powerful hostile reaction is a falsification of a deeply held yearning for that very thing?

So many things fall away from me now, flow away, and I have a sudden memory, a visual memory, of Marian stroking her fingertip through the rainwater on the tabletop. My memory becomes a fantasy, and as it does, the water on the red lacquer transforms into a different fluid, and so finally I realise that it is my own love for blood that has brought me this far.

I know I will go on. I will walk away from this place and do further things before I die. I have the money to do them, and more time than I could wish for.

I get up again and turn back to the girl.

'*Are you going to help me?*'

I see the almost imperceptible; the artery pulsing in her neck.

'No,' I say. 'There is no one to help you now.'

I step towards her.